DEEP BLUE SURRENDER

AN ALLISON HART NOVEL
BOOK 1

ROBIN MAHLE

HARP House Publishing, LLC.

Published by HARP House Publishing
October 2019 (1st edition)

1

Personal agendas, as Allison Hart had come to realize, were what drove most people's decisions. To be fair, not all agendas were self-centered. But in Allison's world, few focused on the greater good. As a woman who hurled along at break-neck speed toward middle age and had survived a divorce after 20 years of marriage, cynicism had become a nasty by-product. It was also what made her good at her job.

Allison was an investigator for the State of Florida. It was up to her to net unscrupulous citizens defrauding Worker's Compensation with false claims. When the topic arose in conversation, eyes would widen and ears would perk up. But on further clarification of her duties, people appeared as though they'd just been doused with cold water. An obligatory smile and nod before they would slink away in search of more interesting conversation. There was nothing glamorous about the job, but Allison loved it anyway. And today, someone had called in a juicy tip. Someone with an agenda, no doubt.

The 48-year-old slender brassy blonde sat behind the wheel of her decade-old blue Honda Civic. The malfunctioning air conditioner spewed warm air from the vents. It was nearing the end of a Tampa Bay summer that carried oppressive air leading into peak hurricane season. Allison rolled down the windows to stem the flow of perspiration that trickled down her face and neck as she drove to a home in a quiet suburban neighborhood.

The tip was from the ex-wife of the target, a term Allison preferred to use to maintain objectivity. None of this was personal. The ex had suggested her estranged husband hadn't at all been suffering from double vision after a blow to his head. A result of a tragic construction site accident. The woman insisted she had witnessed him driving on several occasions, which he had claimed wasn't possible. Allison didn't question how the woman knew this as a fact when she lived in the next town over.

Her job was to collect evidence. What the state did with that evidence was up to them. She rolled to a stop three houses down from the claimant's home along the palm-tree-lined street and picked up her binoculars. Clifford Langston, the man whose name appeared on the manila folder resting on her passenger seat, was due to leave for a regularly scheduled doctor's appointment. With the binoculars pressed against her eyes, she peered at the 1990s beige stuccoed home with terra-cotta roof tiles.

If anyone had told Allison 5 years ago that she would be skulking around a suburban neighborhood in search of schemers, the conversation would've ended with a colorful expletive and a raucous laugh. But 5 years ago, she was still married to Leo. Her marriage collapsed soon after. Their two children were barely teenagers then and the disruption, to put it mildly, had taken its toll. Now that they were college-aged, both had grown used to their new lives.

Charlotte Wells, Charlie to her friends, helped Allison get this position. It turned out, getting back into the job market after not having worked for 20 years was something of a challenge. Regardless, it was Allison's instincts that moved her into the position she now occupied. Razor-sharp intuition coupled with her ability to call bullshit made her the ideal candidate.

Allison fine-tuned the binocular lenses and trained them on the claimant's home. In this line of work, she took her safety seriously and always maintained a comfortable distance. People didn't like to be caught red-handed and often grew unpredictable in the face of it.

Queen Palms flanked the home's entrance and an arched opening led to a small covered porch. The wooden front door was stained dark and adorned with wrought iron details that appeared Tuscan, though the rest of the home looked Mediterranean.

She waited for the door to open and for Clifford Langston to step into his Ford F-150, preferably in the driver's seat. Not that she wanted to catch him committing fraud, but it made for a more exciting day. She would never publicly admit that this was the fun part. A few photos and videos of Langston sitting behind the wheel and pulling away in his nice new truck would do the trick. After that, she could head back to the office where the air was set at a cool 68 degrees. It was the perfect temperature for a woman teetering between hormonal irregularity and the word she had thus far refused to utter...menopause. The hostile condition often found her with her head buried in the employee lounge freezer while her colleagues looked on in abject repulsion.

"There you are." Allison homed in on the door as it opened. A man stepped out. A glance at the file on her passenger seat and she double-checked the photo. "Hello, Mr. Langston."

Langston stood on the porch squinting from the glare of the noon-day sun. He slipped on dark sunglasses.

Another man stepped out from behind Langston and closed the front door. She yanked away the binoculars. "What the hell?"

Allison dabbed at her sticky eyelids, smudging the earth-toned shadow, and redoubled her efforts, tuning the lenses to focus on this new person. "No. No way." She snatched her cell phone from the center console and zoomed in on the two men, snapping photos. "What are you doing here?"

With the video recording, she trained the phone's camera as they continued down the path toward the driveway. The second man, the one who Allison knew was a supervisor in her department, surveyed the area and turned squarely in her direction.

"Damn it!" She ducked below the steering wheel. The jolt caused her to drop the phone to the floorboard. "Please don't see me. Please don't see me." What was worse, her thick blonde hair was stacked on her head a little like Marge Simpson, and hovered above the line of sight. But staying hunkered down was cowardly. Allison pulled up just enough to peer over the dashboard.

The supervisor opened the passenger door for Langston and helped him inside. His eyes darted toward the street but didn't look directly at her again.

"You know I'm here, don't you?" Allison watched as the implausible unfolded.

The truck rolled back out of the driveway with the supervisor behind the wheel. Without Langston driving, she had nothing to use against him. The truck started in her direction and Allison bent over flat along the front seats to stay out of view. After the truck drove by, she sat up again. "Davis Cantrell, I didn't take you for a co-conspirator." She didn't know why Davis was there or how he knew Clifford Langston. But one thing was certain, Davis had seen her.

———

On her return to the office, Allison imagined Davis Cantrell standing in front of her pointing before unleashing a blood-curdling scream in her direction. Just like in the movie. Was she the lone survivor of an alien takeover? It was the only plausible explanation for witnessing his cover-up of a fraud investigation. He must've been a pod person.

The 3-story building that was home to the Bureau's offices was just ahead. Allison couldn't recall how she arrived as her mind had been preoccupied with science-fiction horror. She stepped out of her Honda with long, spindly legs. The black capris clung to her thighs and her white sleeveless blouse stuck to her waist. Allison locked the car and walked to the elevators in her sensible black flats. The doors parted and a blast of cool air smacked her damp skin and raised goosebumps on her arms. With marked hesitation she entered her department and walked straight to Charlie's desk, dismissing everyone in her path. No one had pointed and screamed thus far. "Hey. Can you talk?"

Charlie whipped around with her short and spiky black hair fixed into position. She sized up Allison. "I see you still haven't fixed the A/C in your car."

"Come with me." Allison turned on her heel and started toward the corridor.

Charlie pushed off her chair and trailed Allison with short strides and arms swinging. With each step, her thighs swooshed thanks to the pantyhose she always insisted on wearing. Something about how they chafed otherwise.

Allison waited inside the copy room for Charlie to catch up.

"Okay, I'm here. Are we hiding from someone?" she asked.

"You know I was dropping in on Clifford Langston, right? Gathering evidence."

"Yeah. So?" Charlie replied.

Allison pulled her close. "Davis was there."

Charlie's deep brown eyes sparked with interest and her lips parted. "Davis Cantrell? The assistant director?"

"None other." Allison stepped toward the opened door and searched for eavesdroppers who might be looming in the hall. On her return, she added, "I'm telling you, it was like he knew I was coming. Almost as if someone tipped off Langston."

"What on earth would Davis Cantrell be doing there? How would Langston know him?" Charlie asked.

"I don't know. But he stepped into the driver's seat of Langston's truck and drove him away. I didn't follow. Charlie, I'm pretty sure he saw me. Do you know what this could mean?"

"Davis moonlights as a chauffeur?"

"I'll tell you what it means. It means Davis is protecting Langston. Maybe he knows him personally. And if that's the case, someone on the inside tipped him off that I'd be there today."

"You know how much I love conspiracy theories, Alli, but that doesn't add up. I agree it looks bad. If Davis knows a claimant and that claimant has a file for suspected fraud, that's shady. Maybe the answer is to just ask him. You were doing what they hired you to do. If he wasn't, well, that's on him."

Allison took a step back in consideration. "I think Davis wanted me to see him with Langston, and he wanted me to prove Langston wasn't driving, which I did. He has to know the man personally. There's no other explanation."

"Was Davis the one to sign off on the investigation?" Charlie asked.

"That's a good question. See, I knew there was a reason we were friends." Allison marched out of the copy room.

"I thought it was my witty personality." Charlie jogged to catch up to her. "Hey. Wait up. You brought me into this and I like where it could be going. Davis is kind of an ass."

Allison chuckled. "I dropped the file on your desk. We'll see if Cantrell signed off on it."

They returned to Charlie's desk and huddled together looking like villains twirling their mustaches in search of something to bring down their nemesis. With her index finger, Allison perused the claim for a signature. "Can I borrow your cheaters?"

"Oh, now you want my glasses? I'll remind you of this the next time you make fun of me for wearing these around my neck." Charlie lifted the chain and handed the glasses to Allison.

"Nice try but that won't stop me."

"You're lucky we're friends. What can you see?"

Allison tapped on the signature. "Right there in black and white, Davis Cantrell."

Charlie placed her hands on her round hips. "How does he know Clifford Langston and why would he risk protecting him?"

"That's the $64,000 question." Allison surveyed the maze of cubicles, contemplating a solution when her eyes landed on Cantrell. "He's here."

"What?" Charlie searched for him.

"Shhh. Don't look. Davis is here. He's coming this way." The file slipped from her hands and landed face down on Charlie's desk.

"Allison, Charlie, good afternoon."

Allison noted his exaggerated swagger and smug expression, not at all like a pod person. "Afternoon, Davis."

He placed his hand on her bare shoulder. "I don't suppose you have a minute. I'd like to talk to you about an investigation I know you're familiar with."

She glanced at Charlie and returned her attention to Cantrell. "You bet I do."

"Fantastic." Davis turned on his heel and started toward his office.

Allison followed, but not without a final turn back to Charlie where she revealed a toothy grin and gestured with two thumbs up.

Cantrell held open the door to his office. "Please, take a seat." He motioned to a nearby chair and closed the door behind him. "I won't take up much of your time, Allison. I just wanted to have a quick word with you about a claimant."

She batted her dark brown eyes and feigned curiosity. "Oh? And who might that be?"

Davis lowered himself into his hi-back executive chair and held her gaze. "How do you like your job, Allison?"

"My job? I love it. I can't imagine doing anything else. Don't take this the wrong way, Davis, but why am I here? I don't work for you unless that's changing?"

"I was just curious to know if this was a place you wanted to stay," he added.

"As I said..."

"I heard you." He leaned over his desk. "Just so we're on the same page, Mr. Langston is no longer a concern of yours. You've done your duty and it is appreciated. But I'll be handling his case from here."

"Oh. Do you know Clifford Langston? Is he a friend?"

"It's not your case anymore, Allison. You can send over his file to me and I'll take it from here."

"I don't understand. You're well above my pay grade, Davis. Surely, Langston doesn't interest you. Have I done something wrong in the investigation?"

"Not at all. I just need to oversee this one. That's all this is, I assure you."

Allison wasn't confrontational by nature, but this was leaving a bad taste in her mouth. "I think we both know what this is about."

"Is that so? Please, enlighten me with your insignificant and irrelevant opinion."

Allison stood from her chair. "You obviously knew I was going to be there. You made sure Langston didn't do anything he wasn't supposed to do. I think my being there was part of your plan. God knows why. But I do know you saw me. We saw each other."

"It's been brought to my attention that you have an unseemly habit of setting up claimants to take the fall," Davis said.

"I'm sorry, what?"

"You seem to have set your own quota and that's not how we do things around here, Allison. Suffice it to say, if you like the way things are going for you here, I suggest you get back to the business of finding the real fraud, not something manufactured by an ex-spouse looking to settle old scores."

"Pardon me for saying, but that sounded an awful lot like a threat."

Davis held up his hands. "No threats here. Just honest feedback."

"I don't know who you're getting this so-called feedback from, but I can tell you, I have done my job well. I wonder if my boss knows you were at Langston's house today. He's probably the one I should be taking this to."

Davis smiled. "I've been here a lot longer than you, Allison. People know that I'm an effective leader. What do they know about you?"

"So, if I mention this to anyone, say, my boss, you'll what, come in and tell him what a hack I am? That I've had complaints or something along those lines? Boy, you must be in deep, Davis. I feel kind of bad for you really." She pushed off the chair and started to leave. "Well, there's no better time than the present."

"Where are you going?"

"Me? I have a feeling my boss will be very interested in this conversation." She slammed the door behind her and headed straight for Lou Yancy, her immediate supervisor.

Allison stood in the hall and leaned into his doorway. "Hey, Lou."

He peered up at her. "Allison, come on in. What can I do for you?"

She walked inside and closed the door.

"This must be important," he said.

"It is." Allison regurgitated the events leading up to this moment. She waited for Lou to tell her that Davis would be immediately fired. But people always had an agenda.

"I'll have to speak with Davis on this matter, Allison. You've levied some stiff allegations on an assistant director."

"I understand that, but I'm right. I was there. Davis has a personal connection to the claimant..."

"Okay, okay, you've said your piece." Lou stood. "I'll go speak to him now. You know what, it's getting late in the afternoon already. Why don't you knock off early and I'll take it from here?"

Was this the moment he was going to open his mouth and point his finger? Because it sure felt like she was on the wrong side of this. "Fine. Thank you for hearing me out." Allison left and returned to her desk.

Charlie caught sight of her and quickly approached. "What happened?"

Allison grabbed her bag. "I'm being sent home."

"What? Why?"

"Probably because I just ruffled some very important feathers. Look, I'll call you later when I hear something, okay? I'll be all right."

———

ALLISON HOVERED OVER HER STOVE, STIRRING A POT OF spaghetti when her phone rang. She set down her spoon and grabbed her phone from the kitchen counter. "Lou, thanks for calling. So, what's the good news?"

She wore a smile assuming that vindication was coming her way and that Davis Cantrell wasn't going to win. But as she listened to her boss, his words stumbled as though he couldn't quite say what he'd wanted to say. "Lou, what are you telling me?"

"Allison, I'm afraid we're going to have to let you go. I'm happy to give you a glowing letter of reference."

The smile faded from her lips. The pot of spaghetti boiled over, splattering onto the stovetop behind her. "I can't believe this. I was doing my job."

"I know you were, Allison, but Davis says you haven't been doing the job you were hired to do."

"And you believe him? Lou, I've worked for you for almost 5 years. Are you serious?"

"If you have any questions, you'll need to direct them to HR. I'm so sorry, Allison. It really has been a pleasure." The line went dead.

Everyone had an agenda.

———

THE LEFTOVERS HAD BEEN PUT AWAY AND ALLISON WAS already in her pajamas. It was 7 o'clock in the evening and the sun was just beginning to set. She held the phone to her ear and listened as Charlie ranted.

"So you're giving up? Just like that? Without a fight? I've never known you to be a quitter, Alli."

Allison inhaled a deep breath. "There's no coming back from

this, Charlie. Lou, well, I don't know how Davis got to him, but he did. It's over. I'll find something else. It'll all work out somehow."

"You know you'll have to go to Leo for help, at least in the short term," Charlie replied. "I know how much you don't want to have to do that."

"I have some savings. I'll figure it out. I can't un-ring this bell. But I'll tell you one thing, I'll get to the bottom of Davis Cantrell, that I can promise you."

"And in the meantime?"

"I have friends," Allison replied.

"Like me?" Charlie quipped.

"Well, yes, but in the business, I mean."

"You mean like Shane or Milo?"

"Why not? They know people. Shane's a cop. Milo's a prosecutor. They're bound to have contacts in our industry."

Charlie was quiet for a moment. "Maybe. I hadn't thought about that. You know, with your background, it would make sense for you to transition into something like a private investigator."

"A private eye? Me? Not a chance. I've come across enough of those guys to know they're all money-grubbers who prey on people's insecurities. Get them to foot the bill for tracking down cheating spouses. No thanks."

"That's not all they do, you know. You should think about it. Seriously."

2

Allison was curled on her sofa reading when the doorbell chimed. She set down her paperback and peered through the living room window. "I was wondering when you would turn up." It was 9 pm and late by Allison's standards. The person at her door now was not unexpected, just uninvited. She shuffled to the foyer and gripped the door handle, mentally preparing for her guest. "Well, hello there. To what do I owe the pleasure of this visit? Oh wait, let me guess, Charlie called you."

"She was worried about you and so am I." Leo Hart, Allison's ex-husband, stood under the porch light. Just shy of 6 feet, Leo had an average build but had grown a slight paunch in his middle age. His dark brown hair had begun to thin at the crown, yet his face maintained a youthful glow with only mild crow's feet which deepened as he scrutinized her. "Are you going to let me in or am I going to keep sweating my balls off out here?"

"Did you get permission from her?" Allison stepped aside. "Wouldn't want to cause a rift between you two lovebirds."

"You mean, Jenny? She knows I'm here."

"Then, by all means, come in." She closed the door behind him. "You want a beer or something a little stronger?"

"You know what I like." He set down his car keys on the side table just like he used to when this was his home.

"I thought I did." Allison walked into the kitchen and grabbed a bottle of gin and two glasses. "Maybe I'll join you."

"So Charlie says you quit today." Leo pulled out a stool at the kitchen counter. "Care to tell me what happened?"

Allison poured the drinks and slid one across the white quartz countertop toward him. "That's not exactly what happened. I was let go and she's mad that I'm not going to fight it."

"You? Not fighting? That doesn't sound right." He tossed back a swig of the gin and tonic.

She regarded this man to whom she'd been married for twenty years. Leo had lied to her and had betrayed her, but time had passed and they had evolved since the divorce. Dare she admit they could be considered friends now? Maybe so, but Allison didn't care for Jenny, Leo's latest squeeze. She was young, too young, but that was who Leo was now, a middle-aged man who needed a younger woman to feel virile again, she assumed. Still, it wasn't her concern anymore.

"Something might have happened today to trigger my current state of redundancy." Allison picked up her drink and tossed back a large gulp.

"And now the truth comes out. Well, spill it." Leo gestured with his fingers for her to give up the goods.

"You know I can get—mouthy—when I'm challenged..."

He rolled his eyes. "No, really?"

She returned a scathing glance. "Anyway, one of the assistant directors, a guy who I don't even work for...well, I'm pretty sure he's involved in a cover-up or taking kickbacks. I don't know."

"Kickbacks?" Leo asked before downing another gulp.

"I can't say for sure, but I was checking up on a claimant earlier today..."

"You mean, spying on him?" Leo asked.

"Do you want me to tell the story, or would you like to?"

"I'm sorry. Please, go on."

"I saw this guy at the claimant's home. I think he knew I'd be there. Long story short, the assistant director confronted me about it and essentially threatened me."

Leo pulled upright on the stool and turned serious. "He threatened you?"

"Yes—sort of. I thought it was a threat to either keep quiet or lose my job. So, I went to my boss and guess what? My boss didn't give a rat's ass." She threw back the last of her drink. "So there you go."

"I see. What are you going to do now? What about Nolan?"

"If you think I'm going to ask you for money, don't worry about it. I'll get work. We don't need a handout from you."

"Alli, that's not what I meant. Nolan is my son, too. He still lives here with you. School and his training, it takes a lot of money. We both know that. I'm here to help because he's my son and because, well, because it's you."

"I've held down this job since we divorced. I made good money..."

"I know you did—you do..."

"If things get too tight, I'll ask for help, okay? But until then, I know what I'm doing. We'll be fine."

Leo drank the last of his gin and tonic. "Where is Nolan anyway? I didn't see his car in the drive."

"He's at Joey's house. Said he'd be home by midnight. The kid's 18, I can't tell him when to be home anymore."

"Yeah, yeah. He just needs to remember to keep focused on his baseball. He has a real good chance of making Triple A."

"Just like his dad," Allison replied. "It's getting late, you should go home to Jenny. I'm sure it can't be a comforting thought knowing your boyfriend is hanging out with his ex-wife."

"She's not threatened by our relationship, just so you know." Leo stood. "But I guess it is getting late."

"Yep." Allison led him to the door. "Thanks for coming over. I know you're just checking in and I do appreciate it."

Leo bent over to kiss her cheek. "Just because we aren't together anymore doesn't mean I don't still care about you." He walked out into the night and stepped into his sedan which was older than hers.

Allison watched him drive away. "Too bad it wasn't quite enough."

───────

It was like the first day of summer when the alarm clock rang out yet there was no school. Allison was no longer employed. Getting out of bed early, or at all, was pointless. She wanted to pull the covers over her head and go back to sleep. For most of her adult life, she had been a stay-at-home mom who drove her kids to gymnastics, baseball, and birthday parties. There was always a reason to get out of bed. Right now, Allison couldn't think of one.

She drew up onto the edge of her bed with her long blonde hair pulled into a bun. A burst of laughter, which at this time of morning sounded more like a cackle, broke free.

"What are you laughing at?" Nolan meandered in the hall and peeked into her room.

She hadn't closed her bedroom door since the divorce. "Nothing. What time did you get in last night?"

The young man with brown hair worn a little too long for her liking was as handsome as his father was—even more so. Leo had turned a lot of heads, especially in his twenties when he made it to the Triple A league. His idol had been the great pitcher Nolan Ryan, which was her son's namesake.

"Does it matter what time I got in?" Nolan replied. "Haven't we had this discussion, Mom?"

"We have, but that doesn't mean you don't still have to live by my rules when you live under my roof."

He rolled his eyes so far into the back of his head, that it appeared doubtful they would return. "1 o'clock, okay? I got in at 1. No big deal. I have to leave for school anyway. Aren't you going to work? Are you sick or something?"

She remembered that he hadn't known yet. "No, I'm not sick. Look, Nolan, I'm not going back to that job anymore. I decided to look for something more fulfilling."

His brow knitted. "Okay. Can we afford that? Should I ask for more hours at the Jack in the Box?"

"No, honey. You have enough to handle with baseball and school. We'll be fine. I've already spoken to your father and he'll do what he needs to do to keep your schooling on track."

"But what about you?" He walked inside wearing a look of worry no parent would want to see.

"Don't lose any sleep over this, Nolan. I told you, I'll find something else. It won't take long. Go on. You should go to school. I'll see you tonight. Maybe for dinner?"

"Yeah, sure. That'd be great. I'll see you tonight, Mom." He kissed her cheek.

She smiled as he walked away, not sure how she got so lucky to have a son like Nolan. Both her kids were good. Always had been. They were the best thing to come from her marriage.

———

As it turned out, Allison found a reason to get out of bed. There were two people who had become important in her life and she was on a mission to pay each one a visit. When she arrived at the police station in downtown Tampa, Allison was about to check off the first name on her list. She dressed up for the occasion by wearing a modern grey pantsuit with her hair pulled into a loose braid that rested against her back. This wasn't a job interview, but it sort of felt that way. She approached the administration desk.

"Hey, Allison, how are you?" A hefty woman in uniform and slicked back hair stood behind the counter. "You must be here to see Sully."

"Is he taking visitors today?" Allison began. "I don't have the required gold engraved invitation."

"Today's your lucky day. He's at his desk. You can go on back." Her smile was warm and friendly.

"Appreciate it." Allison headed into the station's bullpen in search of her long-time friend and sometimes partner, Shane "Sully" Sullivan. "Morning. I took a shot you were in and here you are."

"Allison Hart. What are you doing here? Did we have a date I didn't know about?" Shane leaned back in his chair, cool and calm, like nothing ever stuck to him. Of course, nothing ever did.

"Not today. Do you have a minute?" she asked.

"For you? Always. Sit down. What's on your mind?" Shane was an uncompromising bachelor who had just made it to 40. No kids; never wanted them. He was a newly minted detective in the demanding police station and worked mostly minor crimes, petty theft, etc. It took time to get the big cases like robbery or homicide. And he had always been there for Allison since the day they met.

She sat down on the hard plastic chair across from him. "Hey, um, I was wondering if I could ask you a favor?"

"Shoot." He cocked his head, which highlighted his striking jawline.

"I'm looking for a new place to hang my hat," she replied.

"A job? What happened to the one you had?"

"It's a long story that I won't tire you with. Point is, I know you have a lot of contacts and with my background, I thought maybe you might know somebody who could use someone like me." Allison hated asking for favors. She hated asking anyone for anything, but Shane did have connections.

He gazed up at the ceiling, narrowing his brown eyes and rubbing his smooth chin. "Hmm. Someone who might need a fraud investigator." He looked at her again and nodded. "I could make some calls. I know a couple of guys who always need an extra pair of hands. I did meet a chick—sorry—a woman who works for an insurance company. I bet they need fraud people like you too."

"Thanks, Shane. I'd really appreciate you putting in a good word for me if someone's looking."

"Anything for you Allison, you know that. You and me go way back, right?"

"Sure." They went back about four years. "I won't take up any more of your time. I know how busy you detectives can be." She prepared to leave.

Shane stood up, his toned physique on full display. "Hold on a sec. I'll show you out. I'm still a gentleman."

"You don't have to do that."

"Of course I do." He gestured. "After you, ma'am."

"Now you're making me feel old." Allison smiled.

"Well, you sure don't look old and that's a cold hard fact," he replied.

Shane was a player and Allison had figured out that within about ten minutes of their initial meeting. It didn't make him an asshole, it just made him a flirt.

"Thanks for showing me out and thanks for offering to help too."

He led her to the double doors. "I'll get in touch with you just as soon as I hear anything, you got that?"

"I got it. See you later, Shane."

"See you later, Allison."

She could feel his stare while walking away. "Stop staring at my ass, Shane."

"What? Never!"

Allison smiled but refused to turn back and pushed through the doors. "Goodbye."

———

NUMBER TWO ON HER LIST WHICH WAS IN NO PARTICULAR order, was Milo Nash. He was a special assistant attorney in the Fraud and Corruption Unit of the D.A.'s office. That was how Allison came to know him. Some of her cases were sent up the ladder and fell into his lap.

He appeared from the hall of the Tampa District Attorney's Office wearing his signature suspenders. Not everyone could pull off that look, but Milo Nash was born to wear them.

"Allison, what are you doing here? Please don't tell me we had an appointment." Milo checked his watch.

"We did not. I hope it's okay that I popped in." She greeted Milo with a friendly hug. Her arms struggled to reach around him.

"Can you spare a couple of minutes? I could come back another time."

"That's not necessary. I always have time for my friends."

"Since when does a senior prosecutor for the District Attorney's office have any time to spare?" she replied. "I won't keep you. I just wanted to bend your ear about something."

"Of course. Come back to my office." He turned to the receptionist. "Can you hold my calls for a few minutes?"

The young woman looked to be a lawyer in training and replied, "Sure, no problem."

He led the way to his office and waited for Allison to enter. "Take a seat. Tell me what's on your mind. You're looking well." He dropped onto his desk chair.

"And you, Milo. Listen, I'm looking for work." She raised a preemptive hand. "And before you ask, I quit my job and that's all I'm willing to say on the matter."

"Okay. We'll leave it at that then. What kind of work are you looking for? Something along the lines of what you were doing?"

"Yeah, maybe. I think I'm pretty good at what I do." She crossed her long legs and leaned back in the chair.

"And don't you ever doubt it," Milo replied.

He was a few years older than Allison, just over 50, but time hadn't been all that kind to him. The round mid-section and thinning hair gave away his age more than anything else. His eyes were kind, which for a lawyer was an anomaly.

"Well, I could ask around," he continued. "Anyone would be lucky to have you on their team."

"I would appreciate that, Milo, I really would. It's a good time for a change, you know?"

"Sure, sure. And I'll tell you, you got a knack for sniffing out the phonies, I'll give you that." He laughed. "Hell, maybe you should come work for me."

"If only I had a law degree."

He studied her. "Have you ever thought of striking out on your own?"

"What do you mean?" she asked.

"I mean starting up your own thing."

"I'm not sure how that would work. I'd have to have insurance companies hire me as a contractor or something like that, wouldn't I? And then I'd have no benefits. You know Nolan and Micah are still on my insurance." She paused to consider her predicament. "Although now..."

"I mean having people come to you to find whatever it might be that they lost," he said. "Getting to the bottom of things is what you do best, Allison."

She raised the corner of her mouth in a half-smile. "You know, Charlie said something similar to me yesterday and I just sort of brushed it off."

"It might be worth a second look. You got Sullivan over there at the police department. I'm sure he'd be able to refer folks your way. Then I could try and throw you a bone once in a while. I can't say how often, but I've come across situations before that would be great for someone like you."

"I don't know. Maybe you're right. It'd be risky and I'd be starting from scratch, but it's not like I haven't taken risks before."

"You had to start over after you and Leo split up. That's pretty tough. I know because I've been there."

His words were encouraging. Maybe this was something she could do and be damn good at.

"I can put you in contact with a P.I. I've worked with before and I know Sullivan has to know a few too. It is doable, Allison. You should mull it over." Milo checked the time. "I hate to cut this short, but I'm due in court in an hour." He stood.

"Of course, I'm so sorry." She stood in response.

"Don't be. It was good to see you. And I meant what I said. Think about it and get back to me, okay?"

"Okay. I will. I'll think about it."

He showed her out and Allison walked to her car considering what he'd said. Was it really possible? She was pushing 50 and starting her own business at this age. It was beyond a risky proposition. But when she stepped into her car and the air conditioning blew warm air on her face, she knew money was what she needed. Her bills would pile up fast and if her car broke down, well that would be enough to send her into a freefall toward bankruptcy.

Allison pulled out of the parking lot and drove toward the bridge, glancing briefly at the calm waters of the bay. She'd lived in Tampa most of her life but hadn't really begun to live until the divorce. She knew people, influential people. Maybe this was possible—starting her own agency. As crazy as it seemed, Leo would be behind her one hundred percent, and so would her kids and Charlie. What more did she need? "Clients." She laughed. "So I'll get clients. How hard can that be?"

3

Ambivalence was often at the core of failed dreams. Allison never believed herself to be indecisive but the idea of running an agency summoned visions of sitting at her office desk waiting for the phone to ring while the lights flickered off from the unpaid bill. The risks were far greater than any of her previous undertakings, even her divorce. On second thought, maybe that had been a greater challenge but the anger she felt toward Leo then was enough to propel her forward. It wasn't the same this time. She was clear-headed and would have no one to blame but herself if she were to fail.

Allison waited in a small booth inside a favorite dinner spot where she and Charlie often dined. When she spotted Charlie's arrival, a feeling of assuredness washed over her. Charlie had that effect on people. She exuded confidence and given the troubles Charlie had faced in her previous marriage, that was no small achievement. "Hey, thanks for meeting me."

Charlie slid into the booth across from her. "Are you kidding?

Do you have any idea what you stirred up at the office? You were the talk around the water cooler, my friend."

"Really? Do tell." Allison sipped on a glass of Chardonnay. "What do you want to drink?"

"Yours looks good. I'll have the same."

Allison gestured to the waiter. "Hi, could we get another Chardonnay for my friend here?"

"Of course. I'll be right back."

Allison turned back to Charlie. "So, tell me all about it. Is anything going to happen to that slime ball?"

"Davis Cantrell is skating on thin ice thanks to you," Charlie replied.

"Are they looking into his connection to Langston?"

"I don't know for sure yet, but when word got around that you'd been let go, rumors spun like a whirlwind. I don't think I've ever seen so many people buzzing around like little bees. Everyone said it was a sham and that you should sue. Lou's in hot water too. This morning was nothing but closed-door meetings and raised voices. No one's been fired, but according to the grapevine, upper management's going to be looking at not only the Langston claim but others too."

"When did all this happen?"

"Yesterday, this morning, this afternoon. It's a circus on the 3rd floor," Charlie said.

The waiter returned with Charlie's wine.

"Thanks very much," she replied.

"Can I get you ladies anything else?"

Allison turned to him. "Actually, how about the nachos?" She looked at Charlie. "Sound good to you?"

"Let me see...nachos and Chardonnay? Um, yes, please."

"Great. It'll be out shortly." The waiter disappeared.

"As I was saying, there was a big pow-wow around 10 o'clock," Charlie continued. "The directors and department managers."

"I'll be happy to make a statement if it comes to that. I'm not afraid of Davis Cantrell. Anything I can do to help make sure he and Lou get what's coming to them, then I will."

Charlie nodded. "It would probably mean you could get your job back—if you wanted it."

"I wouldn't go back there. Not after they humiliated me like that. Besides, I can't seem to shake the idea you threw out at me yesterday."

Charlie raised a brow. "You mean about becoming an investigator? On your own?"

Allison regarded her half-empty glass of wine and skimmed her index finger around its rim. "Yeah. I mean, I think maybe it could work. I think it's time for me to move on and create something better for myself."

"That's great, Alli. You should. You'd kick ass."

"I wouldn't want to do it alone. I still have to work out the logistics, and probably get a small business loan, but I think you and I should do this together."

Charlie thrust back her shoulders. "You want me to come work for you?"

"Not for me, with me." Allison smiled. "What do you think?"

"Oh, I don't know, Alli." The confidence Charlie radiated when she walked in had all but vanished. "You know how hard it's been for me to keep my head above water. What, with my deadbeat ex and all. I don't know if I could do that to the boys."

"What if I could guarantee your salary? You wouldn't be out anything. And honestly, you're worth a whole lot more than what the state is paying you to work at the Bureau." Allison leaned over the table. Her eyes gleamed with enthusiasm. "Look, it's a risk. I get that. But think of the possibilities. You said it yourself."

"I said *you* could do it. Not *we*."

"Come on, Charlie. There's no we without you." Allison pulled back. "I'll tell you what, I'll work out the financing side of things and come back to you with a proposal. Then you can decide."

"How are you going to get this off the ground?" Charlie asked.

"You already know I met with Shane who said he could put me in touch with some people. I also met with Milo. He came to the same conclusion as you. Said I'd make a hell of a P.I. and should consider starting up my own agency. He has contacts, people who could help show us the ropes. I just need to get an office and some basics set up."

"You've put a lot of thought into this already," Charlie said.

"I couldn't sleep last night, so I had some time to think," Allison replied.

The waiter returned with an enormous plate of nachos. "Here you are. Is there anything else?"

"Two more chardonnays, thanks," Allison said. "We have a lot to hash out." She beamed at Charlie.

THE INITIAL TERMS HAD BEEN SET AND CHARLIE WAS ON board, so long as Allison could secure the funding to lease an office and have enough cash on hand to pay the first three months' salary. Allison wanted to guarantee her more, but Charlie insisted this was more than fair and decided it was worth the risk. After all, she stood behind Allison for long enough and now it was time to stand next to her and go through this together. Allison had convinced her the time was right and Charlie agreed. Though Allison would confirm this again in the morning since the arrangement had been made after a couple of glasses of wine. It wasn't a decision to be taken without a clear head.

Allison returned home, feeling lighter than when she awoke this morning and that wasn't because of the wine. The prospects of what she and Charlie were about to undertake were exciting. She parked the old blue Civic on the driveway and approached the front door. Nolan had forgotten to turn on the porch light, leaving Allison to struggle to insert the key. When she finally opened the door, there was only silence and more darkness. "Nolan? Are you home?" She secured the deadbolt after closing the door behind her.

Allison navigated through to the kitchen and flipped on the lights. In her younger years, she had craved alone time. It came with the territory of being a wife and mother. She was still a mother, but no longer had a child who relied on her. And now being alone only gave her a glimpse into what her future held. It wasn't a pretty sight.

At least she had something to occupy her time. Allison had a new life to embark upon and getting her license to become a private investigator was going to force her to jump through a lot of hoops. Florida law required two years of experience, some 40 hours of schooling, firearms training, and then a test. It was going to be quite an undertaking, but because Allison had been an investigator for the State of Florida, her experience counted for the two years. This left the schooling and firearms training. The idea of taking out some of her aggression at the shooting range seemed appealing.

There were almost 7000 registered private investigators in Florida, meaning there were probably quite a few schools offering the certification. Allison typed in a few keys on her laptop as she sat curled up on the sofa. "Bingo. Oh look, I can apply online.

Done and done." She sat back and admired her accomplishment. "Somehow, I think that was the easy part."

———

SOMETHING ABOUT WHAT CHARLIE HAD SAID DURING DINNER last night tickled the back of Allison's mind. She wondered how Davis Cantrell and her own boss had been placed under such intense scrutiny after only a day. It was as though a little bird whispered in the ear of upper management singing a tune of possible corruption at the Bureau. Outside of Charlie, there was only one other person who Allison had made the slightest mention in passing about Cantrell and that was Shane Sullivan.

"Morning." Allison sauntered to Shane's desk with an astute air and sat down as though this was her second home. "I saw Charlie last night." She crossed her legs and threw her arm over the back of the chair.

"Good morning to you too. How's she doing without you at the shop to keep her company?" Shane leaned back in his chair and laced his fingers behind his head.

"Holding her own."

"I wouldn't expect anything different. So, are you here to collect on the favor?"

"I am, but first I need you to be honest with me."

"Have you known me to lie to you, Allison?"

"No. You are anything but a liar. So I'll start this off differently. I want to thank you for whatever it was you did to get the ball rolling on exposing Davis Cantrell."

"Me? I didn't do anything."

Allison cocked her head. "Sure you did. You're the only one with any authority who I told about it. I mentioned it to Leo but what is a high school baseball coach going to do?"

"Leo, huh? How is the old man? *Ex* - old man. Why he ever let you go..." Shane trailed off.

Allison's cheeks flushed a pale shade of pink. Shane was 8 years her junior and as a handsome man, the compliment was flattering. But Shane Sullivan couldn't be trusted not to break a heart. It might take him a while, but he'd get around to it eventually. "He's fine. And letting me go wasn't his choice, it was mine. Regardless, he doesn't have your connections, so how did you do it?"

Shane's eyes darted back and forth, and he leaned in to whisper, "A magician never reveals his secrets."

Allison drew back in laughter. "Okay, Shane. If you say so." When the laughter between them faded, she pressed on. "I guess if you're going to stonewall me, then I'll just say a heartfelt thank you and move on. As far as taking you up on the offer, absolutely. I can use all the help I can get."

"I'll steer you in the right direction and do anything I can to help. We're friends, right?" He checked the time on his phone. "Listen, I have a briefing I have to get to. Something about some counterfeit Louis Vuitton bags coming into port or some boring shit like that." He pushed off his chair. "I can't wait to get into the real deal. Grand Larceny, murder."

"Ah yes, murder. That is something to look forward to." She stood. "Send over anything you have. I'll be sure to find a way to thank you." Allison started into the lobby.

"Dinner next week would be a good start." He raised his voice as she shrank in the distance.

"We'll see." She shouted back.

Allison returned to her car, which she had now dubbed the sweatbox, and started the engine. Just as she pulled the gearshift into reverse, her phone rang. "Hang on." She pushed it back into

Park and answered the call. "Milo. Hey, I was just thinking about you."

"Good things, I hope," he replied.

"Always. Listen, about what you said yesterday...I decided it's the right move. So if you know of anyone..."

"Actually, that's why I called. I put out some feelers after you left figuring I knew you well enough to know which way you'd lean."

"You do know me well, Milo," she added.

"Indeed. So, I reached out to an old friend of mine. We worked on a case a couple of years back and have tossed tidbits to each other ever since. He needs a hand, someone who can think on their feet if you're interested."

"I do tend to make it up as I go along but yes, absolutely. I would be forever grateful for the opportunity." Allison tapped the steering wheel and silently mouthed, "Yes!"

"Great. I'll text you his information. His name is Tommy Boyce. He's a salty old dog, but he knows a thing or two. Just remember he's old school and you'll be fine."

"Oh Milo, I can't thank you enough."

"Thank me when he pays you by buying me a beer."

"You got it."

"I'll send it to you now, Allison. Let me know if you have any trouble getting hold of him. But I don't think you will. He's one of the good ones, I promise you. We'll talk soon, kid."

She always smiled when he called her kid considering they were only a few years apart. "Thanks, Milo. Talk soon." She ended the call and waited for the text message to come through.

When the message appeared, there wasn't a chance Allison was going to wait and play hard to get. She was going to seize this opportunity.

————

THE HASTY ARRANGEMENT WAS AGREED TO BY THE NO-nonsense Tommy Boyce. And when the afternoon rolled in, Allison prepared to meet with him at The Sail, a laid-back local bar off the Hillsborough Bay. On her arrival, Allison locked the car with the secret prayer that someone might steal it so she could collect the insurance money. The momentary fantasy played out and she entered the bar where a large sunburst mirror was fixed to the wall. She'd been on the go since this morning and catching sight of her appearance left her somewhat repulsed. "Good Lord." Allison smoothed the frayed sprigs of hair that had fallen from her bun.

"Good afternoon, ma'am. How many?" The bright and exces-sively perky young woman batted her eyes.

Allison pulled away from the mirror and walked toward the hostess. "I'm here to meet a gentleman by the name of Tommy Boyce. Has anyone...?"

"Yes, ma'am. He's expecting you. Right this way please." The woman bounded from behind the podium and led Allison to a bartop table under the outdoor patio.

"Thank you," she replied before turning her attention to the man who wasn't exactly as she had imagined. "Mr. Boyce?"

"You must be Allison Hart." He raised from his stool and offered his hand. "Call me Tommy."

With a throaty pitch and pockmarked face, Boyce looked the part. But there was something behind his eyes that separated him from the stereotypical. He looked pained, heartbroken. No sign of this salty dog Milo had warned her about.

"Tommy." She returned the greeting and sat down at the table. "You can call me Allison. I appreciate you clearing some time to meet on short notice."

"Nash mentioned you were itching to get going. I'm happy to oblige. And in all honesty, your timing couldn't be better." Tommy sucked on a fat cigar. "You don't mind, do you? Hardly any places around here let you smoke even outside. These guys take pity on me and look the other way when it's slow."

"Doesn't bother me at all. I am anxious to learn about the business. I don't know if Milo mentioned to you my background."

"He gave me a quick rundown. Pretty impressive. But this is a different ballgame, Allison. In this racket, you won't find people trying to scam the system. Just folks looking to scam each other. But if you know how to handle yourself, you'll do just fine."

The more she listened, the more she believed Milo and Tommy were friends for a reason. They weren't dissimilar. And Tommy seemed like the kind of guy who would give everything so long as he didn't think he was being taken advantage of. She liked him already. "My plan is to get my license and open an agency like yours. Of course, you've been doing this a long time, I don't mean to suggest..."

"I'm not surmising. I get it. But this is no easy gig. It takes hard work, persistence, and thick skin. Speaking of..." He rustled through some files next to him. "Milo told you I needed an extra hand and boy, he was right on the money. So, I think I got something to fuel your fire. You do good for me on this, we'll see if we can generate ourselves an amicable relationship." He handed over a few pieces of paper. "I need someone to check in on this man."

She pulled the papers toward her and slipped on her reading glasses. A picture was paperclipped to the sheets. It was a man, tall, dressed in a suit and tie, and stepping out of a Range Rover. "Who is this?"

"That is Mr. Harlan Goodfellow. But don't let the name fool you. He's no good fellow."

"What'd he do?" She noted Goodfellow's salt and pepper hair, light stubble on his face, and his obvious wealth.

"He's boning his boss's wife."

She deflated all at once. The idea was so cliché. A private investigator trying to catch a cheating spouse.

"This should be right up your alley unless Milo has led me astray," Tommy added.

Allison wasn't easily offended, but the statement seemed to be a loosely phrased personal attack. "I pursued fraudulent claims for the state. I didn't take pictures of adulterers and their liaisons."

Tommy Boyce doused his cigar in a glass of water and set it on a cocktail napkin. The wet tobacco smelled like scorched earth. He captured Allison's gaze with his eyes that were set wide apart from his globular nose. "Look Ms. Hart, I understand that you want to be in the trenches, but ma'am those trenches are lined with double-dealing spouses. It's my bread and butter. There's nothing glitzy about this job. It's dirty and reeks of human misery, and it's better if you understand that right off the bat. This is what I can give you right now. I'm working on some other stuff, sure, but nothing I can hand over to you, someone who isn't even licensed yet. I thought you wanted work. I'm willing to pay you. Take it or leave it."

Allison reevaluated her options and turning down money wasn't one of them. If this was her chosen field, cherry-picking assignments was a pipedream. And if she wanted the respect of others in the business like Boyce, maybe this was the only way to do it. "Okay. I'll take it. I can handle this. Do you have a daily planner or anything that will tell me where I can find Mr. Goodfellow?"

"In fact, I have a comprehensive schedule. Glad to have you on board, Ms. Hart."

4

If Allison ever had the desire to recall what it was like being 19 again and taking a job fetching coffee every morning, this assignment was it. Aside from the fact that she couldn't even see 19 in her rearview anymore. But everyone had to start somewhere, regardless of age. Her reputation, one she hadn't built yet, was on the line. Not to mention she couldn't afford to turn it down.

The paperwork of the alleged cheating spouse and Mr. Goodfellow rested on the passenger seat of her car as she drove home. Tommy Boyce had given her the intel to get the evidence and take it back to his client, a wealthy CEO.

And there was no time like the present. The rendezvous was happening tonight. Allison's plan was to stake out Goodfellow's apartment where the wife was scheduled to arrive, get the obligatory pictures, and then job done. She would take the photos to Boyce and get her first freelancing check in the process.

This should have felt like old hat to Allison. She'd stalked the homes of plenty of scammers, but this was personal no matter how hard she tried to remain objective. If she was going to be any good at this, painting her targets with the same broad strokes as she painted her life experiences was out of the question.

Allison walked inside the house.

"You're home." Nolan sat on the sofa, ramming a sub sandwich in his mouth.

"And so are you." She set her keys on the side table. "Why aren't you at practice?"

"Canceled. Coach said the field was too wet from the storms earlier." He chased down the sandwich with a Big Gulp. "I know we talked about dinner, sorry. I should've picked you up a sandwich..."

"Don't worry about it. I have to leave soon anyway. Just came in for a quick change and I'll grab a small bite." Allison started into the hall toward her room.

"Where are you off to now?" Nolan said as he leaned over to make his voice carry.

"I have a gig."

"A what?" he shouted.

"I'll tell you later if it all works out." Allison made it to her room and closed her bedroom door. She dropped to the bed with the file in her hands and stared at it. "Harlan Goodfellow. Probably not a good idea to put your pen in the company ink. Especially when that ink belongs to the boss."

She stood again and pulled off her pale blue capped-sleeve shirt. From the third drawer in her dresser, Allison retrieved a black shirt with a high neckline and a pair of black shorts. It was too hot for long pants, but the dark clothes would help serve as camouflage.

Her master bathroom was only steps away and she stood in front of the mirror, pulling the elastic band from her hair and the several bobby pins that helped hold the large full bun in place.

Tonight, she would wear it down and tuck it beneath a black base-ball cap that would help her blend in with the night.

She returned to the living room where Nolan had polished off his footlong sub and was slurping down the rest of his giant soda.

"Are you starting a cat burglar business?" He eyed her attire. "What's with all the black?"

"I'm going on a stakeout."

"Wait, what? I thought you quit your job and it's like, what, 7 o'clock at night?"

Allison sat down next to him. "I wanted to tell you this last night, but since you got home at one in the morning..." She paused for effect and when that failed, she continued, "I didn't get the chance and you had school this morning."

"I'm here now. What's going on, Mom?" Nolan asked.

"I've decided to go out on my own. Start my own business. I'm going to get my P.I. license."

Nolan chuckled and tilted his head. "You're going to be a private dick?"

"Really? That's what you want to say to your mother? I can still swat your behind. Don't test me, son."

He held up his hands and laughed harder.

"Are you finished?"

Nolan cleared his throat. "Sorry. Please, go ahead. You want to become a private investigator. I think it's great. What does Dad think?"

"I haven't told him I committed just yet, but I will. I ran it past him, not that I had to, of course. He's supportive."

"And what about, you know." Nolan cast down his sights. "Like what about money and stuff?"

"Well, that's why I'm wearing this. I'm working as an independent consultant for a P.I. in the city. He gave me a job and the money will help tide us over until I can get another job and then another. And eventually, get my license."

Nolan held her gaze. "I think it's great, Mom. I'm proud of you. I know how hard it was when you and Dad got divorced. But you got a job, ran the house just as you always did. And now this. I'm lucky to have you for a mom."

Allison's eyes turned watery. "Well." She cleared her throat and patted his knee. "I better get out there and earn some money. You'll be okay on your own?"

A tsk rolled off his tongue followed by an exaggerated eye roll.

"Sorry. I forgot. You're an adult now." Allison grabbed her car keys and started toward the door. "I don't know how long I'll be, but I'll text you when I'm on my way home."

"Okay, Mom. Be careful. Love you."

"Love you, too, baby." Allison walked through the front door and wiped a rogue tear from her cheek. She clicked the remote to open the car door and stepped inside. "I raised a good kid."

———

THE ADDRESS OF THE APARTMENT LAY ON TOP OF THE paperwork in the passenger seat and Allison glanced at it to double-check it against her phone's map. "This looks like the place." She knew the area, Channelside. An expensive place to live, but she already deduced that Goodfellow must have had money that came with his executive job. And the perks of screwing the boss's wife. She pulled to a stop about 50 yards away from the entrance to the high-rise building adjacent to the Hillsborough Bay. The building didn't have a waterside view but was only a stone's throw away from the cruise port. Fortunately, it was a populated area with several cars parked alongside the road. She didn't stand out unless one was looking for the crappiest car on the block.

Allison rolled down her window and cut the engine. Based on the information in the file, Harlan Goodfellow was due home any minute. And, according to the client, his wife had said she was going out with her girlfriends. The idea was to catch the wife arriving, snap a couple of photos then use her telephoto lens and hope for some shots of the happy couple in Goodfellow's apartment. The unknown variable was whether he liked to keep open his curtains. She could get definitive, if not racy, pictures if he did.

Allison bided her time with the distraction of social media, which she'd only recently begun to use. She struggled to see the point of it all. It was filled with people feigning perfection and happiness. Well, not everyone did that, and probably not the ones she friended. Mainly because she was actually friends with them, not some weird virtual online friend thing. Anyway, nothing special to report in the world of Facebook. She returned her phone to the center console and grabbed a nearby bottle of water, downing a large gulp. Allison pulled back the bottle and recalled her weak bladder. "Better ration this."

The time had arrived that Goodfellow should have been pulling into his parking garage. "Come on, guy. I don't have all night." Her eyes narrowed at a car that had just turned the corner. She shuffled the papers to confirm her suspicions. "Range Rover, black. Gotcha. Now just pull on into the garage and we are golden." She watched closely while the luxury SUV slowed to make the turn. "Yes! Now where is your little girlfriend, Mr. Goodfellow?" Allison eyed Goodfellow's sixth-floor apartment and waited to see a light in the window just to be sure it had been him in the car. Her eyes raised and fixed on the sliding glass door of the unit. "Turn on a light so I know you're home, Mr. Goodfellow." She waited, inhaling a deep breath. And then it happened. "Perfect."

But this was only the beginning. She needed Mrs. CEO to arrive and according to the file, the woman drove a white Lexus convertible. Allison waited; her eyes glued to the street ahead, just itching for that Lexus to arrive.

After a few minutes, her initial excitement waned. "Maybe she was telling the truth." Allison returned her sights to the paperwork and reviewed the car's description just to be sure. Headlights soon shone through her windshield and caught her attention. Allison tensed up and her eyes locked on a small car. "Hold up. A white Lexus?" She squinted to see past the bright headlights. "And check."

The car pulled into the same parking garage and now Allison had to prepare to ensnare her targets. She reached into the back seat for the expensive camera and telephoto lens that would allow her to capture all the action from that distance. It had been an investment made during her time with Fraud Investigations. A worthwhile investment it now seemed.

With her lens trained on Goodfellow's apartment, Allison waited for her chance. Her arms were growing tired and she rested her elbows on the edge of the driver's side door.

The sweat from under her breasts formed a ring through the bra and now appeared on her shirt. She looked down for a moment. "Great. I look like I'm lactating."

The sliding glass door leading to the balcony opened and Allison jumped to attention at the movement. She refocused her lens and a moment later, Goodfellow, and who she believed was Mrs. CEO appeared, her actual name wasn't in the file. Boyce had opted to keep his client's name private. Not that it mattered. She didn't care who these people were, just that Karma was about to pay them a visit.

The two walked onto the balcony holding drinks and rested their forearms on the rail. Allison used the rapid photo setting and snapped at least fifty shots in a matter of seconds. She'd hoped to catch them in an embrace or kissing or something meaningful. So far, they stood about a foot apart from one another. It appeared they were engaged in conversation and Allison captured each one smiling. That was a good sign. She had fully expected clothes to be ripped from one another immediately, but then that was how she imagined it had been with Leo and that girl. It was six years ago and yet it still felt like yesterday. The mind had a funny way of making a person imagine the worst.

The notion that compromising photos weren't in the cards for tonight was growing increasingly certain. Goodfellow turned back and opened the glass doors before they both walked inside.

Allison could still see light through the curtains, but there wasn't a chance she'd get anything more detailed. Not unless he opened them.

She lowered the camera and stared at the balcony. Her eyes shifted from every window in her purview until she reached the inevitable conclusion. "I'm not going to get anymore tonight." Allison laid down the camera on the passenger seat and turned the ignition. She glanced at the unit one last time to be sure all bases were covered.

A flash of light exploded behind the curtain. Then another. "Oh my God." It was the briefest of flashes, like a... "A gunshot." Allison's heart jumped into her throat. Her pulse raced and her eyes scanned about wildly in search of more flashes or movement or anything. But everything became eerily still.

Allison fixed her gaze on the windows of Goodfellow's apartment. "No." She gasped for breath. Someone was alive in there and had just turned off the lights. She swallowed hard and turned to the parking garage.

The echo of screeching tires from inside the garage pierced her ears before wafting out onto the street. She scrambled for her camera again, aiming it at the garage's exit. A silver sedan cut through the echo of the burning rubber. She snapped as many pictures as she could, following the vehicle as it veered right onto the road. "Oh shit." It was coming right at her. She tossed the camera into the back and crouched low, pulling down on her ballcap. "Damn it. I need the plate." It was too risky. The driver would see her. Allison had a family to think about. She eyed her glovebox where she kept her gun.

The rush of air the silver sedan kicked up as it passed by rocked her compact car. Allison shut her eyes praying it would keep on going and that she hadn't been spotted. The gravely whirl of its engine faded and Allison slowly raised again. The road was clear. The shooter was gone. She'd blown it.

Allison reached for her phone and dialed 911. "Yes, I'd like to report gunshots at the Cabana Apartments in Channelside." She listened. "I don't know if anyone's hurt. I only heard the shots. Please, come fast." She ended the call and pulled fully upright. Her sights turned to the balcony. The apartment was dark and all Allison had were some photos on her camera. But were Harlan Goodfellow and Mrs. CEO still alive in there?

5

The application for a private investigator license would include the question, *have you ever committed a felony?* Allison wondered if fleeing the scene of a murder counted as one. Probably so. The engine ran, her hands gripped the wheel and she was paralyzed. But when the wail of sirens filled the street, her instincts kicked in. The cops were coming. They might be interested in knowing why she had been sitting outside the building with a telephoto lens trained on the victim's apartment. There wasn't a single reasonable explanation she could muster. *"Yes, Officer, I was taking photos of the victims. I can't tell you why, you understand."* She would find herself sitting in a jail cell with an answer like that. Her first night as a freelance private eye, Allison had to keep her head above water, or at the very least, keep out of jail.

People spilled out of their apartment buildings standing around in bewilderment. Her window to bolt undetected was closing fast. She rolled away from the curb without turning on the headlights and continued along the frontage road until making her way to a turning. Beyond that turning, Allison would be in the clear but behind her, red and blue lights flashed.

"I have to see Boyce." She reached for her phone and dialed, praying he would answer. "Come on. You sent me out here, buddy. Put down your cigar and answer the call." But it rang through to voicemail. "Damn it." She didn't know where he lived but knew where his office was. There was only a slim chance he would be there, but it was a chance she had to take.

Not knowing whether Goodfellow and his mistress were dead devoured her every thought as she drove through town and headed toward Boyce's office. The idea of contacting Shane crossed her mind more than once. He didn't work Homicide, but he might know what had happened. "No. Just wait. Don't panic."

Boyce's office was situated in a strip mall in a questionable neighborhood and Allison had just arrived. It was after 10 pm and the eye doctor, vape shop, and nail salon that surrounded his office were closed. The entire building was dark. She pulled into a parking space that fronted his unit and stepped out of her car. Allison hurried to the building with the distinct feeling of being watched. On her approach, it was clear something was wrong. She slowed her steps, casting her sights left, then right. The door had been jimmied. She peered through the glass and while it was dark inside, there was no question someone had broken in. A sensible person would've run away but Allison didn't have her senses about her at the moment.

Whatever she thought she knew about the life of a P.I. had just flown out the window. And if Allison crossed the line, there might be no turning back. She stood in front of the office; the glass door was cracked likely from the crowbar used to pry it open. There was no choice. Not if she wanted to do the right thing. Allison walked inside.

If an alarm had sounded, it no longer did and since no cops had roared into the parking lot, she figured they weren't going to now. Allison needed proof and a lot of it. Proof as to what in the hell she'd stepped into. At the very least, Boyce's home address was probably in this place somewhere. She could go to his home and tell him what had happened. All of this was under the assumption Boyce was still alive. And despite her current surroundings, she refused to allow any other option to enter her mind. Since she was making assumptions, she assumed Boyce was smart enough to know if someone might have been after him. He was a private investigator and had probably helped to put away some bad guys. Maybe one had come back. Or maybe this was all tied to Harlan Goodfellow.

She used the light on her phone to guide her through the small office. It had been turned upside down. Papers were strewn around, chairs overturned, computers broken on the floor. The perpetrators had been thorough. If they wanted to scare Boyce, this would send a fairly compelling message.

Allison came across a row of filing cabinets in the back that appeared untouched, which made her think this incident was more of a warning than a search for something Boyce might have in his possession. Her first thought was to look for the corporate papers. They would most likely contain Boyce's home address.

She opened the drawers and discovered mostly closed case files. "Come on. Where's your address." Her fingers worked fast to thumb through the tabs, but nothing. She was onto the next drawer.

The entire parking lot of the strip mall was empty except for her blue Honda. It needed to stay that way. Evidence could mount against her considering she fled the scene of a crime and entered a place that had been ransacked. It was damning enough to raise the eyebrows of overzealous detectives. And coupled with the shooting, it would firmly put her in the number one spot for suspect of the day.

"Got it!" She ripped the file from the drawer and eyed the papers. "This is it." Allison took a picture of Boyce's address and returned the file.

The first rule of being a good investigator was to leave nothing behind. Allison walked to a kitchenette and yanked several paper towels from a holder. With meticulous steps, she wiped down everything she had touched until working her way back toward the entrance.

A final wipe down of the door frame and Allison was back outside heading to her car. Next stop—Tommy Boyce's house.

———

It was well beyond Allison's bedtime to be sure. She was exhausted from the adrenaline that had exploded in her veins and the life-altering decision she had made to leave Channelside. Now, as she arrived at the home of the man who had given her this assignment, she second-guessed herself. What if his family was there and she scared the pants off them by showing up so late at night? "I'll try again." She called his number and hoped for the best. The line rang while she peered at the front door of the house. When the voicemail message began again, Allison hung up. "Well, this can't wait any longer." She tugged on the car door handle ready to open it when her phone rang. The screen lit up and she immediately answered. "Shane? Oh my God, I can't tell you how glad I am to hear from you. Listen..."

He cut her off. "Allison, where are you?"

She hesitated. "Um, in New Tampa."

"You need to come down to the station."

This didn't sound like the same man who joked about staring

at her ass only a day ago. "Shane, what's wrong?" As if she didn't already know the answer.

"Where were you around 9 pm tonight?" he asked.

Her heart skipped. "Are you asking because you don't know or are you asking for confirmation?"

"This is serious, Allison. Where were you earlier tonight?"

She unleashed a deep sigh. "I was in Channelside. Can you please tell me what's going on? You're scaring me."

"I should be asking you the same thing. They traced the 911 call back to you, Allison."

The 911 call she made in front of Goodfellow's apartment building. In her attempt to do the right thing and inform the police, she'd put herself at the scene and identified her as the one to alert the authorities before anyone else.

"You need to come in. Now. I need to know everything before you talk to the detective in charge."

"Are they both dead?" she asked.

"They're dead. The sooner I know what happened the better I can help you." Shane ended the call.

Allison couldn't move, couldn't breathe. How had this all gone so horribly wrong? And now she was sitting in front of the home of the man who sent her to that apartment in Channelside. His office had been ransacked. He wasn't answering his phone. She had no other way to reach him except to knock on that door right now. Tommy Boyce might be the only person who could clear up all of this.

Her mouth was dry and the rest of her was drenched in sweat from the muggy night air. Allison stepped out of her car and approached the home. No porch light burned. No lights were on inside. She would awaken everyone in that house, but the hope that Boyce could help and especially now with Shane demanding she go to the station, Allison needed information.

Allison rapped gently on the door. A moment later, she tried again, a little louder this time. Finally, a faint light shone from behind the closed blinds in the front window. Locks on the door were being unlatched. It opened a fraction of an inch.

"Yes?"

Allison spotted the face of a young woman, a teenager maybe. "My name is Allison Hart. I'm looking for Mr. Boyce. I work for him."

"My dad's not here," the girl said.

"Do you know where he's at? I tried his phone but he's not answering."

"I'm sorry. I don't know where he is. He said he was working late tonight."

"Of course. I'm so sorry to bother you. If you see him, could you tell him I stopped by? It's important I speak to him as soon as possible."

"What was your name again?" the girl asked.

"Allison Hart." She reached into her bag and grabbed an old business card and with a pen, she scribbled on it. "Here's my number."

"Okay. I'll tell him." She slowly closed the door.

Allison stood on the porch as though Boyce would somehow open the door and reveal answers to all her questions. But that wasn't going to happen. She had no choice except to go to the station and see Shane. How he knew about any of this she had no idea but then he was chummy with the other detectives as he tried to work his way up the ranks. Regardless, Allison needed help and Shane was offering.

———

THE LIGHTS OF THE DOWNTOWN TAMPA POLICE STATION shone brightly against the skyline. Most of the high-rise office buildings were nearer to the bay and channel. This was only one of several stations dotted throughout the city and was nearest to the courthouse. That was how Allison met Shane "Sully" Sullivan. The fraud cases she exposed sometimes required her to attend court hearings for the offenders. Shane was still a beat cop the day Allison met him.

It was about a year after her divorce when she had really buried herself in her work. It kept her mind occupied and her dedication brought promotions quicker than others in her field.

A case was due to be heard in front of a judge and Allison walked in dressed in a knee-length skirt and black stilettos, donning one of her now-signature sleeveless button-down blouses. She was about to enter the courtroom when a younger man approached in his uniform.

"Excuse me, Miss."

She had stopped and turned to see this young cop and at first glance felt a bolt of electricity. "Yes?" She noticed he held in his hand a folded piece of paper.

"Is this yours?" he had asked.

She glanced at it and recognized the handwriting on the paper to be hers. "Yes, it is. Thank you." It was a good thing he'd picked it up. The paper had written on it a sum of money the claimant had defrauded from the state as well as personal information on the individual.

"Any time." He offered his hand. "I'm Officer Shane Sullivan. People call me Sully."

"Allison Hart. Nice to meet you." She returned the greeting.

And they became fast friends after that. The spark of electricity she had felt that day was fleeting. Allison had come off a painful divorce and was in no mood to date again regardless of the fact that he had asked her several times. Eventually, he realized she would always reject him and he gave up. Their friendship was important to her and over the past few years, they'd helped each other out with various cases. She now regarded Shane as a close friend. And if he was telling her she needed to get with him so he could help, then this was probably more serious than she knew.

Allison walked inside the station and spotted Shane at the front desk. He appeared stone-faced and as though he'd been waiting for her arrival. "Hi."

Shane took her by the arm not forcefully but not gently either. "Let's go to one of the interview rooms. We don't have long to talk." He turned on his heel and started back.

"Are you going to record me or something?" Allison knew where they were going. The interrogation rooms had cameras and recorded everything.

"No. I just need someplace private. Unless you want to talk about this at my desk in the bullpen?"

Several officers and detectives scurried around the bullpen. It was the last place she would want to have this conversation. "No."

Shane opened a metal door. "Get inside."

Allison walked in and waited for Shane to turn on the lights and close the door. "Please tell me what's happening. Things transpired tonight and I don't know what to do."

"No shit." He sat down at the table. "Tell me everything."

Allison filled him in on nearly all of it. But she left out the one detail that could get her into real trouble. And she would leave out that part until she learned more about what happened to Tommy Boyce and where he was right now.

"Well, the good news is that you didn't kill those people," he said dryly.

"Not this time." Her need to deliver a sardonic retort was what

Shane would've come to expect but it surprised Allison. "Shane, am I in trouble here?"

"I don't know. I assume you have pictures. Where's your camera?"

"Right here." Allison reached into her carrier bag. "I haven't looked at the images. I don't know what I captured yet."

"That's probably what's going to save your ass. But we need to find Boyce so he can back you up. You mentioned you saw a car race out of the parking garage of the building. Do you happen to remember the make and model? And if you got a plate..."

"It was dark and I'll be honest, I was scared out of my mind. I did have sense enough to get pictures of it until it started coming toward me. Then I pushed into my seat and prayed whoever was driving hadn't seen me," she replied.

"Probably the smartest thing you did all night. You might not be here if the driver saw you."

"Whatever I captured; you'll find on here." Allison turned on the digital screen of her camera and opened the files of the pictures from earlier tonight. "Start from here."

Shane reviewed the images. "It's a sedan. Silver. Looks like..." He shook his head. "I don't know. You must've been shaking. I can't tell exactly but it could be a Mercedes." He looked at her. "We'll need to have our forensics team see if they can get any better detail."

"How did you find out about this?" she asked. "Homicide isn't your department."

"I was finishing up a report, a detective returned and started talking about the incident, and how 911 traced the cell phone to you."

"He knew my name?"

"Oh yeah. As soon as I heard 'Allison Hart,' my ears perked up. That's when I figured I needed to get to you first and get the whole story. Those Homicide guys will do what it takes to get answers and they won't be nice about it. They don't like private investigators much."

"None of this should've happened, Shane. I was there to catch a cheater. Nothing more."

"And now you're knee-deep in it, Allison. Look, I'm here for you, okay? This will all be sorted out and you'll be able to go home soon."

"What about Tommy Boyce?"

"He'll have to worry about himself right now."

6

Detective Francisco Montoya was in charge of the investigation into the murder of Harlan Goodfellow and Mrs. Tracy Diaz. She was the wife of Carlos Diaz, one of Tampa's wealthiest real estate investors and CEO of a development firm. According to Montoya, Goodfellow was the CFO at that same firm. It was clear to Allison now how the two lovebirds had met.

Her story checked out. Allison handed over her camera's SD card as well as the file Boyce had given her on Goodfellow. The obvious suspect appeared to be Carlos Diaz. They always suspected the husband. Nevertheless, Allison had been dismissed. She was not going to be a part of this investigation.

"So I can leave now?" It was almost two in the morning and Allison was worn out.

"Yes, ma'am. You can go. I hope we can count on your continued cooperation should we need anything further," Montoya said.

"Of course. Anything you need. You have my details."

Montoya nodded to Shane. "Thanks for your help on this, man."

"You got it. I'm going to show out Ms. Hart." Shane pushed off the corner of the desk. "You ready to go?" He eyed her.

"Yes." Allison stood and retrieved her bag. "Goodbye, Detective Montoya." And as she started to follow Shane, Montoya called on her again.

"Ms. Hart?"

"Yes?"

"Maybe next time, leave the detective work to the professionals."

Shane stopped cold as Allison turned deadpan. "Come on. Let's get you out of here." He led her out into the lobby. "Don't listen to him. He's just stressed because he's got a double homicide on his plate. You were doing your job. Nothing more."

"Sure. My job." Allison followed him through the doors. The air had grown cool in the early hours and the black sky was clear enough to see a few stars. She reached her car. "What happens now?"

He freed an exhaustive breath. "Nothing. You've done your part. It's up to those guys now." He thumbed back toward the building.

"What about Boyce? I have to talk to him." She pressed the remote to open her car door. "I don't care what that detective has to say, I'm going to find him. He wouldn't have sent me there last night if he had any inclination..."

"You have a point. Two people are dead. Look, Allison, I know what you're like. You're very good at what you do but Montoya's right."

"You think I should let the professionals do their jobs too?"

"That's not what I mean."

She folded her arms. "Then please, enlighten me."

"Whatever is happening here is obviously dangerous. I think it's more than you might've bargained for. If Boyce did something, the cops will find out about it."

"Since when do you shy away from anything?" she asked.

"I'm not shying away. Besides, this isn't my case. I'm trying to protect you."

Allison pulled open her car door. "I appreciate what you've done but I don't need protecting." She stepped inside and turned the engine. "You wanna help, great. Otherwise, I'll do what I need to do." She pressed her foot on the gas pedal while the car was still in park, making the engine roar, as much as the four-cylinder engine could. It was enough to give him the hint to take a step back.

Shane stepped away and Allison zipped out of the parking lot.

———

DAWN WAS ONLY A COUPLE OF HOURS AWAY AND ALLISON stood on her front porch, fumbling for the key to the house. The door opened before she could insert it. Nolan stood on the other side.

"What are you still doing up?" she asked.

"I could ask the same thing about you." He stepped aside to let her in. "I was about to call the cops, you know."

"It wouldn't have mattered. I was already with them." Allison walked in and dropped her bag and keys on the side table.

"What do you mean you were with the cops?" Nolan trailed her to the living room. "Mom, what happened? Are you okay?"

She sat down on the couch and raised her hands. "I'm fine. Some stuff happened tonight. Things I wasn't expecting, and I got caught up in something."

"Things, stuff, something. What are you talking about? Mom, please, tell me what happened."

"You know I was given a job by a P.I."

"Yeah." He sat down next to her.

"I was doing my thing. Taking pictures, whatever. Then... You know, honey, I don't need to burden you with this."

"I'm all grown up now, Mom. You can tell me the truth. Please don't lie thinking you're protecting me," Nolan replied.

"You really aren't a kid anymore. Okay. The job was for me to catch a guy cheating on his wife."

Nolan glanced away. He'd discovered all on his own what his father had done that destroyed their family. He overheard something his father had said and that was how he knew. And it looked as though the wound hadn't healed.

"Anyway." She tried to brush away the moment. "I was doing my thing and well, there were gunshots."

"What?"

"Let me finish." She took in a breath. "The people I was watching were murdered. I didn't see who did it, only the flashes of light from behind a curtain in the apartment I was watching. Then a car squealed out of the parking garage and I tried to get pictures of it. The cops are handling it now, that's the important part. I was with them giving a statement."

"And that's it? You're out of it now, right? Not your problem?" Nolan asked.

"Not my problem anymore. So you see, everything is fine. You can go to sleep now. That's where I'm headed." She stood up but Nolan gripped her arm.

"Mom. You're sure that's it? There's nothing else?"

She held his gaze knowing full well that Tommy Boyce had yet to be tracked down. "Nothing else. Goodnight, sweetheart."

"Goodnight, Mom."

———

LIGHT SPILLED INTO ALLISON'S BEDROOM. A NEW DAY arrived and yet the day before had played on a continuous loop and denied her sleep. The echoes of gunfire and thoughts of Tommy Boyce's whereabouts swirled.

Allison had led a sheltered life up to now. A stay-at-home mom for twenty years, working for the state in fraud investigations for the past five years. Being the only witness to a double murder? Not on her bucket list. But she wouldn't take this lying down, literally or figuratively.

Allison tossed her legs over the bed and sat upright. Glancing at the alarm clock on her bedside table, she noticed it was barely 6 am. Nolan would still be asleep, so she stood quietly from her bed and padded into the kitchen.

She brewed a pot of coffee and while it finished, she retrieved her phone from the living room. A text message had arrived from an unrecognized number. Allison returned to the kitchen and rested her elbows on the island countertop, swiping open the message.

"I haven't seen my dad. Can you help?" the message read.

Allison pulled upright again, re-reading it as though she hadn't understood it the first time. It was Boyce's daughter. She had given her a business card from her job at the state and had written her personal number on it. The message was sent over an hour ago. But why contact Allison about this? The girl must've had other family, Boyce's friends, or work colleagues.

Allison typed her reply. *"I can try to help. Do you have other family?"* The coffee maker finished and she poured herself a cup when the phone buzzed with another incoming message. Allison rushed to it, and a few drops of coffee splashed over the cup's edge and onto her shirt. "Damn it." She placed the mug on the counter and swiped a paper towel to blot away the drops, then immediately reached for her phone.

"*My dad's a widower. We don't have any family here,*" the girl had replied.

It never occurred to Allison that Tommy Boyce could've been married or had a child, let alone be a widower who was raising a teenage daughter on his own. Her heart went out to this girl. She didn't even know her name, hadn't bothered asking last night and just felt awful for having intruded.

"*I can come back to your house and we can talk if you want. I don't know your dad well, but he gave me some work and we can probably put our heads together for answers. What's your name?*" Allison pressed send.

"*Lucy. Please come when you can. Thx.*"

It was settled. Allison was going to meet Lucy and get to the bottom of what happened to her dad.

———

THE DRIVE TO BOYCE'S HOME WASN'T LONG ENOUGH TO PULL together a cohesive plan as to where this meeting would lead. Allison was flying by the seat of her pants now. The turn down Boyce's street unnerved her, but she couldn't back out of this one. Lucy Boyce needed to know what happened, at least, as much as Allison knew.

She arrived at the home once again. It looked much different in the light of a new day. Fresh, clean. The fan palms at the entrance swayed gently in the breeze and the grass was a lush green and manicured with care.

Allison stepped out of her car and walked toward the home when the door opened before she made it ten feet onto the pathway. The girl looked younger than she had last night, fragile somehow. She reminded her a little of Micah. There was a resemblance in the eyes. Micah looked almost the same when she learned of her parents' impending divorce. Innocence stolen; heart broken. That was how Lucy Boyce looked now.

"Hi. Thanks for coming." Lucy stepped aside. "Please, come in."

Allison entered. "I'm glad you reached out to me."

"I have some coffee if you want it. Donuts too. They're a day old but still pretty good," Lucy said.

"That'd be great. Thank you." Allison didn't want to refuse the kind offer even if she'd already had three cups of coffee and this fourth would set her nerves on fire. That, along with the sugar rush from the donut, and she was about to be in for quite a ride. "You still haven't heard from your dad?"

Lucy led the way into the kitchen of the modern home. It was much nicer than Allison's house. Boyce had done well for himself.

"No. I guess I was hoping you'd come here with news," Lucy replied.

"I'm sorry. No."

Lucy nodded and reached for a cup in the cabinet. "Cream and sugar?"

"Just cream, thanks." Allison pulled up a stool at the breakfast bar. "Lucy, does your dad usually get called out to work late?"

"Sometimes, but he always tells me when to expect him home." She handed Allison the mug. "I haven't heard from him since yesterday around 5 pm."

"That's about the time I met with him. He did mention he had some work going on, which was why he asked me to cover a quick assignment for him."

"How long have you known my dad?" Lucy sipped on her coffee.

"Honestly? About a day. I met him through a friend. He was

good enough to throw some work my way. I'm sorry. That's probably not what you want to hear."

"I don't know many of the people my dad works with."

"You don't? How long have you lived in the area?"

"About 8 years. My mom passed away two years ago and Dad sort of buried himself in his work. We don't get to spend much time together. I have school at the community college and he has work. But he does his best to keep in contact with me."

Allison was relieved to know that Tommy Boyce seemed to be a good father. "I'm sorry about your mom. That must've been very difficult for you both."

"Yeah. Dad took it pretty hard."

Allison sipped on her coffee and eyed Lucy. "And you too, I imagine. You know, I have a daughter about your age. Her name's Micah. I don't see her much. She goes to FSU."

"Ms. Hart, what can we do to find my dad?"

"Please, call me Allison." She paused for a moment. "Well, I have a few ideas." The thought of telling Lucy about her father's office wasn't appealing. It would only worry the girl even more. "Does your dad keep any of his work files here? Something we can look at that might tell us where he was going last night or who he might have been meeting with?"

Lucy appeared to think about the question. "He does have an office here, but I have no idea what his computer password would be."

Allison nodded. "I see. Well, what about..." an idea began to take shape. "I don't suppose you and your dad have a family locator app on your phones?" She had installed apps on her kids' phones for when they were with their father. Now, she rarely used them and wondered if the kids had deleted them.

"Actually, yeah. Dad's an ex-cop and he doesn't trust anyone.

He said the only way I could get a phone was if he put a tracker on it. I said fine but that he had to have one too."

Allison smiled. "Smart girl."

Lucy retrieved her phone from her back pocket. "I didn't think to check this. I guess I kind of forgot about it till now."

"You've been worried. It's no wonder." Allison waited for Lucy to open the app and take a look at the information. "Anything helpful?"

Lucy peered at her phone, thumbing buttons, zooming in on a map. "According to this, his last registered location was 4562 Channelside Drive. That was at 8:15 last night."

Allison's face drained of color. She knew instantly where that address was because she'd been there last night less than thirty minutes later.

"Do you know that place?" Lucy pressed on.

"Um, no. I know the general location, but it doesn't ring a bell. I could go and check it out if you want. In fact, I'd like to, if you're okay with that."

"Please, yes. If you could do that. I—I could come with you too."

Allison shook her head. "No. No, there's no need for that. I'll tell you what, I'll run down there now and check it out. If he's not there sleeping in his car or something, I have a friend I can see and ask for more help."

"A friend?" Lucy asked.

"A cop." Allison watched as Lucy grew worried. "It's fine. Look, cops are pretty good at finding people and your dad was a cop with Tampa PD anyway, right? I'll bet one of them has heard from him and knows where he is. There's no need for you to worry, Lucy. You said you go to the community college, which one?"

"Hillsborough," she replied.

"My son goes there. His name is Nolan."

"I don't think I know him." Lucy looked at her feet.

"Why don't you go on to school and I'll head over to this address? Then, if all else fails, I'll go and talk to some of the guys who know your dad. Does that sound okay?"

"You'll text me if you find him?"

"I'll do you one better, I'll have him text you himself, okay?"

"Yeah. Okay. Thank you, Ms. Hart."

"It's Allison, remember?" She stood and took a final bite of her donut. "Thanks for breakfast. I'll be in touch very soon, Lucy." She placed her hand on Lucy's arm. "This will all work out. I'm sure your dad just lost track of time or is snoozing away in his car after a long night. Don't worry." Allison started outside and made her way to her car. A final wave to Lucy and she stepped inside, waiting for the girl to close the door.

There was no point in going to that address. She knew what she would find there, a gruesome murder scene. Probably cops and police tape. The question that burned in her mind was why? Why was Tommy Boyce at the very place he'd sent her to stake out? It didn't make sense. She didn't know Tommy Boyce at all. Sure, Milo did, but people always had an agenda. If he had been there, why?

Allison drove away from the home and headed straight to the place she'd left only a few hours earlier, the stationhouse. Shane was going to help her find Tommy Boyce.

7

It was no accident that Allison returned to the station while Detective Montoya was out working the crime scene. He'd made it clear she wasn't to continue pursuing any leads regarding the investigation because, as she recalled, he had said it was better left to the professionals. Allison was a problem-solver and Montoya wasn't going to keep her out of this as long as she had a problem to solve, and that was locating Tommy Boyce.

Allison approached the front desk and caught sight of Shane discussing something that must've been humorous with a young female officer. Before the woman behind the desk could greet her, she interrupted. "I see him."

He noticed her arrival. "Ah, you're back. Good. I've been waiting." Shane turned to the officer. "I'll catch up with you later?"

"Sure." The woman nodded and disappeared into the corridor.

"I hope I didn't interrupt anything," Allison said.

"What? Her? No. Just shooting the breeze," Shane replied.

"Well, as it turns out I could use your help. It's about Boyce."

"Surprise, surprise." Shane pushed off the desk. "Your timing is impeccable, and I have a feeling you intended it that way. Montoya is still at the scene talking to neighbors and building a timeline of events." He started toward his cubicle. "What's on your mind?"

Allison followed him back and the two arrived at his desk. "Tommy Boyce has a daughter. She reached out to me after I made contact with her in the late hours of last night when I needed to find Boyce."

"What did she want?"

"I—um, after what happened, I tried to track down Boyce. I was scared and confused, and I needed to tell him what happened. This was after I made the 911 call, of course."

"Go on," Shane said.

"I knew where Boyce's office was and after my calls to him went unanswered, I drove there. Shane, someone had broken into his office. The door was jimmied. I went inside."

He leaned over his desk. "You went inside? Knowing what had just happened?"

"Yeah. I know it was a risky call."

"Risky? Are you kidding me? Christ, Allison, what were you thinking? Did you leave prints?"

"No. I was careful not to leave a trace. I'm sure of it."

"Funny, you don't sound so sure. If they find evidence you were there, a big shiny spotlight will be sitting right on top of your head."

"They won't find anything. After seeing the state of his office, I assumed it would be better if no one knew I had been there. My point is that someone was looking for something in his office. It all just seems too coincidental for it to have been a run-of-the-mill break-in. I looked for his home address and when I found it in one of the files I drove straight to his house. That's when I met the daughter. It wasn't until after dawn that she texted me and asked for my help because Tommy hadn't returned home. I'm here because I'm swimming in unfamiliar waters, Shane and I promised that girl I would find her dad."

"The first rule of being a good cop is not to promise the families something you might not be able to deliver on."

"Well, as we both know and Montoya so eloquently pointed out, I'm not a cop. There was something positive that came out of my meeting with her."

"Thank God for small miracles. What is it?" Shane asked.

"Her name is Lucy and both she and her dad had a locator app on their phones. According to his last known location, which she clocked at around 8:15 pm, so before the shooting, was Goodfellow's apartment building."

"I'm sorry, did you say that was good news because what I just heard was that Tommy was at the scene of the crime 45 minutes before two people were gunned down."

"It isn't good news in the traditional sense," Allison replied.

"Then please tell me how this is good news at all?"

"I take it to mean he might've been confirming I would show up. You know, checking that I was going to do the job he hired me to do. Then when he realized I was there, he probably left."

"Okay. Where did he go after that? Why was that his last known location?"

"That's why I'm here. I don't know how to track him down and I was thinking maybe you could check the activity on his phone after 8:15. Calls, texts, anything that might tell us where he went later in the evening."

"First of all, this isn't my case. I have no authority to do what you're asking. That would be up to Montoya."

"I can't go to him. He doesn't like me. But you can. You can tell him about Lucy, and she can provide details about Tommy's phone and the app. He'll want to pull records after that, I'm sure."

"That's a possibility. To be honest, she's probably on his list of people to talk to already. Same as her dad. He was hired by the husband, that much is known. Look, Allison, these things take time. I understand you want to jump in and help this girl, but you can't. We are at the mercy of Montoya's investigation. I'll go to him and mention this. But it will be up to him to follow through on it," Shane said.

"Thank you. In the meantime, I'll figure out another approach. Regardless of whether I should or shouldn't have promised that girl help, the fact is, I did. And I won't let her down."

———

MARJORIE PARK MARINA WAS LOCATED NEAR THE CHANNEL district along with other smaller marinas and a nearby yacht club. Randy Newsome had taken off the day from work to take his son on a boating trip.

The seas were a little choppy after the passing of a weak tropical storm and when Randy double-checked his location, the screen on the GPS went black. "What the...?" He flipped the switches to reset it. Nothing. "Come on now." Randy tapped on the screen and still nothing. The 35-year-old father looked at his son who sat in the bow. "Hey buddy, I'm having trouble with the GPS. I think we're going to have to head back in."

"No, Dad. We just got out here. I just got my pole ready." The boy of 15 wore disappointment like only a teenager could.

"I know son, but I don't trust going out any farther without the GPS. I'm sorry." Randy turned the wheel and started back toward the marina.

The boy slunk toward his fishing rod and broke it back down, returning it to the storage under the bench. "Didn't even get to have lunch," he murmured.

They were only a mile away from the marina and as Randy steered, the bay came into view. "Hey son, let's get the ropes ready to tie off, okay?"

"Okay, Dad." He readied the boat to enter the slip which was now just a few yards ahead. As he leaned against the edge of the railing, something caught his eye. "Hey, Dad? It looks like there's something hitting the slip."

Randy faced starboard as he steered the vessel but couldn't see anything. "Here, come take the wheel for a minute and I'll have a look." He waited while his son approached. "Okay, just keep it on this bearing. I'll go see what it is."

When he reached the spot his son had been, he peered over and squinted hard. "What is that?" He removed his sunglasses and looked closer. That was all it took. Randy knew exactly what he was looking at. "Oh no." He shot a glance at his son. "Radio for help."

"What did you say?" the boy asked.

"Radio for help! Now!"

———

Shane stood from his desk to show Allison to her car when he spotted Detective Montoya rush through the doors and hustle upstairs to the Major Crimes Unit. "What was that all about?" He looked at Allison.

"Something's up. Can we go see?"

"Why not? I have no business being up there but what the hell." Shane started toward the elevators.

They arrived on the next floor and continued into the halls. Shane turned to Allison. "Hang tight. I'll see where he went."

The stocky man with black hair and intense eyes arrived at his captain's office. He leaned in the doorway. "Captain, we just got a call from the Coast Guard. Someone found a body floating in the Marjorie Park Marina."

"The Coast Guard?" the captain asked.

Montoya nodded. "They were nearby performing a vessel safety check when a boater was trying to moor up. The boater radioed for help and the Coast Guard heard the call come in. They called us. I need to go out there."

"You're working a double homicide right now. Let Alvarez take this one."

"That double homicide happened a few blocks from there, Captain. I'd like to at least go with him to make sure we aren't overlapping."

"Fine. Keep me posted," the captain replied.

Shane was in the hall several feet away from Montoya and waited there as he started back.

"What's up, Sully?" Montoya asked.

"Did I hear you right? Someone found a body in the marina?"

"Yeah, so? Last I checked, you didn't work in Major Crimes. Besides, Alvarez is taking it, but I'm going with him."

"Listen, I got Hart over there and you know, she's a witness to your double homicide. I don't want to overstep but that marina is damn close to your crime scene. What are the odds there's a connection?"

Montoya regarded Shane. "Why don't you just come out and ask if you can tag along? That's what you want, right?"

"Look man, I'm not trying to step on your toes here."

"I get it. I don't mean to be a prick. I just don't want the P.I.s to think they have some sort of authority to do what we do, you know?"

"Yeah, sure. I get it. But this one over here," Shane thumbed to Allison. "She was just doing her job."

"Then why does it matter to you if there's a body at the marina?" Montoya asked. "What are you not telling me, Sully?"

Shane peered back at Allison.

"You need to clear this with your girl over there or something?" Montoya pressed on.

"No, man. It's just. I get you don't like what these guys do. That they put their noses where they don't belong, but she's different. Look, she just wants to see this through, you know? That's all it is. We can hang back; won't get in your way at all. You can't tell me a body turning up that close to Channelside is a coincidence. You wouldn't want in on it if that was the case."

Montoya shifted his gaze between Shane and Allison who was still several feet away. "Fine. You both can come with, but this is Alvarez's deal unless and until it isn't. You got me?"

"Got it. Thanks, man." Shane stepped out of Montoya's path and quickly walked back to Allison. "Okay. We're going to the marina. A body was found.

"Oh no."

"There's no point in jumping the gun, Allison. We'll know more when we get there," Shane replied.

THE WATERS OF THE BAY GLISTENED AND THE BOATS SWAYED in the breeze. The view would've been stunning to see were Allison not preoccupied with what they would find. The detectives were well ahead of them and had dismissed their presence altogether. There was no point in taking it personally. They were there to do a job and she was lucky to have been allowed to come along.

The squawking of the seagulls, the waves lapping, and the bells clanging made this all seem so normal. But Allison knew this was anything but. Perspiration at the back of her neck dripped along her collarbones and down the front of her shirt. She wiped it away with a handkerchief in her shorts pocket and noticed the detectives ahead reach the location where the body had been spotted.

Alvarez stood beside the boater and his son with a pad and pencil in his hand. "Mr. Randy Newsome? I'm Detective Alvarez. Thanks for sticking around. If you don't mind, I'd like to ask you a few questions."

"Of course." The man placed his arm around his son and pulled him close.

Allison and Shane kept some distance and watched as Alvarez took the boater's statement.

"And you noticed something in the slip, is that right?"

"Yes, sir," Randy replied. "My son spotted it—him—and I..."

"I understand," Alvarez continued.

The Coast Guard officer stood nearby and Montoya approached, pulling him aside. "Thanks for calling this in."

"This one's out of my hands, I'm afraid," the officer replied.

"I know." Montoya approached Alvarez and interrupted. "Mr. Newsome? I'm Detective Montoya. I'm going to be helping out Detective Alvarez. You mind if I listen in?"

"No." The father still appeared shaken up by the incident.

"Did you touch the—body?" Alvarez began.

Randy peered at his son and then at the Coast Guard officer.

The officer seemed to pick up on the father's discomfort. "How about we get you a soda while your dad talks to these fine officers?"

The boy peered at his dad.

"It's okay, son. Go on. We'll just be a minute and then we can go home, okay?"

The boy nodded and the officer led him away.

Randy waited until his son was out of earshot. "We were heading back in after I had some trouble with my GPS. My boy was helping me prepare to dock when he spotted something bobbing in the water. We didn't touch anything. Just called in for help."

Alvarez nodded. "Okay. Why don't you show me where exactly you spotted the body?"

Randy walked to the slip and pointed into the water. "Right here."

Alvarez squatted and peered in between the slip and the water. He shook his head and stood again. "Okay. Let's get him out of there and see if we can ID him." He turned back to Randy and retrieved one of his cards. "If you think of anything else, please give me a call. Whatever small detail it might be, it could still help."

"Of course. Is it all right for me to take my boy home?"

"Yes, sir. Thank you again for your cooperation." He waited for the man to walk away before turning to Montoya. "Why are they here?" Alvarez tossed a glance to Shane and Allison.

"I think we know this is probably tied to the double murders last night. I think Sully might want his girl over there to see if she can identify the body."

"Then you must think it's the P.I. who Diaz hired."

"Could be. You want me to call them over?" Montoya asked.

"Can't hurt anything," Alvarez replied.

"Sully?" Montoya motioned for them to approach. "You two want to see this or what?"

Shane glanced at Allison. "Looks like you're up. You sure you want to do this?"

"I'm here aren't I?" Allison made her way to the detectives and Shane followed. She inhaled a deep breath to calm her rattled nerves and was about to be initiated into an exclusive club. Seeing a dead body, let alone one she might know wasn't a club she ever expected to join. If this was Boyce, hell, whoever it was, it would change her forever. It would change anyone.

"Okay, Ms. Hart. This is why you're here, right?" Montoya asked. "You and I might be on the same page with this one. Go on. Tell me what you see."

Allison squatted low at the edge of the slip. Her legs trembled until she almost lost her balance. The air smelled of rotting fish or maybe it was rotting flesh. It was enough to turn her stomach.

The plump body rolled and bounced with each wave, sometimes crashing into the nearby pillar. Montoya walked around the edge with another officer. "Can you guys harness this and pull him out of there? We need to get a better look."

"Sure thing." The officer gathered two other men.

One of them was in a wetsuit and plunged into the water. He wrapped a harness around the wide midsection of the body and gave a thumbs up, attaching the end to another rope. "Here." He handed it to one of the officers on the dock. "Let's pull him up."

Allison looked on with a sense of dread weighing down her shoulders.

Shane placed his hand on her back as she remained crouched low. "You okay?"

She didn't look at him, only nodded and watched the body rise from the water.

It went limp. The arms fell to its side, the head dangled from the neck and the legs swung as they heaved.

She stood up and covered her mouth. Her eyes welled and tears streamed down.

"Ms. Hart," Montoya's tone was much softer. "Do you know who this is?"

Allison nodded and finally pulled away her hand. "It's Tommy Boyce."

"You're sure?" Alvarez asked.

"As sure as I'm standing here, yes. That's Tommy."

Montoya nodded. "Okay. Then we have ourselves a bigger problem now."

———

ALLISON GAZED THROUGH THE PASSENGER WINDOW AS SHANE drove them back to the station. "How am I going to tell Lucy? She has no one else. No one here in Florida anyway."

"I understand that you're concerned about Boyce's kid but I'm more concerned for you right now. This is a big deal. You were working for Boyce and now he's dead, and you were there when his targets were killed. Who put you in contact with him?"

"Milo," she replied.

"Nash? From the D.A.'s office?"

"Yeah."

"How would he know Tommy Boyce?"

"I have no idea. Milo's been around a while. Their paths must've crossed at some point." Allison turned to him. "Looks like I picked the wrong time to change careers."

He chuckled. "Yeah." Shane gripped the steering wheel and appeared at a loss for words. Then he began, "I think the right thing to do now is let Montoya in on everything."

"I already gave him a statement," she replied.

"He needs to know about Boyce's office and his kid. That's the way it has to be, Allison."

"He's going to shut me out. How will I be able to help Lucy?"

He shifted the car into Park and stepped out, waiting for her to join him. "I'll do what I can to keep you in the loop, okay? But I need you to see how dangerous this is. Whoever killed Boyce is likely to be the same one who killed the other two. We're talking about professionals here."

They walked toward the entrance of the station.

"What do I do about the girl?" she asked.

"You can't be the one to tell her about her dad. It needs to come from the authorities. Montoya or Alvarez will do the dirty work."

"I saw the car, Shane. Maybe not well enough but I don't want to sit on the sidelines."

"I said I'd do what I could to keep you in the loop. You'll have to trust me on this, Allison. I won't let you down. You should know that by now." Shane opened the door and waited for her to enter.

"I do trust you. But since when have you known me to back away from a promise?"

8

T he directive from Shane for Allison to elaborate on her original statement only served as fodder for Detective Montoya's already low opinion of private investigators. Allison wasn't a P.I. yet, but he already lumped her in with the rest.

However, pointing out that Tommy's office had been turned upside down on the same night jumpstarted Alvarez's investigation into Tommy's death. Two murders and now a third had made for a complex case.

Allison was left with no choice but to rely on Shane to keep his word as to the detectives' progress but in the meantime, there was something she could do to keep her promise to Lucy and that was to visit Milo Nash. He had put her in contact with Tommy Boyce. If he hadn't known what happened, he was about to.

Allison entered the District Attorney's office and walked to the front desk. It was tough to shake the melancholy, but she did her best to conceal it. "Afternoon. Hey, is Milo around by chance?"

"He is. I'll let him know you're here, Allison." The receptionist made the call and relayed the message before turning back to her. "He'll be right out."

"Thanks." She wandered aimlessly inside the lobby.

"Allison," Milo said. "How are you?"

"I've been better. But by your expression, I'm guessing you must already know why."

"I do. Please, let's go to my office." Milo started back. "I got the call from Shane a short while ago. He said I should expect your visit."

"Did he?" she replied.

Milo stopped and turned back to her. "He's worried about you."

"I'm worried about Tommy's daughter. That's why I'm here."

Milo held open his office door. "Allison, if I'd known..."

She walked inside. "How could you have? I know you'd never do anything to put me in a dangerous situation." Allison waited for him to sit at his desk. "I'm here because I need to ask you some questions about Tommy. Can you tell me how you met him?"

Milo appeared to think on the question. "He was a cop with Tampa PD for a short while, then retired. He'd been a cop for years prior to moving here. We crossed paths during his stint with our force. He and his family moved to the area, oh, I don't know, maybe 8, 10 years ago. After he retired, he started his own agency. Shortly after that, his wife passed. Honestly Allison, I'm just beside myself over what happened."

"Me too."

"Anyway, we got along well and next thing you know we were having beers together and became great friends." Milo's grief appeared to catch up to him. "I can't believe he's gone."

"Milo, is there anyone you can think of who might've, I don't know, maybe held a grudge against him? Was looking for payback?"

"If I knew that I wouldn't keep it to myself, that's for damn sure. I know how the game is played, Allison. I've been keeping score for a long time."

"Look, I realize this is something I should let the detectives handle, but they have their hands full and I just can't face Lucy Boyce without bringing something to the table. I'm here because I want to know if you can put me in touch with any of his associates. Someone who was familiar with Tommy's current caseload."

Milo turned to his computer. "Let me see what I have in here. Last I talked to him, well, before I mentioned you, he said he'd been keeping pretty busy. We know some of the same folks in the business." He continued to search. "Yes, here it is. You might want to write this down."

Allison pulled a sticky note from a pad on Milo's desk and grabbed a nearby pen. "I'm ready."

"Finley Dawson. He goes by Fin and he's a private eye too. I've worked with him once or twice, but I know he and Tommy were real close." He looked away. "Criminy, I wonder if he knows yet."

"If they're as close as you say they are, he probably does," Allison replied. "Not that I want to be the one to tell him."

"I'll tell you what, I'll give him a buzz and let him know what happened if he doesn't already know. Then I'll tell him to expect your call. That will make it easier on you, I think." Milo regarded her with concern. "Allison, the police do know what they're doing. Are you sure you want to go down this road? I don't know anyone who would want to harm Tommy let alone kill him, but whoever did this is probably someone you don't want to be messing with. You're charting a new course for yourself, Allison. This could derail you."

"You're one of the toughest prosecutors I've ever seen, Milo. If you thought you could help, wouldn't you?"

He nodded. "Well, all I'm saying is be careful."

Allison stood from her chair. "I'm a divorced, middle-aged mother of two. I'm everyone's worst nightmare. They should be worried about me."

Milo laughed. "Probably so."

———

MATERNAL INSTINCT WASN'T SOMETHING THAT COULD BE turned off like a faucet. Allison was desperate to reach out to Lucy and offer love and support. Regardless of the obvious parallels to her relationship with Micah, Allison was going to do everything she could to help Lucy even if the two had only just met.

Allison returned home to catch her breath and collect her thoughts. She had identified the body of a man she knew. It wouldn't be easy to overcome something so traumatic. Although it was nothing compared to what Lucy Boyce would suffer when the detectives knocked on her door.

Nolan walked into the living room. "Hey mom. How are you doing?"

"I'm fine. Just a little tired. What are you doing home? What time is it?"

"It's 4. My last class was at 2." He sat down next to her. "You sure you're okay? I mean, after what happened..."

Allison placed her hand on his knee. "I'm fine. I had to go back and talk to the police about what happened. But it's all over now. What do you have going on this afternoon? No practice?"

"Tomorrow. I think Dad said he was going to stop by in a little while. I kind of mentioned what happened and he got worried."

"Oh, honey."

"I know. But he still cares about us, Mom."

"Of course he does, but this doesn't involve him." Allison held his gaze. "Nolan, honey, I need to make a quick call."

He stood up. "Sure. Okay. I'll leave you alone. Let me know when Dad gets here?"

"I will." She waited until he returned to his room and closed his door.

Milo had texted her on the way home telling her that Finley Dawson was expecting a call and that he relayed the devastating news. Allison felt like a vulture ready to eat roadkill, pouncing on a grieving man like this, but there was no point in delaying it. A murderer was free. He would understand, she hoped.

"Hello?"

Allison picked up on his placid tone. "Is this Finley Dawson?"

"Who is this?" he replied.

"My name is Allison Hart. Milo Nash mentioned to you I would be calling?" She waited for a reply but there was only silence. "I understand you were a friend of Tommy Boyce?"

"I was, yes," he replied flatly.

"I'm so sorry about what happened. I don't know how much Milo told you, but I helped the police identify him..." she trailed off, wishing she had never made this call now.

"Why are you calling me, Ms. Hart?" he asked.

"I understand you also worked with Tommy on occasion. I was sort of hoping we could meet up to talk."

"About what?"

This wasn't going as Allison had planned. The awkward exchange had grown uncomfortable and she felt like an intruder. "I was hoping you might know what Tommy had been working on. What his caseload was like before..."

"Tonight. I can meet you at 6 o'clock. Do you know the Wave Rider?"

"I do. I'll see you there. Thank you, Mr. Dawson." Allison ended the call and took in a breath. Then the knock on the door came. "Leo." She pulled up and shuffled to the foyer to open it. "Hi."

"Hey. Can I come in?"

"Why not?" Allison stepped aside.

"Nolan told me what happened. I came to see how you were doing." He continued inside and offered her a peck on the cheek. "I'd like to talk about it if you're up to it."

Allison headed to the kitchen and opened the refrigerator. "You want some water?" She pulled out two bottles and met him at the breakfast island. "There's no need to worry, Leo. Everything's under control."

"Everything's under control?" He eyed her. "When were you going to tell me you witnessed the murder of two people? I had to hear it from our son?"

"First of all, I didn't technically witness it. I only heard gunfire —and saw the flashes of light. You don't know about Boyce then?" she asked.

"Who's that? And no, I don't. Maybe you should fill me in on the past couple of days."

"I'm not in any danger and neither is Nolan."

"I certainly hope not."

"You knew about the job. I have to work, Leo. It's not like I can sit at home and expect you to pay my bills. Hell, you're a high school baseball coach, you can hardly pay your own bills." She winced at the biting comment. "I'm sorry. That wasn't fair. I just didn't think I had to tell you everything that was going on in my life. We aren't married anymore."

"I know that, but we share two children, in case you forgot."

"Oh, I haven't forgotten. By the way, Micah's tuition is coming due in two months."

"I'm aware." Leo walked around to the other side of the kitchen island and stood inches from Allison. "Whatever's happening, Allison, it is so far removed from anything you've ever dealt with before. This isn't some guy defrauding the system. This is murder. Two murders. And I can see the look in your eyes. You're afraid, even if you won't admit it. This shouldn't involve you, okay? It scares me."

Allison firmed her stance. "This is what I want to do, Leo. I know I'll be good at it. You know how much I loved my job. This is just an extension of that."

"I disagree. Not that you loved your job. I know you did. But what you want to do is a whole different ballgame. And who is this Boyce, anyway?"

"Well, if you're concerned about my involvement in the double murders, then you're really going to be pissed about this. Tommy Boyce was the man who hired me to get pictures of the cheaters, they were the ones who were murdered. Unfortunately, he was found dead at the marina only blocks away earlier today."

"What?" Leo paced the kitchen. "That seals it. You're not going to be a part of this anymore."

She seized his gaze with a look of derision. "You have no input, Leo. You don't get to tell me what I can and can't do. Look, I'm going to find out who killed Tommy Boyce. He was a good man as much as I knew. And he has a daughter. I promised her I would help. I won't renege on that promise. I went to see Milo today..."

"Milo? What does he have to do with any of this?" Leo asked.

"He referred me to Tommy Boyce, the man who hired me for the freelance work."

"Oh, well, great." He threw his hands in the air.

"Can you please calm down?" Allison peered over her shoulder to be sure Nolan wasn't alerted. "Milo gave me the name of one of Boyce's counterparts. I'm going to meet with him tonight.

Leo, I understand that you're scared. Maybe I am too, a little. But I've come a long way since our divorce. I can do this. I need you to have faith in the fact that I would never allow anything to happen to either of our kids. If I feel like I'm getting in too deep, I'll ask for help. I have Shane and Milo on my side. And Charlie." She sighed. "Geez, Charlie. I have to tell her what happened." Allison returned her attention to Leo. "She's going to be a part of the plan. I want her with me. Once all this is settled, I'll get my license and open an agency. I have to know that you'll stand behind me on this, Leo."

He held her gaze. "You're so damn stubborn, you know that?"

"So you always tell me." She reached for his hands. "Do you trust me to make the right call?"

"Of course I do. Trust was never an issue. I mean..." He seemed to realize he had been the one to break the trust in their relationship.

"I know what you meant. Thank you, Leo. I won't let this get out of hand."

"You're assuming you'll have a choice in the matter."

———

ALLISON ENTERED THE BAR AND SEARCHED FOR THE MAN named Finley Dawson. She knew nothing of his appearance but examined the bar for one who seemed distraught or otherwise forlorn.

There was one who matched that description. Although he seemed to have masked his feelings well enough. Her only real clue was that he was alone and staring at the entrance as if waiting on someone.

Allison's lips parted slightly at the sight of him. The blonde-haired man appeared positively adolescent. Maybe that was a slight exaggeration. He was probably in his early thirties. And now her insecurities awakened like an angry lion. Suddenly, every joint cracked with each step she took and her arm flab wobbled like Jell-O. There were times in Allison's life, as much as she hated to admit it, when she became acutely aware of her age. It was generally in the presence of younger, attractive people. Finley Dawson, with hair that skimmed his shoulders, a square jaw, and well-defined arms, was the most attractive man she'd seen in some time. And that was just what she could see while he sat in the booth.

Allison tugged on her form-hugging blouse and pressed lightly on the bouffant bun on her head. His magnetism had reduced her to an awkward teenaged girl and in the face of what she had been through today, was wholly inappropriate. "Mr. Dawson?" She approached the booth.

"You must be Allison Hart." He raised just enough to offer a greeting. "Please, call me Fin. Have a seat, Ms. Hart."

She slid into the booth. "It's Allison. Pleased to meet you. And thank you for seeing me on short notice. I'm sure you're very busy."

"Not as much as you might think." A hint of regret flashed across his face. "I can't wrap my head around it—losing Tommy. He was a good friend and associate. This isn't how I thought the day would turn out but now that it has, I have to ask what it is you want from me."

"I have no doubt the police will get around to speaking with you about your relationship with Tommy. I'm sure they'll want to talk to all of his friends and colleagues. But Mr. Dawson..."

"Call me Fin."

"Fin, I don't have that kind of time."

"You mentioned on the phone you didn't know Tommy well," he added.

"No. I wish I had. I only just met him yesterday afternoon. It all happened so fast. He asked me to do a job for him and I did. The problem was, the people he asked me to stake out ended up being murdered. Then today Tommy turned up dead too."

"I'd say that's a problem," he replied.

"I agree. That's the real reason why I'm here. I'd like to know if you can shed some light on what Tommy was working on, apart from the assignment he handed to me."

Fin raised a finger to garner the attention of the waitress. "I'd like a Land Shark, please." He turned to Allison. "Can I get you a drink?"

"I'll take the same. Thank you."

"Two Land Sharks. Thanks." Fin returned his attention to Allison. "I do know he had a full plate. I can't say anything in particular stands out. Just the usual P.I. stuff."

"Like taking pictures of cheating spouses," she replied.

The beers arrived and Allison tossed back a long, slow drink.

Fin watched with mild concern. "Exactly."

"I'll be the first to admit that this is all very new to me," Allison began. "I won't bore you with my background except to say that I do have some experience that related to the work Tommy asked me to do. I don't pretend to have the knowledge you do or that Tommy had. But I need to tell you that it's starting to look like someone was trying to set him up. The work he gave me, he was supposed to do it. He was supposed to be there and instead, I was. And I met his daughter. She said Tommy's last known location was the very place where the murders happened—where I was."

"You met Lucy?" he asked.

"It was sort of unintentional, but yes. She's a very sweet girl and I feel just terrible for her. Fin, you don't know me from Adam, and I wouldn't blame you one bit for walking away from me right now. But I could really use some help in finding out who Tommy had been in contact with."

Fin tossed back a swig before holding her attention. "Let me ask you something, Allison, are you working this case or are the cops?"

"Let's call it a parallel investigation. I have no intention of getting in their way, but I will see this through. You were his friend. I'm sure you'd like to know what happened to him and why."

"Why are you so interested? He wasn't your friend. You didn't know him well."

"Sadly, no. I'm doing this for Lucy," Allison replied.

"I might be able to help but you'll need to come with me to my house."

"Your house? I see." She nodded. "Is this how you go about picking up women?"

"First of all, you called me. And secondly, do I look like I need to strong-arm women to come back to my place?"

She averted her eyes for just a moment. "I'll have to plead the fifth on that one."

Fin chuckled. "I work out of my house, Allison. All of my files are there. I can tell you what I know about Tommy's cases and who he might've been working with recently. If you want my help, that's what I can offer."

9

The home of Finley Dawson was exactly as Allison would've predicted. His looks alone evoked visions of riding waves and popping open a cold brew next to a bonfire on the sand. It was everything life was supposed to be living in this part of the country. She admired the lifestyle. Carefree, unattached. It wasn't something she'd ever expected to admire or possibly envy.

"You'll have to excuse the mess. The maid doesn't come until tomorrow," Fin said.

"You don't have a maid, do you?" Allison replied.

"No, I don't. Come in." He pulled open the blinds and revealed a dusky sky. "It's too bad you didn't get to know Tommy. He was intimidating as hell but once you got to know him, he would do anything for you."

"That's what I hear." Allison followed him to the living room. She eyed the futon couch and the recliner next to it. A small rattan coffee table was placed in front of the futon and a flat screen television was mounted on the wall; its wires hanging down to the plug.

"I think you might have been destined to meet him when you did. Someone or something must have seen fit to put you on this path," he said.

"Funny. I never would've taken you for a destiny or fate type of guy."

"There's a lot you don't know about me, Allison." Fin stood in the center of the living room. "That's my office over there." He headed into the short corridor to the double doors that opened into a room filled with boxes and papers. A laptop rested on a folding table with a rolling chair beneath it. The beige tile floors were sprinkled with grains of sand.

"How often did you work with Tommy?" Allison observed the slight disarray.

"This year? Probably three, maybe four times. Usually only if he needed some help with the cops. He was a retired officer himself but had rubbed a few of the guys the wrong way. I could usually smooth things over if I had to. I know some guys with Tampa PD."

"Oh yeah? Me too. Who do you work with?" she asked.

"I doubt you'd know them. They work in Vice mostly."

"I lean on Detective Shane Sullivan, mostly because of my previous job and now this. We're close. He made sure I was in the loop on identifying..."

"Tommy? Lucky you." Fin walked to his desk and sat down. "Let me see what I can find here and try to help you out."

Allison examined the room. Pictures on the walls of Fin surfing, a few medals she assumed he won as a result of that surfing. Then she spotted a framed photograph sitting near the printer. It was Tommy, Lucy, and Fin. She picked up the frame. "You've met Lucy?"

"I have. The Boyces were here for a few years before Tommy's wife passed. That was taken before she died not long after I met him."

"Forgive me, Fin, but it seems like you were very close to Tommy and yet I get the impression you would rather not get involved."

He turned away from his laptop. "We all deal with grief in different ways. You'll excuse me for not opening my heart to a woman I just met who was also one of the last people to see Tommy alive."

Allison returned the photo to the table. "You're right. I'm sorry."

"Yeah, well..." Fin returned to his laptop and reached for a pad of paper. "I don't have much, but I have one name for you." He scribbled it down. "He was Tommy's go-to guy for his surveillance equipment." He handed her the slip of paper. "I'm sure he would've been the one to help Tommy out on the last gig. The one you worked on."

"I appreciate it, Fin. Thanks. I'll give him a call." Allison examined the slip of paper. "Listen um, if I run across anything, would it be all right if I reached out to you—for guidance?"

"I might not express my feelings well, but Tommy was my friend. And Lucy. I don't know how she will get over this, especially after losing her mom. But I will tell you this, these cops, they know what they're doing. I don't want to stop you from looking into this, but you should know there's going to be trouble just waiting for you. So, I guess what I'm saying is, yeah. If you find yourself in a jam, I'll do what I can to help out. Just don't expect miracles, okay? It doesn't work that way."

"I understand. Thank you."

He stood from his chair. "You have my number. Call me anytime."

———

CHARLIE STOOD OUTSIDE ALLISON'S FRONT DOOR WITH HER arms folded against her body and a grimace on her face. The night air was heavy and appeared to add to her foul disposition. She watched Allison step out of her car and head toward her. "Well, well, well. It's about time you showed up."

Allison wore her guilt like a cloak, eager to hide beneath it. "I'm sorry I'm late. The meeting went longer than I expected." She keyed the lock and opened the door. "I thought Nolan would have been here to let you in."

"Nope." Charlie tapped her foot. "Been waiting here for half an hour."

"Why didn't you call me?" Allison asked before stepping inside.

"Uh, hello? I did." Charlie followed. "It went to voicemail."

"Oh." Allison dropped her keys on the foyer table and retrieved her phone. "I didn't hear the call, I'm sorry. I must not have had a good signal where I was."

"Weren't you at that bar?" She trailed inside, still in a huff.

"That was where we started but then we went to Fin's house." Allison walked into the kitchen. "Now before you go ape-shit, let me tell you why."

"Oh yeah, you'd better. Tell me what happened with, what did you call him? Fin? With everything that's happened, you went to a guy's house who you don't even know."

"I wasn't in any danger. Trust me. If you met this guy, you'd understand. He was an associate of Tommy Boyce and had some information. The guy works out of his home. What do you want me to say?"

"Oh, I don't know. That 'hey maybe I should call ol' Charlie and tell her where I'm going.' You know, in case someone finds you in pieces in a body bag."

"How long are you going to be mad at me? Just so I'm prepared," Allison replied.

Charlie exhaled an exaggerated breath. "Fine. Did you at least get something worthwhile?"

"I think so." Allison retrieved the slip of paper. "This guy here. Fin said he was Tommy's go-to guy for surveillance equipment. He has to know what Tommy was working on so I'm going to contact him."

"Are you sure this is what you want to do?" Charlie pulled out a barstool and sat down. "Alli, I'm not going to lie. This is scary. Maybe you do need to let the police handle this. You can always ask Shane to keep you posted. People are dead. You get that, right?"

"I'm not oblivious to that fact. Consider this trial by fire. If I run away from it, what kind of private investigator will I be?"

"A living one."

"Be serious, Charlie." Allison retrieved a Pepsi from the fridge. "You want one?"

"No, thanks."

She popped it open. "I'm not dismissing your concerns and apparently, you're not alone. Leo said virtually the same thing."

"If you tell him I said this, I'll take you out myself. But Leo could be right. Three people are dead, including the one who hired you to photograph the other two."

Allison turned squarely to Charlie. "You didn't see his daughter. Lucy's just a kid. Reminds me a lot of Micah. I told her I would help her find out what happened to her dad. I have to do that. You know me, Charlie. I'm not a quitter."

"Which was why you stayed in your marriage longer than you

should have." Charlie peered at her sternly. "Okay then. Fine. But you're crazy if you think I'll let you do this alone."

Allison smiled. "I figured you'd say something like that. We're the same."

Charlie folded her arms across her chest. "No, we're not."

"Oh yeah, we're the same."

———

IT HAD BEEN TWO DAYS SINCE THE DEADLY MURDERS AND Detective Montoya's only person of interest was the husband, Carlos Diaz.

Shane sipped on his coffee steaming from its paper cup when he noticed the senior detective looming toward him. "Montoya. What can I do for you?"

"Sully, we got a problem." He dropped a file onto Shane's desk. "You mind telling me what your friend's prints were doing all over Tommy Boyce's office?"

"Despite what you might think, I actually have a lot of friends. You want to help me narrow it down?" Shane asked.

"I'm not dicking around, man. You know I'm talking about Allison Hart."

"If I recall, she mentioned to you she went there that night looking for Tommy."

Montoya's veins bulged on his neck and forehead. "She also said she didn't go inside. Now I find her prints? She contaminated my scene. That's not okay."

"No, it's not. I'll find out what happened. Hey um, did any other prints come back?"

"Not yet. Hers were in the system because of her previous job. We're still waiting for any others."

Shane nodded. "Look, Montoya, I get you're pissed but Allison's not withholding information from you. What can I do to help?"

"Remind your girlfriend who's in charge. It's bad enough she's all over that office, I don't want to discover her prints or anything else of hers anywhere near this case or I'm going to have no choice but to include her as a suspect."

"I get you. And hey, let me know if you need anything. I'm here to help. I mean that," Shane replied.

"Just keep Allison Hart away from my investigation." Montoya turned on his heel and disappeared beyond the corridor.

Montoya didn't know what he was asking. It was like asking a shark to avoid the school of fish heading right toward him. Allison wasn't going to give up because he said so. Nevertheless, Shane would need to take care to keep Allison and Montoya at arm's length from one another. He'd known her long enough to under-stand that if Montoya pushed, she would push back—harder. It was dumb luck she had gotten away clean that night. By all rights, she should be dead too. Allison was in deep now and Shane would have to help her not only play it safe but stay safe.

———

FINLEY DAWSON JOGGED INTO THE SURF WITH HIS BOARD under his arm. The waves had been forecasted at between 5 and 6 feet this morning; perfect for him to catch a few before work. His sandy blonde hair went dark as he plunged under the water before springing up and laying on his board with ease and agility. With his arms gently paddling, Fin watched the rolling wave approach and in one swift motion, he jumped to his feet and rode the wave back to shore. When the surf dumped him near the shoreline, he bobbed for a moment until reeling in his board. Upon resurfacing, he spotted a woman standing on the shore only feet from him. The glare of the morning sun made it difficult to identify her, though her silhouette was lean. She waved to him.

Fin squinted and placed his hand on his brow to shield the glare. "Allison?" He paddled to shore and carried his board to meet her where she stood. "Allison, what are you doing here?"

"I was wondering if you could sit down with me for a minute." She pulled down her sunglasses. "There's a coffee stand up the street."

"Sure." He rammed the bottom of his board into the soft sand and followed her. "How did you find me?"

"I tried your phone, then checked your house and figured at this time of morning, this was the most logical place to try next."

"No wonder why Tommy liked you."

Allison smiled. "I don't know if he liked me, but I do know how to read people." She continued toward the small booth near the oceanfront. "Morning. Two coffees please."

The man inside the air-conditioned kiosk leaned over. "Cream and sugar?"

Allison turned back to Fin. "Well?"

"Both. Thanks."

She turned back to the man. "Both, yeah, thanks."

"That'll be right up." He disappeared inside.

"What did you want to talk about?" Water droplets clung to Fin's chest and his wet hair curled up into ringlets.

Allison tried hard not to stare. The sunglasses offered an effective disguise. "The man you told me about. I tried to reach him last night."

"Good. Was he helpful?"

"Well, I had hoped he would be but according to his voicemail, he's on vacation. And unfortunately, he didn't give any time frame on his return."

The man inside the booth held two cups. "Here you go, ma'am. That'll be $8.75 please."

Allison handed him a ten. "Keep the change."

He glared at her with mild contempt.

"Hey buddy, I'm unemployed. Wish I could do more." She reached for the cups and handed one to Fin.

"Thanks. I can pay for this," he said.

She raised her hand. "Don't worry about it." Allison sat down at one of the tables where Fin joined her. "I don't suppose you would have any idea where this guy would vacation, would you?"

Fin sipped on his coffee and chuckled. "I'm afraid not. I'm sorry it didn't pan out."

"I should probably clear up something. I want you to know I'm not after your clients or your contacts. My only goal is to find out who killed Tommy Boyce. It would be helpful if I knew who his enemies were."

"Allison, I wish I could help you. I really do. Look, I was friends with Tommy and I'm sorry as hell he's gone. It hasn't really sunk in yet, but I told you everything I know. If you think I'm threatened by you, then you've totally misread my intent."

"One thing I failed to mention last night was that I went to Tommy's office after the shootings. The detective in charge just got the report of my prints in his office. He wasn't happy that I'd been there."

"I'm sure. But why did you go?" Fin asked.

"After what happened, I knew I had to talk to Tommy. He wasn't answering his phone, so I went to his office. Unfortunately, someone beat me to it. The place had been tossed. My point is, I got a call early this morning from my detective-friend. He said Montoya, who's running the investigation, hasn't received any other reports of fingerprints back yet. Just mine."

"And this is a concern for me why?" Fin asked.

"After I identified Tommy's body yesterday morning, my friend and I went back to Boyce's office in search of any new details that would tell us what the hell happened. He took his kit with him and pulled prints. And when he ran them through the system, he got back more than just mine. I don't know how or when you did it, but you should've told me you had been to his office too." She sipped on her coffee and eyed him, waiting for a response.

Allison just stepped on a landmine. She had no such evidence and neither of them had returned to Boyce's office. She was playing the odds, and in a moment, she would know if the land-mine would explode in her face.

"I told you I worked with Tommy on a regular basis. It should come as no surprise my prints were found in his office. What is surprising is that your buddy pulled prints in the first place. This isn't his investigation." Fin eyed her for a moment. "Why don't you tell me the real reason you tracked me down this morning, Allison? Somehow, I don't think it was to check out my surfing skills."

"If I'm going to find out who's responsible for killing Tommy Boyce, I'm going to need your full cooperation," Allison began. "You were at Tommy's office. Makes sense. But then why act like you didn't know anything? Were you helping him with the Diaz case?"

CHARLIE WELLS STILL WORKED FOR THE BUREAU AT THE state agency. The ordeal regarding Davis Cantrell was ongoing and the man had been placed on administrative leave, with pay. Had it been any other of the staff it would have meant immediate dismissal or at the very least, leave with no pay. Typical upper management crap as far as Charlie was concerned. But she had a job, for now. Although the prospect of moonlighting with her closest friend, Allison, sent her mind soaring. It would be an incredible opportunity and allow her to finally leave this joint and move on to something better. Something more exciting and maybe someday it might help her toward retirement.

Charlie plugged away on her computer when she spotted a surprise visitor. "Shane, what are you doing here?"

"Hey, Charlie. Don't suppose you've heard from Allison?"

Charlie turned stone-faced. "No. She should be at home. Why? Did something happen?"

"Nothing happened. Everything's fine. That I know of." He glanced around for any eavesdroppers. "I need to find her, though and she's not home. She's not answering her phone either. I was hoping you knew what she had going on this morning."

"I haven't talked to her yet. She can't just up and disappear like this." Charlie's tone was laced with fear. "I'll go tell my boss I have an appointment or something. Give me one minute." She marched through the hall leaving Shane at her desk.

"I have an emergency." Charlie stood in the doorway of her supervisor. "It's one of my boys. I have to pick him up from school." Almost everyone in her office, including her supervisor, was well aware of Charlie's trouble with her deadbeat ex-husband and how she was pretty much on her own where her boys were concerned.

"Of course you can leave. Maybe shoot me a text later to let me know everything's okay?" the woman said.

"I will. Thank you." Charlie marched headstrong back to her desk where Shane waited. She reached in a drawer and grabbed her purse and started away. "Let's go."

"Where to?" He jogged to catch up with her.

"We'll figure that out in the car."

10

The question lingered for far too long and made the hair on Allison's neck stand on end, even in the heat of a rising sun. Fin appeared caught off guard by her question of his involvement with the Diaz case that brought an end to Tommy Boyce.

"I'm not sure what it is you think you know, Allison, but I worked with Tommy regularly. We exchanged information on a variety of cases. Frankly, I don't know you. Tommy didn't know you. If you think I'm going to hand over sensitive details to someone whose motives I haven't figured out, then you're mistaken."

The young surfer who could melt the heart of any woman with a blink of his eyes had hardened in an instant. But Allison wasn't just any woman.

"You can dance around it all you want but the sooner we get on the same page, the sooner we'll find out who killed Tommy and maybe who killed the couple." As strong as Allison portrayed herself to be, there was a hint of fear beneath the surface. This man who had seemed so open to helping her earlier had withheld vital information either to protect himself or someone else. Maybe she didn't want to consider the alternative. Maybe Finley Dawson had something to do with Boyce's murder.

"I got the heads up from Goodfellow's housekeeper about the wife showing up that night," Fin conceded. "Tommy knew from what the husband had said about her visiting friends, but he wanted something solid and asked me to check around. He needed some extra hands, as you know. And I found Harlan Goodfellow's housekeeper. She said she'd been instructed to clean that day and stock the fridge, including alcohol. She was also instructed to light candles and whatever else he wanted to impress his mistress with. So, I figured the two would be found at his place that night."

"Why didn't you tell me this from the start?" She tipped back the last of her coffee that had already cooled. "You're right. I didn't know Tommy. But he trusted me enough to hire me for the task. You say you were close to him, then you should've known well enough to trust his instincts."

"Fine. Maybe I was wrong, okay? I'll admit it. I don't see how this helps you get any closer to finding out who killed him," Fin replied.

"It doesn't. I just need to know what I'm up against. I don't profess to be some great detective with a nose for clues, but I am good at what I do."

"Which is?" Fin added.

"I'm good at exposing the liars. Now, you can sit on the sidelines or you can get on the field and we'll find out who killed Tommy together."

———

"So tell me, oh wise one," Shane began. "Where will we find the elusive Allison Hart on this fine morning?"

Charlie glanced at him from the driver's seat of her car. "There's only one other person, besides you and me, who Allison would confide in."

"Milo," he replied.

"You got it." She grabbed her cell phone. "I'm going to find out if he's talked to her today." Charlie dialed the number and waited for the line to answer. "Hey Milo, it's Charlie Wells."

"I was wondering when I'd hear from you," Milo replied.

"Let me guess, you've talked to Allison this morning?" she asked. "Please tell me you know where she is. I'm with Shane and we need to talk to her."

"I haven't talked to her, actually. Not since yesterday when I offered her the name of one of Boyce's associates."

"Was that Finley Dawson?" she asked.

"The one and only."

"Do you know how I can reach him?" Charlie added.

"I'll text you his number. Let me know if you hear from her, okay?" Milo said.

"I will. Thanks, Milo." Charlie ended the call. "She might be with this guy she met last night."

"A guy she met last night?" Shane asked.

"Yeah. Tell me about it. Anyway, his name is Finley Dawson and I guess he worked with Tommy. Milo's sending over his number now."

"I should try her phone again. The detective working the case came to me this morning. He said Allison's prints were all over Boyce's office when his team went through it looking for evidence. I covered for her, but if that detective gets a wild hair, she'll be the one under the microscope."

"Allison did say she was there that night," Charlie began.

"What she told me was that she was careful and didn't leave behind prints."

"Sounds like she wasn't as careful as she thought," Charlie said. "I just want to find her. We'll figure out the rest afterward."

———

ALLISON PULLED OFF HER SUNGLASSES AND EXAMINED HER phone. "I need to take this if you don't mind?"

"Go ahead," Fin replied.

"Charlie, what's going on?" She said into her phone as she stepped away from the table. "I'm kind of in the middle of something."

"You're in the middle of something? Shane's been trying to get hold of you. I've been trying to get hold of you. Where are you, Alli?"

"Calm down. I'm fine. I'm at the beach."

"What? Why are you at the beach?" Charlie asked.

"I'm meeting with someone. Tell Shane I'm sorry for not answering but I'll call him back later. Is that all you needed?"

"Is that someone Finley Dawson?"

Allison raised her brow. "How'd you know?"

"Lucky guess. Look, do you know anything about this guy?"

"I'm learning." She peered at him and revealed a brief smile. "Charlie, I'm going to have to call you back."

"Wait. Shane needs to ask you something." Charlie handed him the phone. "Better make it quick."

"Allison, it's Shane. Montoya approached me first thing this morning. He said your prints came back all over Boyce's office."

In light of the imaginary scenario she had presented to Fin, this seemed unreal. "That's not possible. I told you I was careful."

"I know. That's why I needed to talk to you. Somehow your prints are there and yet you didn't leave them."

Allison glanced at Fin who was drinking his coffee. "No, I didn't. I'm sure I was careful."

"We need to put our heads together. Maybe you should excuse yourself from that meeting of yours and come to the station. Look, I covered for you with Montoya—for now. But we should get a handle on just who Finley Dawson is before you put all your eggs in one basket."

"Sure, okay. I'll wrap things up here and meet you back at the station. Give me just a little bit."

"I'll see you later. And Allison, be cool. Don't let Dawson pick up on the fact he was the topic of conversation," Shane said.

"Sure thing. I'll be cool." Allison ended the call and returned to the table. "Sorry about that."

"Everything okay?" Fin asked.

"Just peachy. But I will have to cut short this meeting. What's your answer?" Allison leaned over the table and waited. In the back of her mind, she wondered how she had been careless enough to leave prints. Maybe it didn't matter now, but Shane's hackles were raised about Dawson. She had faith that Tommy was a good guy and so were the people he surrounded himself with. But she didn't really know.

"You're asking me to break into the office of a dead man," Fin said. "If there was anything to be found it would have been uncovered already."

"Maybe. But what I'm looking for the cops might not have found. You know more about Tommy than I do. What are the odds that we'd find surveillance footage at Boyce's office? Tommy was smart. I have no doubt he had cameras everywhere. Probably in places the cops wouldn't think to look."

He inhaled deeply. "He had cameras. That much I know. And

there's a slim chance they were tucked away where the cops wouldn't find them. You want to go to his office to look for video evidence? Is that what you're saying?"

"As clearly as I possibly can," Allison replied. "I'd like to do this tonight. The sooner, the better. Preferably before the cops get around to looking any harder."

He nodded. "Tonight. 9 pm. We'll meet at his office."

———

Allison walked into the stationhouse and removed her sunglasses. "Hey Jan, is Sully here?" she asked the desk clerk.

"He's waiting for you, Allison."

She started into the bullpen where she noticed Shane at his desk. "You got Charlie worked up over this?"

"Take a seat, Allison. We need to talk," he replied.

"Yes, sir." She folded her arms tightly across her chest as she sat down.

"Relax, I'm not reprimanding you," Shane said.

"That's not how it feels from this seat."

"We need to know more about Finley Dawson before you get too chummy with him. You understand that, right?"

"I know all I need to know. He's a kid who thinks he knows everything. But I set him straight."

"You set him straight?" Shane's brows raised.

"I told him we needed to come to an understanding and work together if we're going to find Boyce's killer."

"Okay, okay." Shane raised his hands. "I'm going to have to stop you right there. Detective Montoya and Alvarez are responsible for finding out what happened to Boyce. You aren't a cop, Allison. You aren't even a private investigator yet. I can't let you..."

She cocked her head. "How long have we known each other, Shane?"

"A long time."

"Okay. And in that time have you ever known me to go off the rails? To jump to conclusions or, I don't know, put myself into situations I can't get out of?"

"Well, no."

"No is right. Then why do you think this time is any different?"

"Because of the scope of this thing, Allison. You've never dealt with murders before. You handled people who took money from the state when they shouldn't have. That's a far cry from homicide."

"I get that, Shane. But that doesn't mean I'm careless or ignorant. I know what I'm doing here and Finley Dawson knows something. I'm going to get it out of him one way or another."

"And what about Charlie and your big plans to start an agency? Is all that down the drain now?"

"I haven't forgotten it. If anything, I'd consider this my first case. It's just that no one's paying me." She unveiled a wry smile.

"I just want you to be safe, Allison. If anything were to happen to you..."

"Nothing will." She held his gaze. "Now, do you want to do a background check on Dawson or keep wringing your hands with worry?"

Shane pulled up straight and typed on his keyboard. "I'll start with his license first and see if there are any complaints against him." He started typing. "So what did you talk to him about this morning anyway?"

"Well, after I tracked him down at the beach, I got him a coffee and asked him about his relationship with Boyce."

"What did he say? By the way, how did you find him?"

She smiled. "I can be industrious when necessary. How do you think I found most of my fraud cases? They weren't always in their homes and so I dug around social media or what have you and figured out a location. Dawson is all over Instagram posting about surfing and whatever one posts about on that site. I wouldn't know. Point being, he'd posted that he was headed to catch some big waves. So, I checked the forecast and Clearwater was expecting a pretty good surf this morning."

"She shoots, she scores," Shane said.

"And you were worried about me."

"Well, Charlie did mention you went to the guy's house yesterday."

"She told you that, did she? Traitor."

He continued to type until coming across something, Allison couldn't quite tell. "What is it?" She leaned in.

"He's fairly new to the game. He's only had his license for a few years. Oh, and look at this, he mentored under Boyce." Shane turned to her. "That's noteworthy."

"He already claimed to have a close relationship with Boyce. He's chummy with the family too."

"Okay smarty-pants, how do you think the two came to know each other?" he asked.

"Something about when Tommy was a cop. I can't recall exactly."

"Dawson's a native. Born in St. Augustine," Shane continued. "Meaning he's been around. He must know people. How or why would he attach himself to Tommy Boyce who'd only moved here, what did you say, like 8 years ago?"

"I'm not following," Allison said. "I don't get why this is important. I figured Dawson was born here. He had to have come across Boyce like anyone else, through contacts in the business."

"Maybe. I'll have to keep looking into that because something's not right there. But onto the next thing. Let's see his employment history." Shane continued to punch in commands on his keyboard until the information appeared on his screen. "He graduated USF in 2010. BA in business. Okay. Not criminal justice or anything like that."

"He must've found his calling later in life," Allison said.

"Sure."

Allison waited for Shane to have some sort of a-ha moment. Some major revelation that would set the course for her continued participation in this case, over which she had no authority and neither did Shane for that matter. "I understand you want to know who Finley Dawson is so I don't get any surprises, but I feel like we're wasting our time a little, don't you? The man is who he says he is. It doesn't matter how he came to know Boyce, just that he knew him."

"Say you're right. What is it you plan on using him for?"

Allison cracked a smile. "Why, information, of course. What did you think I was going to use him for?"

11

A virtuoso of words and ideas, a confidence man persuaded people with the delivery of said ideas. The more Allison considered Finley Dawson, the more she questioned whether she had been taken in by him. He spoke of his friendship with Tommy Boyce and his daughter, Lucy. She'd seen pictures of them in his home. Yet he hesitated to jump on board with finding Tommy's killer. Maybe she was a better friend than he had been because if something had happened to Charlie, she would've been the first to get to the bottom of it.

Now, as the hour approached 9 pm and the time to meet Fin had arrived, she pushed back her doubts. It was time for her instead to turn the tables on Finley Dawson. To learn more about him and why he withheld fundamental details about Tommy and his history with him.

"I don't know, Alli, I don't like the idea of you going alone." Charlie sat at Allison's kitchen island toying with her phone.

"I won't be there alone," Allison replied.

"Oh, that's right, a guy you hardly know, a guy who has

already misled you once, will be with you. Sure. That makes me feel a whole lot better."

Allison studied her. "Then come with me. You and I are going to be partners, right? Why not start now? If you're worried about this, then we'll have strength in numbers."

Charlie appeared to consider the idea. "I could. Do you think Dawson would have a problem?"

"Does it matter? I agree with you. It should be the both of us. What do you say?"

"That we can do anything boys can do." Charlie laughed.

"You're damn right we can. Let's go."

———

ALLISON'S HONDA ROLLED INTO THE PARKING LOT NEAR THE front of Boyce's office, which still had police tape across it, but now the front door was boarded up. "Here we are." They stepped out and Allison searched the lot. "Looks like Fin is already here." And when her eyes landed on the man with the sandy blonde hair strolling along the sidewalk, she nodded. "Yep. That's him."

"That's Finley Dawson?" Charlie stopped in her tracks. "Wow."

"You can pick up your mouth off the ground now. Don't go all googly-eyed over this guy. He knows all too well how attractive he is and he uses it." She started toward him. "I hope Shane's wrong about him, though."

"What do you mean?" Charlie asked.

"You'll see." Allison brushed away the beads of sweat that dribbled down her neckline.

Charlie caught up to Allison and leaned in to whisper. "He's looking at us."

"I know. He looks concerned that you're here. Good. I want

him to know he isn't controlling the outcome." Allison led the way toward the door of the office where Fin waited. "Thank you for being on time."

"Allison." He nodded. "Who's your friend? I didn't know we were bringing friends to this party."

"This is my partner, Charlie Wells. Charlie, this is Fin Dawson, an associate of Tommy Boyce's."

Fin offered his hand. "Charlie. It's a pleasure to meet you."

"Right back at ya." She returned the greeting.

"Partners, huh?" Fin asked. "Good for you. There's a door around back. As you can see, the cops have this boarded and taped. Follow me."

Allison nodded to Charlie and they followed him around to the back entrance where a metal door stood. "Do you have a key? Because we aren't getting in through here otherwise."

"I do happen to have a key." Fin pulled it from his pocket and opened the door.

"Can I ask how that came into your possession?" Allison said.

"How else did you think we'd be getting in tonight? I told you Tommy and I were friends."

She eyed Charlie before they followed Fin inside. The office was still overturned but it was obvious that some items had been removed. No computers remained and any paperwork that had been laying around was gone too.

"Cops did a pretty good job cleaning out the place," Fin said.

Allison surveyed the office. "If I were Tommy and wanted to protect myself with video surveillance, where would I keep it?"

Fin stepped carefully around the office. "If it was me, right back here, inside this broom closet." He made his way to the door and pulled it open. "But not anywhere too noticeable. Maybe up here on this high shelf?" He raised on his tiptoes and felt with his hand behind the boxes. "Just a little more." His fingers stretched out farther. "Oh, I think we might have something here."

"You need a stepladder?" Allison asked.

Charlie approached one of the desks and pushed a chair toward the closet where Fin waited. "This is as close to one as you'll get."

"Thanks, Charlie," Fin began. "That's a cool name." He flashed a bright smile at her that highlighted the dimples on his smooth cheeks.

Charlie's face turned a pinkish hue and she turned away.

Allison noticed the exchange and uttered to Charlie under her breath, "told you."

Fin stood on the chair and rustled around the top shelf until recovering the server that had been tucked away. "We're lucky the cops didn't see this."

"But you found it right away. I'm impressed." Allison was more concerned than impressed.

"Tommy and I were a lot alike. He was my mentor. And I'll bet we'll find cameras inside the smoke detectors. Probably under the eaves outside. That's where I would've put them."

"I'm sorry. This must be pretty tough for you," Charlie said to him.

Fin stepped off the chair with the server in his hands. "Yeah, well. We should get this hooked up to a computer. Anyone bring a laptop, by chance?"

"I don't want to stay here long enough to get caught." Allison peeked out through a side window. "Can we go back to your office and take a look?"

"Smart call." Fin started toward the door but stopped short. "I don't know what we'll find on here, but I think it would be wise to keep it to ourselves."

"Why would we do that? Whatever it is could help the cops find Tommy's killer," Charlie said.

"Tommy had a lot of friends in the department," Fin began. "But he also had a lot of enemies. I don't want to risk this falling into the hands of someone looking to cover up what they or someone they know might've done."

Allison furrowed her brow. "Do you really believe that could happen?" Fin was talking about enemies. He had a key. He knew where the video server was kept. Allison was starting to feel like Fin Dawson knew everything.

"Don't underestimate any of this, Allison. Neither of us has any idea what this is really about."

Allison wasn't convinced that was the case. She suspected he knew much more than he let on. Maybe Shane was right to want to look into Fin's background before she got too close. "We should probably go."

"We'll meet back up at my place." Fin walked to the rear entrance and waited for them to catch up. "Drive safely, ladies."

Allison and Charlie headed into the parking lot and Allison peered back. "He's locking it up again."

"I certainly hope so." Charlie reached the car and stood at the passenger door.

With the keys in her hands, Allison unlocked the car and slipped behind the driver's seat and once Charlie was inside, she started the engine and pulled away. "I should call Shane and let him know how it went. I know he's going to worry."

"I can see what you mean about Fin. He makes it easy to get you to trust him."

"Yes, he does. It helps when you look like him too."

"Was it me or did you think it was a colossal fluke that Fin happened to find the surveillance system in a manner of seconds?" Charlie asked. "Is he that lucky?"

Allison glanced at her. "It was anything but a coincidence."

"That's what I thought. Where's his house, anyway?"

"We're almost there, actually." Allison reached for her phone and pressed Shane's contact. "Better talk to Shane now before we arrive." She waited a moment until he picked up the line. "Shane, hi. I know it's getting late..."

"Late for who?" he asked.

"For me, I guess." Allison watched as Fin pulled onto his driveway and she was close behind. "I said I'd check in with you and well, we just left Tommy's office. We're about to go inside Fin Dawson's house. He found a server connected to some cameras. We're going to take a look at the files now. I have Charlie with me."

"Oh, geez. You two are at his house?" Shane asked.

"It was my idea if that makes you feel any better. Fin wanted to look at the videos right there in Tommy's office, but I was afraid we'd get caught."

"None of this makes me feel better, Allison." Shane was quiet on the line for a moment. "Just let me know when you leave there, okay? I won't sleep until I know you're both safe."

"If I didn't know any better Shane, I'd say you sound an awful lot like a worried parent."

"You mean, like you?" he replied. "Do what you have to do and get out of there. Call me when it's done. I hope to hell it's worth it."

"It will be." Allison noticed Fin peering at them as he stood next to his car. "I gotta go. Talk to you later." She ended the call. "Ready?" She asked Charlie.

"He worries about you even if he won't admit it," Charlie said.

"The last thing I need is another man to look after me. Let's go before Fin thinks something's up."

They stepped out of the car and caught up with him.

"What took you so long?" Fin asked.

Allison noticed suspicion had masked his face. "Just getting our ducks in a row."

"Sure, although it looked to me like you were on the phone." Fin walked to his door and keyed the lock. He pushed it open. "Welcome to my humble abode." He walked inside and switched on the lights, illuminating the sparsely decorated bachelor pad.

Charlie looked around the home as if assessing a value to it. "Gee, I can't imagine why you're still single."

Fin turned back to her. "Maybe this place just needs a woman's touch."

He might as well have batted his eyes at Charlie. Allison watched the exchange and jumped in with a retort. "A touch, a hit over the head, whatever works."

Fin smiled at her. "You want to come back and look at this or keep trading barbs?"

"Trading barbs. Hands-down." Charlie followed Allison and Fin to his office in the back.

Fin turned on the lights and opened the laptop on his desk. "Let's see if this was all worthwhile." He connected the server to his laptop and waited for the files to load.

Allison moved behind him and peered at the screen.

Fin looked over his shoulder. "What are you hoping to find on here, Allison?"

"I'm not sure. I guess maybe I thought if Tommy was being threatened by anyone or maybe whoever drove the car I saw that night will show up."

"What car?" he asked.

"We're pretty sure it was a Mercedes that flew out of the parking garage where Harlan Goodfellow lived and died," she replied. "If that's the case, we might get lucky enough to get a good look this time. And if the Gods are smiling on us, maybe we can pull a plate. I wasn't able to get it the first time."

"You're already assuming that whoever killed Tommy also killed the people he hired you to photograph," Fin said.

"Who else could it be?" she added.

"Anyone," Charlie replied.

Fin used his index finger and tapped it on his nose. "Bingo. Although, I suppose we're all about to find out."

"Too bad we don't have any popcorn," Charlie added. "Sorry, I don't mean to make light of it.

"Don't worry about it. I like your sense of humor, Charlie." Fin opened the files for the previous week's video. "This is going to take some time. You two might as well get a front row seat."

———

Midnight loomed near and Victor Esposito nursed his third gin and tonic from the comfort of his sofa. The anticipated knock on the door arrived. "I'm coming." He stood in socked feet and shuffled to the door. When he opened it, a tsk rolled off his tongue. "It's about time you showed up. You'd better have some news for me. I've been waiting for hours."

"Take a chill pill, dude. I'm here now. You want to let me in, or should I tell you out here?"

"Get in." Victor moved aside and closed the door behind him. "What did your buddy say about the cops having a sit-down with Diaz tomorrow? Is it a go?"

"That would be a full-on affirmative."

"What about Boyce?" Victor returned to his sofa and a low grunt escaped him as he sat back down. The overweight fifty-something felt older than his age. Too much booze and bad food tended to do that to a person. "Oscar sit, would you? I'm straining my neck here."

Oscar Nunez was a tall man with a thin build and only in his twenties. Cocky but smart, he was Victor's trusted associate. "Sorry, man." He dropped to the sofa with ease. "Cops found him floating in the bay."

Victor nodded. "Then let's keep our focus on Mr. Diaz. If they're talking to him tomorrow, we need to be sure he toes the line."

"He didn't need to bring in the private eye. It put us in a bad position," Oscar replied.

"No shit. If we remind Diaz what's at stake, we'll be able to keep him on a short leash. Let the cops piss away time looking into the affair," Victor added.

"I'll call Diaz in the a.m. and leave a friendly reminder before he sits down with them," Oscar replied.

"Good. Now get the hell out of here. I need some sleep. You can show yourself out."

"No probs." Oscar pushed off the couch and started toward the door. "You let me know if this gets to be too much for you, buddy. I'm happy to pick up the slack."

"I'll bet you are, kid." Victor threw back his drink.

———

SIFTING THROUGH THE VIDEO FILES FROM BOYCE'S OFFICE had evolved into a daunting task. About half had been scoured so far and yet nothing damning had been discovered.

"If I was Detective Montoya, I would do my best to get Carlos Diaz to hang himself." Fin opened another file on his laptop.

"What do you mean?" Allison had pulled up a dining chair and sat on one side of Fin while Charlie was on the other.

"Like any good detective, he should be looking at the husband. Especially a man like Diaz. Wealthy, powerful. And Montoya will want to tie this up with a nice neat little bow and move on to the next case," Fin replied.

"Regardless of how I feel about Montoya, he's not stupid. How could Carlos have killed them?" Allison began. "That would've meant he hired Tommy to be there when the murders happened under the pretense of obtaining evidence of his wife cheating."

"That's true," Charlie added. "Except he wasn't there, you were."

"And Tommy's phone was last located near the scene 45 minutes before the shooting," Allison said. "I can't explain that one. But that still puts Carlos nowhere near the vicinity."

"That's what it's been made to look like," Fin leaned closer to the screen. "What have we got here? Are you two seeing this?"

Allison and Charlie leaned closer before Allison began, "It's a silver car."

"Looks like a silver Mercedes to me," Fin said. "Allison, you mentioned a car like this. Is this the same one you saw coming from that parking garage?"

"It does look like it. I'll be honest, I was terrified at the time, but it could be. Where's the time stamp?" She pointed to the screen. "There. Two days before the murders."

"Let me see who's about to step out of this car." Fin waited while two men emerged in the footage and walked inside Boyce's office. "I don't recognize them."

The idea they could be the same men she saw that night sent Allison's nerves on end. "They're going in."

"I have to switch to the other cameras. Hang on." Fin opened another file and pulled up the time stamp to coordinate with the outside camera. "Okay, let's see what these guys are doing. There's Tommy, at his desk."

"He's checking them out," Allison began. "It doesn't look like he knows them."

"He looks pretty calm about the whole thing," Charlie replied.

"Just hold tight," Fin said.

The two men approached Boyce's desk and loomed over him.

"Turn up the audio," Allison said.

Fin complied.

"We're all set for tonight?" A young man asked Tommy.

"Yes, sir. I've put my best person on the job."

"Wait, you ain't going to be there?" The older man added.

"Something else popped up tonight. But don't worry, you're in good hands. I promise you that."

The men traded glances at one another before the younger man added, "If you say so but this isn't what we talked about. It isn't what Carlos wanted."

"So he does know them," Allison added.

The video continued and Tommy began, "I understand and I'm happy to call him to get his authorization if it would make you feel better."

"I'm sure he'll trust you're doing what needs to be done." The older man turned to his colleague. "Let's leave Tommy to do his work."

"You got it, boss."

"You be sure and get Carlos those pictures just as soon as you have them," the young man said.

"This isn't my first rodeo, kid. It's under control." Tommy kept his eyes on the men as they walked out.

"That's it?" Allison asked. "We don't know any more than we did an hour ago."

"I disagree," Charlie said. "First of all, we have the car. That's something huge. And those men knew Tommy wasn't going to be there. They acted like they worked for Carlos too."

Allison eyed Charlie. "I wonder if that means Carlos Diaz

knew Tommy wasn't going to be there either. So who the hell are they?"

"I hate to put this out there," Charlie began, "But what are the odds Carlos was the target? Those men knew the job was to get pictures of the cheating couple. They expected and maybe Carlos did too, that Tommy would be the one doing it." She looked at Allison. "What if Carlos was supposed to be killed and Tommy was going to be framed for his murder?"

Fin peered at the women. "It sounds a little farfetched especially since Carlos was nowhere around. But right now, I wouldn't rule out anything. I will say this, I think that might've been the end of Tommy right there. As soon as they knew he wasn't doing the job, that was it."

"And the car. They had to be the killers," Allison said.

"Let's take a step back for just a moment," Fin began. "You said yourself you weren't positive of the car from the parking garage. So let's work on getting more details before we pin this on a couple of guys who happen to own a silver Mercedes."

"Fair enough. But is it possible that if they expected Tommy to be there, they might've killed him when they killed the wife and Goodfellow?" Allison asked.

Charlie nodded. "If they weren't working for Carlos directly, maybe that was their plan, but Tommy wasn't there. You were."

12

Carlos Diaz owned one of the newest and costliest high-rise buildings in all of downtown Tampa. When Detective Montoya arrived on this Saturday morning, he admired the grandeur of it all. But in the back of his mind, it was one more nail in the coffin. The very wealthy, he believed, thought they were above the law.

The building must've been operating with only a skeleton crew today and Carlos had preferred the meeting be at his office. A red flag for Montoya. The reason for the location, according to Diaz's attorney, was so that his neighbors wouldn't see the detective near or in his home. Montoya wondered why Diaz would be so concerned about his neighbors when his wife had just been murdered. Seemed to him that his neighbors would offer their condolences, not their judgments.

The detective entered the building through a revolving door and stepped onto the deep grey wood-grain-like tile. His dress shoes echoed in the vast lobby that was adorned with photos of the company's development projects. Diaz headed up the largest development firm in the city, maybe even the state. His company was responsible for the revitalization of much of downtown.

"Detective Montoya. I'm here to see Mr. Diaz." Montoya retrieved his badge and presented it to the guard at the front desk. "Tampa PD."

"Of course. Just one moment please."

Montoya sized up the guard while he made the call to Diaz. Early twenties. Probably the kid's first job. Nervous.

"He's on his way, sir." The young man presented a tense smile. "May I get you some water or coffee?"

"No thanks, kid. And there's no need to be nervous. I'm not here for you." Montoya started toward the corridor where he expected Diaz to emerge.

Carlos Diaz drew near with an unnaturally broad smile and gleaming white teeth. His hair was pushed back and gelled into place. His tan skin was clear and revealed only minor lines. Botox? Probably. Diaz was 50 but didn't look a day over 40. Nevertheless, what struck Montoya the most was that he didn't appear to be a man mourning the loss of his wife.

"Detective Montoya. I can't thank you enough for juggling your schedule to meet with me this morning." Diaz offered his hand. "I'm sure it's not how you would want to spend your Saturday morning."

"It's no problem, Mr. Diaz. I'm here to find out what happened to your wife. Justice doesn't care about the time or day." He returned the greeting.

"Of course. Please, follow me. We'll talk in my office."

Montoya followed him, making note of Diaz's gait and his body language. He looked for any reason not to believe a word out of this man's mouth. That wasn't how justice worked but that was how Montoya worked.

"Here we are." Diaz ushered Montoya inside. "I wasn't sure if you had eaten yet, so I had bagels and coffee brought in."

"I'm fine for the moment, Mr. Diaz, but thank you."

"Why don't we sit over here? It'll be much more comfortable." Diaz showed him to a sofa and chair with a small coffee table in the center near his desk. He gestured to the chair while he made his way to the sofa. "I hope you don't mind. I haven't eaten."

The food and drink were placed on the table and Diaz took his time pouring a cup of coffee and spreading cream cheese on his plain bagel. He was wasting time.

"I'd like to start off with a few questions." Montoya retrieved a digital recorder. "You don't mind, do you?"

Diaz eyed it. "I thought this was going to be an informal inquiry. That's why my lawyer isn't here. We didn't want to give the wrong impression."

"I prefer to record the responses rather than write them down. That way, there's no mistaking what anyone might have said. But it is your right not to be recorded." Montoya held his gaze.

Diaz yielded. "I guess it's fine."

———

SHANE SULLIVAN ARRIVED AT THE STATION AND WAS OFF-duty. He knew Montoya was questioning Carlos Diaz this morning and decided now would be a good time to look for answers. Montoya didn't like to share and especially not with another detective who didn't work in his department. He had already torn Shane a new one about Allison's prints being found at Boyce's office. Shane wanted to know who else had been there and the prints should have come back by now.

He made his way through the corridor and up one flight of stairs.

Homicide was part of the Major Crimes Bureau which encompassed the entire floor. Sometimes, it was all Shane could think about—working in Homicide. At his age, he should've been there already, but he didn't join the force until he was almost 30. Shane was a late bloomer and it took him a while to figure out what he wanted to do with his life. For now, his work in Investigations and Support was all well and good but Major Crimes was the big leagues.

When the elevator doors parted Shane noticed far more people than he had expected. Of course, crime didn't stop because it was the weekend. He stepped off the elevator and nodded politely as he passed by a variety of staff, some administrative, some detectives, all too busy to pay him any notice. Montoya's desk was down the corridor and to the left. But as he strolled the halls like he belonged, Alvarez's cubicle appeared. He was in charge of Tommy's investigation and the cases overlapped. "I'm already here." Shane darted into the cubicle and eyed the desk. Papers were neatly stacked in a bin; a few files were placed on the edge of the desk. But as Shane glanced at the tabs, he realized neither was the Boyce file or the Diaz/Goodfellow file. He looked at the two drawers beneath the desk and tugged on each one. "Damn it."

"Can I help you with something?"

Shane flinched at the voice behind him. "Oh, hey, I was just looking for something Alvarez was working on."

The woman looked him up and down with judging eyes. "You don't work in Major Crimes. What's he got you doing?"

"Prints. I was looking for the file so I can get him an ID on some prints that came back on a case he's working."

"I don't think he's coming in today so you can either wait until he gets back, or you can run down to the lab and check with the technicians."

Shane beamed at the idea she had just handed him. "Do you know who in the lab would be working the Boyce or Diaz cases?"

"Not a clue but there's only a couple of techs working prints on the morning shift. I'm sure one of them can help you."

"Great. Thanks. I'll do that." Shane started walking but stopped short. "I'm sorry, I didn't catch your name. I work downstairs and don't get to see a lot of you guys."

"Leigh Mills. And you are?"

"Shane Sullivan but everyone calls me Sully," he replied.

"You mean like the airline pilot?"

"Yeah. Without the 'having saved hundreds of lives' thing going for me." He started again. "Thanks for the info, Mills."

"You got it, Sully."

Shane continued toward the elevators and rode to the first floor again. The Forensics lab was in the far eastern corner of the building. He walked inside the dimly lit area packed with desks and equipment. There were special rooms designed for identifying bullets and even a room used to stage reenactments of murder scenes just to be sure their coordinates were correct. The techs he searched for were in a corner in a room behind a glass wall.

He pushed through the door. "Morning. I'm helping out Alvarez and Montoya concerning the Boyce investigation. It's tied to the Diaz/Goodfellow case. I'm not sure if you're..."

"We know the case." One of the technicians kept her back to Shane while she worked on her computer. "What do you need?"

"Montoya is in the field and he and Alvarez have been waiting to see if any more prints had come back from the office of the victim, Tommy Boyce."

She glanced at her colleague. "You see anything come back on that yet?"

"Let me check." The man typed in commands on his computer. "Looks like. Yeah, actually. We just got a match on two more sets this morning." He turned to Shane. "Finley Dawson and Franklin Perry."

Dawson. That figured. But who was the other guy? "Is there a file on Franklin Perry?" Shane asked.

The man shuffled through the report. "Perry's in the system because his company has been contracted with the city on public works projects. I don't know any more than that."

"Thanks, man. This is great. I'll pass it along to the guys," Shane replied.

———

ALLISON OPENED HER FRONT DOOR TO A BRIGHT MORNING and the sun glaring in her eyes. "Thanks for coming over." She stepped aside.

"After you called last night letting me know you were home, I wanted to get to the station first thing this morning and see if they had all the prints back." Shane brushed by her and walked into the kitchen. "Please tell me you have coffee?"

"In the pot." She followed him. "So, are all the prints back?"

"Two more sets were recovered. Your buddy Fin Dawson popped up."

"He's not my buddy. And the other?" Allison grabbed a mug from the cabinet and handed it to him.

"A guy by the name of Franklin Perry. I don't have a background on him yet but apparently, he was involved in a couple of public works projects for the city a while back. That's all I know right now. You have that video from Boyce's office?"

"I left it with Fin." Allison perched on one of the stools while Shane stirred his coffee.

"You left it with Fin? Why? Allison, I need to see it. What if one of the men in Boyce's office was this Franklin Perry guy? We have his prints. It wouldn't be hard to confirm facial-recognition from that video with any other surveillance Montoya might find down the road. What if he was the killer?"

"We left it with him because there were still several more hours of files to go through. Fin said he'd get with us this morning when he finished reviewing it all."

Shane threw back his head and moaned. "How can you put such blind trust in this guy, huh? You don't know him. He's going to have to turn it over to us. That's all there is to it. You said you thought you'd seen the same car in that video too. I mean, come on, Allison."

"Shane, I know you're one of them..."

"One of them. You mean a cop?" He held her gaze. "Allison, this isn't up to you to decide. This could be evidence. Critical evidence. Do you want me to lose my job? Because that's what's going to happen if we don't turn this over to Montoya."

"We don't even know if it's the same man or the same car. Shane, I don't know what I saw that night. I wish I did. I told you, I —I froze. I've never been so scared out of my mind before. I don't know if the car that pulled up to Tommy's office was the same one I saw that night. It could be. And two men entered his office, not one. I only caught a minor glimpse of the driver coming out of that garage. I saw no passenger. There are similarities, yes, but I just can't be sure."

"Then let me take you off the hook here. You don't have to be sure, okay? It's a possibility and that's enough to run on," he replied.

"Fin mentioned he was going to see if the plates on that car were visible in any of the remaining footage as well. He knows someone at the DMV who can run plates."

"I can run plates. And it would be legal. You're stalling, Allison. Why?"

"Montoya doesn't want me within a mile of his investigation. You either. He has made that crystal clear. If we hand over the video, we're out. Both of us. You and I know he's laser-focused on Carlos Diaz. He's not paying attention to what happened with me or the car I saw because I didn't give him enough detail."

"That could change depending on where the leads take him," Shane replied.

"Sure. But we can run with this now. If we don't get a plate or can't identify the men in the video, then I'll make sure to hand the footage over to Montoya myself." Allison reached for Shane's hand that he had pressed on the countertop. "I would never put your job in jeopardy. If it comes down to it, I'll say you knew nothing. I won't let you take the fall for my decisions. But Montoya could be overlooking the obvious. I don't think he or Alvarez are looking into Tommy's murder the way they should be."

"That's not a fair assessment."

"Maybe not, but that's how I see it. Just a day, maybe two. Can you give me that? Let me do what I promised Lucy I would do. I'm not interfering with their investigation. I'm not getting in their way."

Shane held her gaze. "On one condition. You're not doing this alone."

"You, me and Charlie. I couldn't ask for anything more."

———

DETECTIVE MONTOYA SCRATCHED HIS TEMPLE AND EYED Carlos Diaz once again. "Why did you go to a private investigator when you had concerns about your wife's fidelity?"

"As I said, I wanted proof she was cheating."

"You didn't think to just ask her if she was having an affair?" Montoya pressed on.

"I have a lot to lose, Detective. I'm a wealthy man. Evidence would be necessary to move forward on divorce proceedings and ensure Tracy wouldn't see a dime of my money."

"Of course. And the fact that she was cheating with the man who you trusted most with your company's finances, that didn't play into your equation?"

"Of course it did. The easy solution would have been to fire him. Again, I needed proof and I chose to hire a private investigator to obtain it for me, which is within my legal rights."

"Mr. Diaz, did you suspect Harlan Goodfellow of embezzlement or otherwise trying to harm your organization?"

Diaz pulled upright and thrust back his shoulders. "No. I had full trust in him."

"Then it must have been very difficult to learn of his deeply personal betrayal."

"It would throw anyone for a loop, Detective Montoya, I assure you."

"I have no doubt." Montoya pressed the stop button on the digital recorder. "Mr. Diaz, I can't imagine what you must be going through right now. Learning of your wife's betrayals and then knowing that she was murdered along with her lover. A double blow like that can make a person feel hopeless."

"What is your point, Detective?"

"I want to find your wife's killer, Mr. Diaz. That is my number one priority. And in order to do that, I'm going to need to dig deeply into your relationship with her. I have to rule out the possibility of you being a suspect."

"How can I possibly have done such a thing?"

Montoya raised a preemptive hand. "Crimes of passion are nothing new, Mr. Diaz. But my point is, you're going to need to turn over everything you have regarding your contact with Tommy Boyce, who, I'm sure you're already aware, was found dead the day after your wife and her lover were killed."

"I am aware, yes," Diaz replied.

"I have reason to believe Mr. Boyce was acting on behalf of another when working the task you hired him for." Montoya watched as Diaz appeared confused. "What I'm saying, sir, is that this is a two-pronged approach. I need to look at why Boyce was targeted in addition to your wife and Mr. Goodfellow."

"I will tell you everything I know about Tommy Boyce, Detective. My wife is dead. Regardless of her betrayal, I would never have wanted this to happen. You have to believe me."

"Then I will also ask for your help regarding Mr. Goodfellow."

"Anything," Diaz added.

"You two were close friends and colleagues. I'm going to need any records you have. Receipts of hotels, purchases, whatever, that your wife might have made in conjunction with their affair. I'll need Goodfellow's employee records, any stocks he held with your company, anything relating to his work here too. And I'll need to know if Mr. Goodfellow had enemies."

"Unless he was also screwing someone else's wife, I can't think of anyone who would have wanted him to be murdered."

Montoya nodded. "Before I turn on the recorder again, I need to ask you a final question and this will be off the record, so I need you to be as straight-forward as possible."

"Okay," Diaz replied.

"You already stated your whereabouts on the night of your wife's murder. Your alibi checks out. But what I want to ask you is when you last saw Tommy Boyce."

Diaz eyed the recorder. He returned his sights to Montoya. "I did go and see Mr. Boyce earlier in the day just to confirm everything was on track. However, on my arrival at his office, he wasn't there. I tried his cell phone too."

"Did you notice if his office had been broken into when you arrived?"

"No. It was locked up and everything looked fine. Why?"

Montoya nodded. "It had been broken into later in the night. We're working on getting Boyce's phone records so any calls you made to him will show up just so you're aware. Let's continue." Montoya turned on the recorder once again.

13

Lucy Boyce was alone. Her mother was gone and now her father. For the girl of only nineteen, returning to normal seemed desperately out of reach. In the eyes of the law, she was an adult. The burden of dealing with the estate fell on her. Not that there was much of an estate. The house, the car, her dad's business. This was what she had to deal with now, along with arranging for her father's funeral. There was extended family to whom she'd already made the heart-breaking phone calls. An uncle, her father's younger brother, and a cousin who lived in New York. The uncle offered to help Lucy through the painful time but Lucy, being her father's daughter, refused the help and insisted only on his attendance at the funeral at a time and place to be announced soon.

An impossible weight to endure, Lucy had no other choice than to confront the duties head-on. She recalled the time spent sorting through her mother's belongings. Now it was time to rifle through her dad's bedroom and figure out where he had left off. What bills had been paid, what tasks were left undone.

It was almost noon on Saturday. It was the day she and her father sometimes sat around watching movies or going out for lunch on the beach. That was over now. This day, she stood in the kitchen with her eyes still swollen from two days of tears and steadied herself enough to enter his room. He had a desk inside where she knew he kept files. His laptop rested on it. So far, Lucy had only been approached by a detective named Alvarez. She gave him her statement and hadn't heard anything since. She supposed these things took time but was surprised by the detective's lack of interest in her or their home. He seemed more interested in the office where she hadn't yet had the conviction to visit since it had been broken into the night he disappeared.

The time since the death of her mother was long enough such that when she entered the bedroom, Lucy no longer saw it as her parents' room, only her dad's. The two had long ago rid themselves of all that belonged to Lucy's mother. He couldn't handle the pain of seeing anything that she had touched. Lucy kept a picture and old photo albums in her room, out of sight from her dad.

With a deep intake of breath, Lucy made her way to the small desk pressed against a large picture window overlooking the screened-in pool. She opened his laptop and peered at the sign-in screen. Tommy never kept secrets from his only child, but Lucy didn't know his username and password. This was the only computer that hadn't been turned over to the police. She knew they had his laptop from the office and the other two desktop computers. They also had plenty of smart people to figure out how to gain access to those computers. She didn't have that sort of expertise. So, her only solution was to search for someplace he might've written down the details, if he had written down anything.

She started first with the drawers in his desk and rummaged through them to find any clues. "Of course there's nothing." She continued to search, making her way to his bedside table. The drawers contained nothing out of the ordinary and nothing that gave away his passwords. "Come on, Dad. I could use some help here," Lucy pressed on.

She walked around to the other nightstand where a photo of the two of them sat in a frame on the top. A tear fell down her cheek and she set down the frame again before opening the top drawer. Her brow knitted as she delved through the papers inside. "Letters?" Her lips quivered. She discovered several letters written by Tommy addressed to her. "Dad, what are these?" She opened the one on top and began to read. Her eyes consumed the words as they welled with tears. "Oh my God. You knew something was wrong. You knew something was going to happen."

In the letter, Tommy instructed her on what to do with the house, his car, everything he owned, including where he kept his will. "Dad," she cried. And at the bottom of the letter, there it was.

"You'll need access to my laptop, assuming you still have it, so here's my password."

Lucy wiped away the tears and walked over to his computer again. This time, she entered the password.

File folders dotted the screen's wallpaper which was a photo of her and her dad sitting at a table overlooking the beach. Tears streamed on instinct. Lucy sat down in the chair gazing at the files and wondering if any of this meant anything.

She hadn't known what case he had been working that night. They didn't talk about it in any great detail. Lucy only knew he had been working on an affair situation, which was the bulk of his work anyway. She never thought much of it. Upon studying the screen, she spotted the names of the people who were probably his clients. There were too many to know which were or were not important. Maybe she could ask the woman who had seen him last that night. Allison Hart had been kind and helpful. Her dad had trusted Allison, so maybe she should too.

———

"I'm on my way." Allison ended the call and swiped her keys from the entry table. She peered into the living room where Nolan had just awakened. "I'm heading out. I won't be long."

He slowly turned his head to her, confused. His sleepy eyes and disheveled hair looking almost comical as he sat in front of the television holding a bowl of cereal. "Okay."

She didn't stop to explain, only opened the door to a blast of tropical air and started toward the driveway. Lucy had reached out to her. That alone was enough to add fuel to her fire to keep pursuing Tommy's death no matter how hard Shane tried to hold her back. A murderer was still free.

The house she had visited twice now was just ahead. Allison pulled to a stop along the front of the home and cut the engine. She peeled herself off the driver's seat and started toward the front door. But before she could knock, the door opened. "Lucy. Hi."

"Hi, Ms. Hart. Thank you for coming." She stepped aside. "Please, come in."

"Thank you, Lucy. It's good to see you." Allison noticed Lucy's puffy eyes and reddened cheeks. She had been crying and it was no wonder. "I'm so glad you called me."

Lucy closed the door. "You've been so kind to try to help me and I was hoping that maybe you could take a look at something for me?" She walked into the hall. "The last time you were here, I mentioned I couldn't get into my dad's laptop. Well, as I was starting to clean out his room, I found where he had written down his password. So, I opened his laptop and saw a bunch of files on there. They look like case files, but you might know better than me." Lucy continued to Tommy's bedroom. "Please forgive the mess. I only just got started."

"No apologies necessary." Allison followed her inside. It was strange to stand in the bedroom of a man she hardly knew but whose daughter tugged so hard on her heartstrings.

Lucy made her way to the laptop and signed in again. She stepped aside and waved over Allison. "Will you take a look?"

"Absolutely," Allison drew near.

Lucy pointed to the home screen. "I'm pretty sure these folders are all cases he worked on. I couldn't tell you how far back these go, but the reason I wanted you to see this is that I'm wondering if any of the names on these folders might mean something to you."

Allison pulled her reading glasses from the handbag that still hung off her shoulder. She leaned in for a better look and examined the names. There must have been fifty at least; all crammed onto the screen in seemingly random order. "Let me see." She recalled the names of the people she photographed that night, Harlan Goodfellow and Tracy Diaz, and looked for them. "This is it." She looked over her shoulder at Lucy who gazed intently at the screen. "Diaz. Your dad hired me to photograph the wife."

Lucy nodded. "Okay. I guess we should open it then." She clicked on the folder and a list of file names appeared. "There's a lot of information here. Should we give this to the police?"

"That would be the right thing to do. Lucy, I'm not a cop, but that doesn't mean I don't want to find out who killed your dad. I feel responsible."

"Please don't. You couldn't have known what was going to happen," Lucy replied.

"Be that as it may, yes, you should hand this over as soon as possible. But with your permission, I'd like to copy the files before you do."

"Why?"

"I'll be honest with you, Lucy, there are other people involved in this that the cops aren't focusing on just yet. But I think they could be key players. I guess you could say it's a hunch that I would really like to pursue without getting in the way of the police. I'll tell you what, I have a friend who happens to be a detective, and I know he'd be just as interested in seeing what's on here as I am. We can take a look, copy anything we think could be important, then I'll hand over the laptop to him. He'll see to it the detective in charge gets it. But I want you to be a part of this if you'd like. I think your dad would've wanted it that way."

"Like now?" Lucy asked.

"The sooner the better. I can have him meet us at my house if you'd like to come over. I'm sure you don't want people here right now."

"Not really. I suppose having him take a look would be a good idea," Lucy replied.

Allison smiled. "I agree."

———

ALLISON OPENED HER FRONT DOOR. "THANKS FOR COMING. There's someone I'd like you to meet." She walked back into the kitchen. "Lucy, this is Detective Shane Sullivan. He's a good friend of mine. Shane, this is Lucy Boyce, Tommy's daughter."

"I'm very sorry for your loss." He offered his hand. "It's nice to meet you and thanks for letting me be here."

"It's nice to meet you as well. Should we take a look at these files now?" Lucy asked.

"No time like the present." Allison pulled up to the counter and Shane stood next to her.

Lucy opened the laptop once again and clicked on the files. "I don't know if there'll be anything important in here or not."

"That's what we're here to find out," Allison replied.

They began to examine each file and each one seemed insignificant to the murder of Tommy Boyce.

When Lucy came upon the Diaz file, she opened it. "This was the client who hired him, right?"

"It is," Allison began. "Hey Lucy, can you open this one here." She pointed to the file named "City Deal."

Lucy clicked on the file and copies of contracts appeared. "What is this?"

"Perry Construction. What does this have to do with the affair of Diaz's wife?" Allison added. "Lucy, do you mind if I set up my printer on this? I'd like to print this out to get a better look."

Lucy turned the laptop toward Allison where she connected her home printer.

"Okay. Let's print out this puppy." She pressed the button and in the back hall somewhere came the sound of a printer spitting out paper. "I'll go get it."

On Allison's return to the kitchen, her brow furrowed as she peered at the document.

"So?" Shane asked.

"It's a copy of a contract with Perry Construction." She looked at Shane. "Franklin Perry? And it's also signed by the City of Tampa and Carlos Diaz's development firm."

"It has to be Franklin Perry. That name can't be a coincidence. And it's included in the Diaz file. Why?" Shane asked.

"I have no clue." Allison leaned in closer to the laptop. "Is there anything in there regarding the Diaz firm?"

Lucy listed the files again and scanned the names. "What about this one? It says, 'Pay Deal.'"

"Sounds dubious," Allison began. "Open it up."

Lucy clicked on the file and an image of a bank statement appeared. "You want me to print this out too?"

"Yes, please." Allison started back into the hall again to retrieve the document. And, getting the first look at it, she already spotted the problem. "Oh, no."

"What is it?" Shane asked.

Allison set it on the counter. "There's a $50,000 deposit on here." She continued to examine the statement. "It's from an anonymous account and this account belongs to Carlos Diaz. See for yourself."

"Payment for a construction contract? Does it match with this document here?" Shane pulled the other paper toward him and reviewed it again.

"I don't think you're understanding me," Allison added. "This money went into Diaz's *personal* bank account. Not his business. Look." She pointed to the name on the account. "And it doesn't have his wife's name on it either. But what's scarier is that we don't know where it came from. The payor is unidentified."

"A bribe." Shane's tone turned flat. "Why would Boyce have had this? He was hired by Carlos Diaz to get proof to use against his wife. That's not what we're looking at right now."

"Do you think this was why my dad was killed?" Lucy turned solemn. "Did his own client kill him?"

Allison placed her hand on Lucy's arm. "Oh, honey, I think your dad might have stumbled onto something bigger than what he bargained for. But we can't jump to conclusions just yet. This is going to take some research." She turned to Shane. "What do you think?"

"Lucy, I think your dad found something important. What it means yet, I can't say. However, I'm willing to bet there's more to this than what we're seeing right now. It could mean Carlos Diaz was into a shady deal and murdering his wife was someone's idea of retribution."

"I know you and Montoya aren't exactly buddies but what are the odds you can get copies of Mrs. Diaz's cell phone records?" Allison asked Shane.

"Why hers?" Lucy asked.

"Well, I think the only way your dad would have this was if Mrs. Diaz gave it to him," Allison replied.

"And so by getting her phone records, you'll try to find out if my dad was in contact with her directly?"

"Yep. And others who could be important." Allison turned to Shane again. "Getting Tommy's phone records would be helpful too."

Shane nodded. "If Tommy Boyce was in direct contact with Tracy Diaz, that changes everything."

14

Milo Nash understood that control was slipping through his fingers. His friend was dead, and he shouldered the responsibility. This was his operation. And now the special assistant attorney was at the mercy of outside influences.

He was alone in the office on a Saturday afternoon and had arranged for a meeting. The other person attending this meeting had just knocked on his door. "It's open." It was time to navigate this landmine Milo had set for himself and make it to the other side without taking anyone else down with him. He eyed his door when it opened. "Franklin. It's good to see you. Thank you for coming down."

"Milo," Franklin Perry offered a greeting.

"Have a seat." Milo shook his hand and sat back down. "Franklin, as you know, the Diaz organization is in the midst of troubling times."

Perry scratched at his thick grey hair and winced, accentuating the wrinkles around his eyes. "That's a bit of an understatement,

Milo. None of this has gone the way we had hoped. I'm not sure how much longer I can protect my people."

"You're not the only one with folks to look out for," Milo replied.

"Then what do you suggest we do to bring this to its conclusion before anyone else gets hurt?"

Milo leaned back in his chair and laced his fingers behind his head. "I should've stopped Boyce earlier."

"How could you have without jeopardizing the operation?" Perry asked. "How long do you think it'll take for the cops to find out what Diaz was up to? And what if they tie it back to me? The last thing I want to be accused of is obstructing an investigation."

"It's not just Diaz we should worry about. You and I both know there are people much higher on the food chain who will do everything they can to shield themselves. Right now, Tampa PD is working a double homicide."

"Triple," Perry added.

"Yes. Their focus is on Carlos Diaz and a possible crime of passion. We need to make sure that's all they focus on in the short term until we can get more details. I also have a very good friend who I know is looking for answers. I've offered her crumbs and want to see where they lead her."

"And if this friend ends up like Tommy?"

"She's off their radar for now. I'll keep it that way. Franklin, do you have any idea who was in the driver's seat that night?"

He shook his head. "I've done my best to get you some answers. I wish I had something for you. But I am working on it."

"You'll have to work fast. It's the proof we need to end this. I want it before any more of our people end up in the crosshairs."

Perry took in a deep breath and pushed off the chair. He stood at a respectable 5 feet 11 inches and was thinner than he should've been. "I have to maintain distance between the investigation and my interactions with Diaz. If Carlos gets a whiff of what we're doing..."

"He's under a microscope right now and for the foreseeable future. The timing is opportune for him to dig himself a deeper grave. That's what you should be focused on right now. Let me handle the rest."

———

CARLOS DIAZ TRAVERSED HIS OFFICE WITH NERVOUS ENERGY. His jawline sprouted black whiskers and his eyes were weighed down by heavy bags underneath. "I didn't kill my wife. Detective Montoya doesn't believe me. I could see it in his eyes. He's already picturing me in a 6 by 8 cell."

"Just calm down, Carlos." Franklin Perry took him by the arms and captured his gaze. "I'm here to help. You're innocent and the evidence will show that."

"I'm not so sure the cops care about evidence right now. I hired Tommy Boyce to get proof of Tracy's infidelity. That's all. I didn't kill her or Harlan. I swear it. And now Tommy's dead too." He returned to a small heather-grey sofa in his office and sat down. "I'm losing it, Franklin. What am I going to do?"

Franklin sat down in the chair across from him and leaned over with his elbows on his knees. "Carlos, you're doing everything in your power to cooperate with the police. They see that. You can't worry about the other stuff. They aren't looking at your finances, your business dealings, nothing like that."

"They'll have my phone records in a matter of days, if not sooner," Carlos replied. "And Tracy's."

"All they'll find is a man desperate to understand why his wife was cheating on him," Franklin replied.

"Can you guarantee that? I think that might be beyond even your reach, Franklin."

"If you show Montoya that there's something to worry about besides Tracy, we all lose. We can't afford to let that happen."

Carlos twisted his face in anger. "I realize that, okay. Jesus!"

"Flying off the handle isn't the sign of a man who's keeping his shit together. I'm going to need you to calm down and then we can talk rationally about a solution."

"Yeah, okay. I'm sorry. I'm just..." His eyes welled and tears spilled down his hollow cheeks. "My wife's dead. Tracy's dead."

"She was cheating on you, brother," Franklin replied.

"That doesn't mean I didn't love her." Carlos swiped at the tears. "What do I need to do, Franklin? How do I keep the cops away from the business? Harlan was the only one I could rely on. Now he's dead too. He would've made sure the cops didn't see anything they shouldn't."

"Here's what you're going to do," Franklin began. "Move the money to some offshore account."

Carlos scoffed. "Are you serious? There's no such thing anymore. All those so-called 'off-shore' banks are cooperating with the US and have been for some time."

"Then cash out. Get the money and put it someplace safe. Close the account. So far, no one knows about that personal account and we're going to keep it that way."

Carlos eyed him with suspicion. "And what about the money they gave you?"

"I'm not the one under investigation, Carlos. This isn't about me."

"Not yet."

Franklin's eyes narrowed and the muscles in his face tensed. "Is that a threat?"

Carlos retreated. "No, man. I'm sorry. I didn't mean anything. I'm..."

"You're under a lot of stress right now. Just do as I say. Hide the money however you can. If the cops find it, then you're screwed. Like you said, they have no evidence you killed Tracy or Harlan."

"That's because I didn't."

Franklin raised his hands. "I know. But if they find the money, they'll follow the trail. And you and I both know that will direct them to the one we believe is the real killer."

"I don't know who did it," Carlos insisted.

"Oh, I think maybe you do. I think we both do. But it's too late now. First and foremost, we get you out of Montoya's crosshairs and then we'll fix everything else. We'll make sure the ones responsible pay the price. But remember, Tracy died because she knew what you were doing, and she was going to use it against you. Harlan was dumb enough to try to play the knight in shining armor and help her find a way out. Except that he was caught in the crossfire. Asshole shouldn't have been screwing your wife in the first place."

Carlos dropped his head into his hands. "I'll move the money." He raised his sights to Franklin and continued, "you're going to have to get me a name. I need to know who killed her. I have to know if it was them."

———

ALLISON WALKED LUCY TO HER DOOR. "I WANT YOU TO CALL me if you need anything, you understand? Day or night."

"Thank you, Allison." Lucy hesitated, finally turning back. "I'm afraid."

"I know you are. But I want you to know that you're not in any danger."

"Someone broke into his office. This seems like the next logical place to look, doesn't it?" Lucy added.

She reached for Lucy's arm. "Detective Sullivan and I wouldn't leave you here if we thought, in any way, there was a chance you might be in danger. I think your father was a casualty of something else. I think he got in the way and they wanted to silence him. But that doesn't mean anyone will be after you. In fact, it's a good idea to keep doing what you're doing. It's best if no one suspects anything's changed."

"Except that my dad's dead. How am I supposed to keep that a secret?" A stray tear skimmed down Lucy's cheek.

Allison embraced Lucy as though she was her own daughter. There was nothing more she could say to this girl and her words of reassurance were hardly founded on solid ground. "There's nothing for you to worry about. We will get to the bottom of what happened to your dad. Today was a good day. We learned a lot. There's more work ahead of us and both Shane and I and a couple of my closest friends will do what's necessary to assist the police and work to find Tommy's killer. In the meantime, you know how to get hold of me."

"You'll keep in contact, though, right?"

"You know I will. Just take care of yourself. Let me handle the rest. Goodbye, Lucy."

"Bye, Allison."

Allison returned to the kitchen where Shane waited.

"Is she going to be okay, you think?" he asked.

"No. Not for a long while." Allison held his gaze. "I think you should turn in the laptop to Alvarez. But I might leave out the fact that we already looked at it. Don't point anything out. He has a team of forensics people for that and I'd prefer if we stayed just a step ahead of him for now."

"I have no intention of telling him we copied the files," Shane replied.

"And I think I need to see Finley Dawson."

"You'll be getting that video back, right?" he asked.

"I will and I'll see if he found anything else."

"I'm sure he'll be very forthcoming with information," Shane huffed.

She turned to him. "Jealousy doesn't become you, Shane."

"Jealous? Of what? That wannabe cop-slash-surfer? Look, Allison, I don't trust the guy. Sorry, but I don't. I know you think he's the be-all-end-all, but I don't. And I'm not so sure he wasn't trying to set you up to take the fall for the break-in at Boyce's office."

"That's a stretch and you know it. You're looking for reasons not to trust him. I don't think he's the all-important lynchpin to this investigation and you're wrong about him, Shane. I know he's arrogant but he's smart. Fin has something to offer. He can be of value. And besides, we need all the help we can get. Which reminds me, I need to call Charlie."

"We're getting too many fingers in this pie. The more people who know, the more danger those people might end up in."

She held her phone, ready to dial up Charlie. "Well, that puts me at ease."

"I'm not trying to ease your conscience. If this is what we think it is and there are people willing to kill to keep their secret, then make no mistake, this is dangerous."

Allison pressed on. "I get it, Shane. But you and I alone don't have the resources necessary to delve into this the way it should be. Montoya will keep you placated by tossing you scraps and nothing more. He has no reason to keep either of us in the loop. You might be able to buy a favor from Alvarez, but we'll see."

"I'll use what we know now to get what we need later," Shane said. "Boyce's laptop will come in handy."

———

ALLISON WAS IN HER KITCHEN WITH THE PHONE TO HER EAR when the knock came. "Hey, Charlie, hang on a second, would you? Shane just left and I think he's at the door. I'll bet he forgot something." She pressed the mute button and opened the front door. "Shane, what did you.... Oh, Milo, what are you doing here?"

"Allison. You mind if I come in?" Milo could often be too humble for his own good and right now, he carried that humility in spades.

"Not at all. Please come in." She closed the door and returned to the call. "Charlie, I'm going to have to call you back. Milo just showed up." Allison ended the call and turned to him. "You arrived just in time."

"Is that so? By the sound of it, I interrupted a phone call." He continued inside.

"I'll call her back." Allison started into the kitchen. "Can I get you something to drink?"

"I'll take a coffee if you got it."

"So long as you don't mind it being reheated." She reached for a mug in the cabinet.

"Not at all. Listen, I'm sorry to just drop by. I normally would've preferred to call but this was something I needed to discuss in person. And it couldn't wait."

Allison placed the re-heated coffee in front of him. "In person, huh? That sounds alarming."

"How is everything going with Finley Dawson? Was he able to offer help regarding Tommy's caseload?"

"He was. We've been putting our heads together. Why do you ask?"

"Obviously, with what happened to Tommy and of course the people he hired you to photograph..."

"Uh-huh." She watched him stare at the mug with unusual intensity. "What's going on, Milo? Cageyness isn't your style."

He looked at her with notable concern. "There are details I omitted when I passed along Tommy's contact information. At the time I thought it was unnecessary and unrelated to address your goals."

"Don't lawyer up on me now. Just say what you mean to say."

"I knew Tommy needed help," he continued. "He was getting buried in some of the more mundane aspects of his work and I thought, why not see if he could use your skills? I gave him a heads up and he said, 'great, send her over.' Nothing more than that. But..."

Allison's face hardened. "But..."

"I also knew if things went south you were, hands-down, the best person to handle it."

"Oh, I don't think they could've gone any farther south. Milo, what do you know about Tommy and his involvement with Carlos Diaz other than investigating the affair?"

"I knew Diaz hired him to get evidence he could use in a divorce, yes. But what I didn't know, evidently, was that Tommy would end up dead because of it."

Allison detected a sense of foreboding and it drove her pulse higher. "You're talking in circles now."

"What I mean to say is that I knew Tommy was working on something big. What I couldn't possibly know was that it would end up ensnaring you."

"But it did," Allison replied.

"You're tough as nails. I've known that since we first met in the courtroom that day."

"Enough, Milo. What did Tommy get himself tangled up in? I have to know. I found out a few things…"

"Things?" he asked.

"Tommy's daughter, Lucy. She asked me to take a look at some files she found on her dad's laptop. That was just this morning. There was something on there that we don't know much about yet. But by the sounds of it, maybe you do?"

"The money," Milo replied.

Allison shook her head. "So you did know?"

"I suspected it. Tommy was working on getting proof of a bribe of some sort. It must have happened fast because he would've come to me with it straight away. Allison, if you have that proof it's important that you turn it over to me."

"He hadn't told you about it?"

"Like I said, I can only guess that he'd just received it. We were supposed to meet up the day after…" Milo trailed off for a moment. "He was probably planning on telling me then. Where is this information now and what exactly did you find?"

"I'll be happy to tell you what we found if you give me everything. Look, I'm in up to my knees, Milo. You have to tell me everything."

15

Milo had laid it all on the table. All the events leading up to this moment and it was now on her shoulders to decide if she could continue. "You know I love you, Milo, but how could you do this? How could you get me involved in something like this? Forget that Tommy's dead. Forget that he has a daughter. What if I was killed? Nolan, Micah? At the very least, you should've told me what I was getting myself into. It should have been my decision to make."

He closed his eyes in regret. "There was no way I could have foreseen what happened that night, Allison. It wasn't even in the same ballpark as what we knew Tommy was doing at the time. You have to believe me. I would never put you in harm's way. And I didn't think Tommy was in that sort of danger either. The arrangement was Tommy was going to continue working for Carlos Diaz and do exactly what he asked regarding his wife, Tracy. And in the background, I, along with another, would continue to build a case against Carlos. There was no reason Tracy or Harlan Goodfellow should've been in the crosshairs, let alone Tommy Boyce."

"Well they were. Someone knew enough about them to be concerned and they ended up dead." Allison folded her arms and clenched her jaw. "How much do you know about the wife, Tracy?"

Milo shook his head. "No more than I should, I suppose. She wasn't part of the plan. It was Carlos we were after. The affair was a sidebar. It fell into our laps and we used it as a way to keep Carlos distracted and that was when I brought in Tommy. I facilitated their meeting."

"You keep saying 'we' and 'they.' Who else knows about this?"

"I think it's best if you don't know that just yet. And that's strictly for your protection, not because I don't trust you."

Allison nodded. "Sure. But you know, if Tracy Diaz was like most other women, she would have confided in a close friend."

"About the affair?" Milo asked.

"Yes. And maybe other things too. I'll have to find out who was in her inner-circle. I want to know how long the affair had been going on and what she told her friends."

"What will that accomplish?"

She held Milo's gaze. "Let me ask you something. Do you think Carlos Diaz killed his wife and his right-hand man?"

Milo pursed his lips. "Not in the least."

"Neither do I. First of all, if he had he would be behaving much differently and from what Shane has heard on the grapevine, Carlos seemed genuinely heartbroken. And then we have the car, which we're pretty sure was a Mercedes. It blew past me that night, straight out of Goodfellow's building."

This wasn't payback for Milo withholding details from her, but Allison didn't want to mention the possibility it had been the same car they had seen in a video outside Tommy's office. Then again, maybe it was payback and she was being petty. Regardless, that was going to be her ace in hand in case she needed it later.

"I didn't get a good look at the driver, but I can guarantee you it wasn't Carlos Diaz," Allison continued. "If he was a passenger, I sure as hell didn't see him."

"I suppose he could have been in the backseat," Milo said.

"Sure. But for the moment, let's go with our assumption that he didn't kill the couple. Then that would lead me to believe Tracy opened her mouth to someone, a friend maybe, about Carlos' business dealings and her affair. You can't tell me she wouldn't have known what he was up to. Harlan Goodfellow was Carlos' CFO and close friend."

"Harlan could have told her," Milo added.

"Can't rule that out either. But let's get back to Tracy because I think she might hold the key as to who let it be known where the happy couple was planning their tryst that night. Is it possible to get a list of names of her closest friends?"

"If Montoya is worth his salt, he would've already talked to her friends. I don't know the man personally, but you don't get to be a homicide detective without knowing what you're doing. So, it's possible he could forward that information on if he was feeling generous."

"Not likely. He doesn't think much of me. He's not going to give me the time of day, let alone details I have no business having. Shane either. So who else might know?"

"Sounds morbid as all hell, but what about the upcoming funeral?" Milo asked.

Allison crinkled her nose as though a terrible smell wafted in front of her. "The funeral. Of course. I hate funerals. But that would be the place to go if I wanted to know who Tracy's friends were."

"As you know, I work for the D.A.'s office so I can't exactly encourage you to pursue this avenue. But if I were you and I wanted to know if Tracy Diaz spilled the beans to a close personal friend, and maybe said friend let it be known, then the funeral may be all you have to work with." Milo cocked his head. "Now that I've given you that, it's time you tell me what evidence you have regarding the suspected bribe."

———

THE POPULAR BAYSIDE RESTAURANT WAS BURSTING AT THE seams as Saturday night rolled in. Allison sat in the booth. The music was loud, and the patrons were louder. She watched Charlie's eyes glaze over with a blend of repulsion and anxiety. "I know it's crazy, but I think it's the only way. I talked with Milo about it and he agrees."

"Milo agrees?" Charlie scoffed. "That can't be right."

"Look, Charlie, I get that it's a little macabre, but we have to know who she talked to. Who her friends were. Tracy Diaz might have been murdered for something her husband was doing. Maybe she threatened to talk, I don't know. But if we can't uncover who her friends were or who she may have confided in, I don't know where else to go. It's the last option before we have to trust that Montoya will figure it out. Or Alvarez will offer up valuable phone records. I'm not going to hold my breath for either outcome. What's worse is that neither detective knows about any of this. And for now, Milo wants to keep it that way."

"Hold up. Milo, an attorney for the D.A.'s office, doesn't think this should be brought up with the investigating officer? Why?"

"Because it'll end his own investigation. People he has working for him will be exposed. Milo knew about the money. I told him what we found on Tommy's laptop and now he has a copy of it. He's more determined than ever to see this through. And if Montoya catches wind that Tracy Diaz knew her husband had some shady deal and took a bribe or something, Milo thinks Carlos will be gone in a heartbeat and then no one's going to know what happened to any of them."

Charlie shook her head. "This doesn't feel right, Alli. What if we're breaking the law? You want your license, right? Well, if all this comes out that you did nothing about this, what chance do you stand of making that happen?" Charlie asked. "What does Shane think about all this?"

Allison picked up her glass of iced tea and sucked on the straw, averting her eyes.

"He doesn't know," Charlie said. "You haven't told him this cockamamie idea, have you?"

After a final, loud slurp, Allison set down the glass. "No, but not because I don't think he would go for it."

"Really?"

"Maybe he wouldn't but point being, Montoya is trying to find who killed Tracy and Harlan Goodfellow. As of right now, he has no reason to look into Carlos's business dealings. That could change, and probably will. Which is why we don't have a lot of time to figure this out."

"How do you know? Are you there with Montoya questioning Diaz?"

"Well, no," Allison replied.

"No. You're not. You don't know where his investigation is leading him or to who. And for you to jump in and somehow make nice with Tracy Diaz's friends? That is a rabbit hole, my friend."

"I know this is way off base from where we started."

"Sister, we are so high up in the bleachers, I can't see the field let alone the bases. We started this because you wanted to help that girl. An admirable goal. Now you want to help Milo catch Carlos Diaz in what, a bribery scheme or something?"

"It's all tied together. I promise you, Charlie, it is. Boyce knew what Diaz was up to. We found proof on his laptop. Diaz was on the take with someone and it involves a company called Perry Construction. Milo says it's all intertwined."

"If Milo wants you to handle it this way, then he must have a hell of a lead on something huge. But we aren't doing this without Shane's guidance. You're going to have to tell him." Charlie picked up her barbecue bacon cheeseburger and held it to her lips. "And I'll need a black dress."

———

GIVEN THE MEDIA ATTENTION TO THE MURDERS AND THE social and business standing of Carlos Diaz, blending in at the funeral was a piece of cake for Allison and Charlie. No one questioned if or how they knew the deceased.

The service was only minutes from commencing and the Sacred Heart Catholic Church in Tampa was filled to capacity. The ornate cathedral had a long and storied history in the city. It was the perfect choice for the wealthy Diaz family. Allison and Charlie were donned in appropriately dark attire and were just about to enter.

"Let's hang out here in the back and see who approaches Carlos. Particularly women. They're most likely to be Tracy's friends." Allison smoothed down her long tresses. It was rare that she wore her hair down, but it felt right today; respectful. "Are you ready?"

Charlie tugged on her black blazer. "I should've gotten a smaller size. I look like a rotten sack of potatoes in this. And I'm sweating."

"You look very—conservative." Allison smiled.

They stood in front of the church steps ready to ascend them when Allison set her sights across the street. Between the many cars that lined the road, she noticed Shane standing in the spindly shadow of a tall palm tree. He nodded.

"We've just been given permission to enter." Allison took the first step and made her way inside.

Charlie was right next to her.

"I see Carlos Diaz in the front," Allison whispered.

"He looks like hell," Charlie replied. "Not at all like a man who murdered his wife."

Allison directed Charlie to a pew near the back of the church and both took a seat wedged between other mourners. She retrieved her phone and placed it in her lap, covering it with her hands.

Charlie eyed the phone. "What are you going to do with that?"

"If the opportunity presents itself, I'll take pictures."

"Seriously? Here?"

"If I get the chance, yes, I'm serious. Charlie, I have to be able to identify these people. How else can I do that?"

"Not sitting in a pew, my friend. If you ask me, it's like we're wedding crashers only this is way creepier."

"I'll be discreet and only take the pictures if I'm sure no one is looking at me. I'm not a complete fool."

"Just a partial one." Charlie snickered softly.

"You might have a point." Allison revealed a sly grin.

The mood quickly turned somber when the services began. The two sat quietly in the back amid the gentle sobs and occasional blowing of noses. It had been many years since Allison attended a funeral. Not since her grandmother passed and that was almost 10 years ago, back in the days when she and Leo were still married, and the kids were still young. A lot had changed in those 10 years.

When the service finished, Carlos Diaz, along with his two teenaged children walked into the aisle and toward the vestibule.

The music echoed when the doors opened into the lobby that was complete with tall ceilings and stained-glass windows.

The mourners stood. Allison and Charlie fell in with the rest and clasped their hands at their fronts and lowered their eyes while the family walked by. But Allison couldn't look away. She wanted to look in Carlos's eyes. Would there be remorse or guilt, or would his eyes be empty, void of any emotion at all?

Allison saw his eyes. She knew then that if Carlos Diaz had intended for his wife to be murdered, he didn't show it. Allison finally cast away her glance, feeling more determined than ever to understand how Tracy Diaz was involved and how it had led up to her death. More importantly, how Tommy Boyce became embroiled in it.

Several others approached the casket at the end of the service and Allison took a mental note of each woman who appeared to have been roughly the same age as Tracy. These women would most likely have been her friends, possibly family.

"We should probably leave now, don't you think?" Charlie whispered.

"I want to wait in the lobby." Allison glided out of the pew with Charlie close behind. She made her way through the crowd who appeared to aimlessly wander the lobby in search of a place to be told where to go. "Did you notice the women who approached the casket?"

"I did. I also noticed you didn't take any pictures," Charlie replied.

"What can I say? You made a convincing argument. But we're out here now and I'd like to try to talk to one of them." Allison squinted for a better look as Carlos was approached by a woman. "Who's that one there?"

"I have no idea. She was near the front of the church. Family, maybe?" Charlie replied.

"Maybe." Allison pulled close to Charlie and whispered. "Look at how close she's standing to him. Her body language. This is not a friend. Not Tracy's friend, anyway."

"You could be right. Her hand gestures," Charlie began. "It's like she's flirting almost. Gross. Who would do that to the man whose wife just died?"

"She's the mark. And she's walking away from Carlos. It's now or never."

"Alli, are you sure..." Before she could finish her sentence, Allison started toward the woman. Charlie cursed under her breath but played along and stayed a step behind.

Allison tilted her head and offered a tender smile as she encountered the woman. "I'm so sorry for your loss. Tracy was a beautiful soul." The words rolled from Allison's tongue as though she'd practiced them for the last hour, natural, genuine and the woman was responsive.

"Tracy was exactly that." The woman with auburn hair and puffy brown eyes studied Allison. "How did you know her?"

"We met a few times in passing. But with everything that's happened, I felt the least I could do was pay my respects. Are you with the family?" Allison was polished and unfettered in her response.

"She was my best friend. Well, Tracy had a lot of best friends, but I've known her since before she and Carlos were married," the woman replied.

"Well, I'm sure you were grateful to have been so close," Allison said.

"Yes, thank you. I'm sorry, what did you say your name was?"

"Emma Stone."

Charlie's eyes widened and anyone within 5 feet of her would've heard the gulp in her throat.

"Like the actress?" The woman asked Allison.

"Um, yes, actually. I am obviously much older than the actress, so I tell people she stole my name." Allison remained unflappable in the face of her major faux pas.

"Oh. That's funny. I'm Laura Young." She turned her head when a man touched her shoulder.

"We should probably go," the man said.

Laura placed her hand on top of his and turned back to Allison. "It was very nice to meet you, Emma Stone. I apologize, but I have to..."

"Of course. It was my pleasure, Laura. Please, take care." Allison held a sympathetic eye while Laura and the man she was with walked away.

"Emma Stone?" Charlie asked.

"I know, I know. I messed up. If I hadn't just watched that damn musical she was in."

"Sure, okay. Maybe we should go too?" Charlie reached for her arm and gently tugged, but Allison wasn't moving. "Alli, you did good. We have a name."

"Laura Young was with another man but the way she was acting with Carlos. Something's weird there. And you know, there are others here. I should try to meet them."

"What? And introduce yourself as Emma Stone again? Some of them could be friends with that woman. You can't risk it, Alli. This is good enough. You did what you set out to do."

After a moment of hesitation, Allison relented and followed Charlie outside. She spotted Shane now standing in front of his car.

Several of the cars that had lined the street earlier were now leaving when they met Shane at his car.

"How'd it go in there? It lasted longer than I expected." Shane pushed off the passenger door and stood inches from Allison.

"I have a name."

"Just one?" he asked.

"I sort of made a mistake when I introduced myself and well, Charlie thought it best to get out while we were ahead."

Shane eyed Charlie. "I knew there was a reason why I liked you."

"You can call her Emma from now on." Charlie nudged Allison and chuckled.

"Why is that?" he asked.

"Don't worry about it. It's nothing." Allison eyed her friends. "So, how do we go about getting information on Laura Young?"

———

FINLEY DAWSON SAT DOWN AT HIS DESK WITH HIS PHONE IN hand. The view of the ocean was outside his window and sometimes when he was stressed out, he could lose himself in that view. Thoughts about riding the waves and soaking up the rays were relaxing. But that wasn't on the cards for today. There were far more pressing matters to attend to. The first one being Allison Hart. She had seen the video and he'd convinced her not to take it to her detective-friend. It seemed he had earned her trust. But how long that would last would depend on how much she could figure out on her own. Allison was smart. He knew that the moment she found him on the beach the other day. Tommy had made a good choice for himself. But this changed things for Fin and the people to whom he answered.

"It's Dawson. Thanks for taking my call. I know how busy you are." Fin peered again at the view from his office. "Listen, we might need to come up with a plan of action. Things have developed more quickly than I would've thought, and I'm concerned about your exposure." He paused to listen. "Of course. I can be there tomorrow. Thank you, sir. Goodbye."

16

From the office of his high-rise, Carlos Diaz stood with the phone at his ear. He peered out over the city. The waters of the bay shimmering in the bright sun. He regretted all of it now. Tracy hadn't deserved to die, although his feelings for Harlan Goodfellow, a friend and his CFO weren't as remorseful. That man had been screwing his wife and Carlos couldn't have cared less about the fact that he was dead too. None of this was supposed to go down the way it had. Tommy Boyce was another in a long line of his missteps and misjudgments.

Carlos needed a way out. His partner in this scheme, Franklin Perry, had dumped everything on his shoulders. *"Hide the money,"* he'd said. So that was what he was going to do.

"Yes, I'm still here." He said to the person on the other end of the line. "Thank you. I don't mind holding." Carlos inhaled deeply. It was the bank in Panama where he was about to move the money. He didn't know if transferring the funds and closing the US account would be traceable. And while he had people who could guide him with such a transaction, it was too risky to involve anyone else. Carlos was on his own this time.

It was just supposed to be a way to make a quick buck. He'd lost so much in the market collapse years earlier and that money helped refill his coffers. All he had to do was ignore certain aspects of the development project. What did he care if there were so-called "conflicts of interest?" That was how things went down everywhere. Greasing palms wasn't exclusive to him or Franklin Perry.

"Yes." Carlos returned his attention to the phone. "Of course, yes, that will be fine. It needs to happen today, you understand?" He nodded as he listened. "Thank you for your help. It is very much appreciated and won't be forgotten." Carlos ended the call and dropped his phone into his pants pocket. He peered again through the window overlooking the city's skyline. If this didn't work, it might be one of the last times he would get to enjoy this view. The next view might be through a 1-foot by 1-foot window lined with bars.

———

THE POLICE STATION BULLPEN WAS CRAMMED WITH OFFICERS and detectives and Shane sat at his desk searching for a way to get Montoya or Alvarez to copy him on the victims' phone records. He was sitting on a ticking time bomb. Diaz was the recipient of a wad of cash from an unknown benefactor. And there was the video of the car at Boyce's office which he felt fairly confident was the same one Allison had seen, a silver Mercedes. All Shane had left in his bag of tricks was the laptop offered up by Lucy Boyce. It just so happened to contain the fuse that would detonate this bomb.

"No time like the present." Shane marched toward the elevators and to the Major Crimes division where the real detectives worked. "Hey, Alvarez," Shane approached him at his desk. "Can I talk to you for a minute?"

"Sully, what's up?" Alvarez turned away from his computer.

"Listen, I was wondering if you and I could work together on something. Something I think could make a difference to your investigation into Tommy Boyce's murder."

Alvarez creased his brow and studied Shane. His hardboiled features, black crew-cut hair, and square lines made him appear perpetually angry. "What kind of difference?"

Shane cast a suspicious glance before sitting in the chair across from Alvarez's desk. "I might have something for you."

"Sully, whatever it is you have to say, you might as well just say it. I'll tell you after the fact if I'm interested."

Shane conceded. "Okay, fine. I'm going to have to trust you." He shifted in the seat, pulling one leg over the other. "I have some evidence pertaining to the Boyce investigation, and I was hoping we could do a little quid pro quo."

Alvarez raised the corner of his mouth in a brash smile while folding his arms across his narrow chest. "If you have something, you better spill it."

Shane pushed back his shoulders. "Like I said, quid pro quo."

"What do you want?"

"Tracy Diaz's phone records. Tommy Boyce's too if you're feeling generous," Shane replied.

"This isn't your case. You don't even work in this department. Why the hell would you want those records?" Alvarez's interest appeared to grow. He leaned over his desk; his elbows planted in front of him. "What do you have, Sully? And more importantly, how did you get it?"

"Look, you know I have a good friend who was doing some work for Boyce the night he was murdered."

"The Hart chick," Alvarez replied.

"She was contacted by Boyce's daughter who asked for some guidance," Shane replied.

"I talked to the girl. She didn't know anything."

"Not at the time," Shane added. "Not until she started going through her dad's things. She found another laptop. It might prove useful to you."

"You have this in your possession now?"

"Will you share the phone records with me or not?" Shane didn't have a leg to stand on because one way or another, he would have to hand over the evidence or risk losing his job.

"Are you trying to clear Hart of her association with Boyce? You know her prints were all over Boyce's office. Does she have something to hide?"

"No. Whoever is behind all this—and there is an 'all this,' they want you to focus your efforts on Allison and anyone else associated with Boyce because it gives them time to cover up whatever it was they were doing."

Alvarez nodded. "I'll share the records with you out of the kindness of my heart. And I'll even forget that you used evidence as leverage because I like your style. Now hand over the computer."

———

ALLISON HAD HER OWN WAY OF GETTING TO THE BOTTOM OF things. The past few years had been spent catching people in the act of defrauding the state. It took a certain stealthy behavior and learning how to bypass the system to do it. This was how she knew she would make a good private investigator when the time came.

She perched on the edge of her sofa with her laptop resting on her knees. It was almost 6 pm and Nolan would be home soon from practice. She'd promised a home cooked meal, but that promise had already evaporated. Allison had made progress on Laura Young. It was almost too easy. The 34-year-old posted her entire life on social media. There were even pictures of Laura outside the church just before the funeral of her so-called closest friend. It was a shame to see something so personal as grief be splashed across Facebook, Instagram and any other social platform she could use.

As regrettable as it was, it gave Allison what she needed. Laura had just checked into a restaurant that was about twenty minutes from Allison's house. She wondered if it might be too soon, but Allison didn't know how much time she had before the people who killed Tommy learned about the laptop. The time was now if she wanted to ascertain the relationship Laura had with Tracy Diaz.

Allison closed her laptop and stood in a long stretch. She whipped around, nearly pulling a muscle, at the sound of the front door opening. "Nolan."

"Hey mom. What are you doing?" He dropped his gym bag to the floor. "Yoga or something?"

"No. I was actually getting ready to head upstairs. I'm going to be running out in a few minutes."

"So, you didn't make dinner?" Disappointment masked his face. "I wish you would've said. I could've picked up something on my way home. I'm starving."

Allison moved toward him and stood on her tiptoes to kiss his cheek. "I'll tell you what, I'll give you some cash for dinner—this time. Since I did promise you a homecooked meal."

"Fine." He offered a smile as though this result had been his intention all along. "So where are you off to?"

"Oyster Bay."

"Nice. Are you meeting someone?"

"Are you keeping a diary?" she replied. "I'm only kidding but now you know how it feels."

"I know you've been busy lately and it seems like you've been really stressed out. I can't imagine what it would be like to know that a guy you were working for was killed. I just want to know that you're doing okay. That's all."

"I'm fine, baby. I'm meeting Charlie there for dinner. I don't know when I'll be home but I'm sure it won't be late." She patted his shoulder and walked up the stairs.

Allison slipped into a red floral summer dress that landed just above her knees. Though she could easily get away with something shorter, there was something to be said for modesty—and middle age.

She walked into her bathroom and ran a brush through her hair that was still down from the funeral. With an elastic band between her fingers, she worked her magic and in seconds the massive amount of hair was piled on her head. Allison grabbed her phone from the counter and she sent a text to Charlie. *"Meet me at Oyster Bay in 20."*

A text appeared on her home screen. *"You assume I'm free? Just kidding. See you there."*

Allison returned downstairs. "I'm leaving. Don't wait up."

"Hey? Where's my money?" Nolan asked from the couch.

Allison reached into her purse and pulled out a twenty. "Don't spend it all in one place."

"Gee, thanks." Nolan laughed. "JK. This is plenty. Night, Mom."

"JK?" Allison scoffed. "Goodnight, honey." She started out the door and into the dusky light of an early evening. Allison pulled out of the driveway in her old blue Honda and headed toward the restaurant. As she negotiated through the neighborhood and out onto the main roadway, she noticed a car in her rearview. A quick glance and it appeared to be narrowing the gap between them. Her pulse quickened as she continued to watch the vehicle behind her while staying on course. "Stay calm." The highway was just ahead and she turned onto the onramp. The car was gone. "Damn it." Allison slammed her palms on the steering wheel. "I should've gotten the plate."

The restaurant was only minutes away now and her pulse slowed again. There was a slim possibility she was being paranoid or naïve, neither was good. The good news was that it hadn't been the silver car. She chalked that up to a win.

On arrival at the restaurant, Allison stepped out of her car and assessed the area for anyone who might be watching. "You are being paranoid." She continued inside and noticed Charlie in a booth.

"Good Lord Alli, you're white as a sheet. Are you feeling okay?" Charlie asked.

Allison slid into the booth. "I think someone might have been following me."

"What?" Charlie leaned in. "Did you get a plate? What kind of car was it?"

"I didn't think to get a plate. I only thought that I needed to get away from it, so I pulled onto the freeway and it didn't follow after that. All I know was that it was a newer white Toyota Camry."

"Did you tell Shane? He might be able to get more details," Charlie pressed on.

"No. It literally just happened. I'm a little shaken up though."

"I'll bet. Alli, I don't like this. What if it was a warning? The kind that says you're getting too close."

"I've been threatened before, Charlie. You know how many times people stood toe-to-toe with me after I caught them red-handed?"

"This is different. This isn't some asshole taking disability payments from the state." Charlie caught sight of the waitress and raised her hand.

"Hi. What can I get you ladies to drink?" She wore a pleasant but tired smile.

"I'll take a vodka cranberry. Alli?"

"Same but make mine a double."

"Right away," the waitress replied.

"Have you seen her yet? Laura Young. Is she here?" Allison noticed the concern on Charlie's face. "I can't dwell on the car right now. I'm sure it was nothing. I need to be seen by Laura so I can accidentally bump into her."

"She's over there." Charlie thumbed over her shoulder. "I don't know how long she's been here. I made sure she didn't see me."

"Good. I'd rather be the one to run into her. I think it'll play better."

"Whatever you say."

The waitress returned with the drinks. "Can I get you two something to eat?"

"Would you mind coming back in a few minutes? We could use a little more time," Charlie said.

"Of course."

When the waitress left again Charlie picked up her drink and tossed back all of it."

"Geez, you must have been thirsty." Allison studied her again. "Look, I'll tell Shane about the car after we leave here if that will make you feel better. This is too important. If we can find out what Tracy might have said to her friend, that could change everything."

"And you really believe you can befriend that woman quickly enough to get her to spill her guts—tonight?"

"Hey, if I can ply her with enough booze..."

Charlie was stone-faced.

"Relax. Please. You look constipated," Allison replied.

Charlie finally cracked a smile. "Who says I'm not?"

Allison finished the rest of her drink and slid toward the end of the booth. "Order me another, would you? And maybe a plate of nachos?"

"No problem. So this is it?"

"It's now or never, my friend."

"That's the second time you've said that. Just know that I chose never. I will always choose never," Charlie replied.

Allison stood up and headed toward Laura pretending to search for the restrooms. A casual glance at the woman's table and she stopped cold. "Laura?"

Laura gazed up at her. She was sitting with another woman Allison hadn't seen before.

"Yes? Wait a second." Laura squinted as if that would bring Allison's name to the tip of her tongue. "It's Emma, right?"

"Kind of hard to forget the name, I know." Allison smiled.

"I'm surprised to see you here. Um, this is my friend, April. April, this is Emma Stone."

"Emma Stone?" April laughed. "She's not Emma Stone. She's way older." The young woman looked at Allison. "I'm so sorry. I didn't mean it that way."

"It's okay. I'm not the actress. I just share her name. Lucky me."

"I'm so embarrassed." April's face put that embarrassment on full display. "It's nice to meet you, Emma."

"Same here." Allison returned her attention to Laura. "How are you holding up?"

"All right. Thanks for asking. And you?"

"Doing okay." Allison peered back at Charlie and looked again at Laura. "Listen, I'm here with one of my girlfriends. If you two would like, maybe we can sit together?"

Laura glanced at her friend who shrugged her reply. She turned back to Allison. "Um, sure. That would be nice."

"Great. We have a nice big booth. Why don't you two join us over there?"

"Of course." Laura stood from the chair. "April?"

"Oh, yeah, sure. Let me grab my purse."

Allison led the way back to Charlie. "Hey Charlie, this is Laura from the funeral. And this is her friend, April."

"Yes, hi. Fancy meeting you here." Charlie appeared to wait for Allison to take the lead on this awkward exchange.

"I asked them to join us. The more the merrier, right?"

"Absolutely." Charlie scooted down the booth. "Come on in."

The ladies sat down, and Allison returned to the booth.

"So Emma, you must get a lot of flak for your name?" Laura asked.

Allison shot a glance to Charlie as a reminder of her alias. "Initially yeah, but it wears off depending on the number of drinks."

The women laughed.

Allison raised her hand. "Speaking of. How about I order us a round?"

17

Four gin and tonics. It was a record for Allison, not taking into account her college years. She didn't keep track in those days. But that was 30 years ago. Nowadays, two drinks were sufficient to take off the edge. Laura Young and her friend, April, had demonstrated their prowess for drinking others under the table. Even Charlie struggled to keep up. The upside was that the restaurant was closing soon.

Allison was just clear-headed enough to recognize she hadn't reached her objective and time was running out. Laura veered away from the topic of Tracy Diaz on multiple occasions. Maybe it was because the subject hurt too much, or Allison had misread the situation and the two women hadn't been as close as she predicted. Allison's window was closing. If she didn't strike, all of this would have been for nothing. And the subsequent hangover would be an annoying reminder of her failure.

Allison set down her empty glass. "I have to pee. Anyone want to come with?" She eyed Laura.

"I'll go. April?" Laura replied.

"Charlie and I can go when you two come back. That sound okay with you, Charlie?"

"Absolutely."

Allison scooted out of the booth and waited for Laura to stand. She locked arms with her new-found friend. "Come on. I need you to keep me steady."

"You're not much of a drinker are you, Emma?"

In her current state of inebriation Allison almost forgot she was using a fake name and regarded Laura with a furrowed brow. "Oh. No, not really. But I'm having a nice time."

"Good. Me too. It's a nice distraction," Laura replied.

As they entered the restroom Allison was quick to do her business before stepping out again. In front of the mirror, she examined her face and blotted areas where makeup had smudged. She peered into the mirror at the stall Laura was in and waited for her to reemerge.

The door swung open and a swaying Laura stepped out.

Allison remained in front of the mirror. "I'm really glad I met you, Laura. I know what a difficult time this is for you. Tracy really was a wonderful person."

Laura stood in front of an adjacent basin. "I already miss her so much."

"You two must have been close," Allison pressed on.

"We were."

"It's nice to have someone you can talk to and confide in. That's what I have with Charlie."

"She does seem nice." Laura dried her hands and turned to Allison. "I think the hardest part of all this is knowing I won't get to have those conversations with Tracy anymore, you know? We spent a lot of time together. I wish I could've helped her."

"There's no way you could've known what would happen," Allison said. "You can't blame yourself."

"No. You're right. I couldn't have known she would be murdered. But Emma, I knew what she was facing, and I didn't take it seriously. It didn't occur to me that it was all that important. I just figured they were headed for divorce and Tracy was just venting. Everyone goes through that, right? If only I had done something—anything—it might've changed the outcome."

"What do you mean?" Allison asked.

"It makes no difference now." Laura started toward the door.

Allison was losing her. She had to act. "No, hang on." She gently grabbed Laura's arm. "Was she in some kind of danger?"

"No. I mean, I don't know..." Laura trailed off. "Do you know who her husband is?"

Allison nodded.

"He was into some stuff—I don't know—stuff that made Tracy think twice. I mean, look, she wasn't perfect by any means. But she was a good person and what Carlos was doing..."

"Did he hurt her?" Allison asked.

"No. Nothing like that. It was his business. He, well, like a lot of developers, right? They're all a little shady. Carlos was the shadiest and Tracy knew it." Laura sighed. "Never mind. We should get back out there."

"Sure. Yeah. You're right. But I thought you and Carlos were good friends the way you consoled him at the funeral," Allison said.

Laura stopped dead. "I'm sorry, what?"

Allison overstepped and needed to salvage this—fast. "I'm sorry. I didn't mean anything...you know, we should get back. Maybe we can order one more drink before last call?" She locked arms again with Laura and the two returned.

Charlie appeared to study Allison's demeanor as though wondering if her friend had been successful.

Allison lent a subtle nod before slipping back into the booth. "So, should we order a final round?"

"Way ahead of you," Charlie replied.

The idea of clinging to a toilet bowl for the rest of the night wasn't appealing and Allison was sure that was where she was headed. Nursing the final drink would make no difference. Her fate was sealed.

The conversation was about anything and everything except what Allison had wanted to discuss. At least she knew that Tracy was aware of Carlos's dealings. And getting evidence of the bank account was probably the catalyst that sealed her own fate.

Laura glanced at her phone. "It's getting late and I think they're about to close. We should get out of here."

"Probably best," April replied. "I'll get us an Uber." She snatched her phone and requested the Uber on her app. "Says two minutes. Let's go wait, Laura."

"Okay." Laura stepped out of the booth. "How are you two getting home?"

"Same." Allison looked at Charlie. "Uber?"

"Oh yeah. We'll walk out with you and order one."

Allison led the way through the virtually empty restaurant. "I can't tell you how much I needed this tonight, ladies. Thank you."

"I'd be happy to do it again sometime, Emma. You're a hoot," Laura replied.

They were in a trendy part of town that was surrounded by other hot night spots, and Ubers and Lyfts lined the streets. Allison looked on before she pulled Laura aside. "I'd love to grab drinks again but if you'd like to have coffee and just unload, I'm here for that too."

"Thanks, Emma. I'll definitely take you up on that. I bet Tracy thought you were a hoot too."

"I don't know about that. She was pretty great, though."

"You never did tell me exactly how you two met," Laura said.

Allison promptly sobered. She had been vague on purpose because of course, she had no idea what Tracy Diaz was like or how she could possibly have come to know her. Allison recalled her initial response when she had mentioned a charity hoping that would suffice. "I think I mentioned before. It was through her charity." Allison had no idea what sort of charity but assumed a woman of Tracy's standing would have been involved in more than one.

Laura returned a smile. "Of course. Tracy loved the children. She couldn't have any, you know."

"I didn't know that," Allison replied. "So, the kids with Carlos?"

"Her step kids," Laura replied.

At that moment April tapped Laura on the shoulder. "That's our Uber."

"Well, I would love to meet up again soon, Emma. Call me anytime." She reached for her cell. "What's your number? I'll put it in my phone now."

Allison relayed her phone number. "I look forward to us becoming fast friends. Get home safely." She offered a tender embrace and watched the two women step inside their ride.

As it pulled away Charlie called out, "Our ride is here, too, Alli."

"Good. Oh, hey, remind me to change my voicemail."

"Why is that?" Charlie asked.

"Because I just gave her my cell number. The name, Allison Hart, can't be on the message."

"Good catch. Oh, by the way, I like how I didn't get an alias. Just you."

Allison started toward the Uber. "Only because I was the one working for Tommy Boyce. I didn't want to risk it."

"Sure. Yeah, I get it. I didn't rank highly enough to warrant protection." Charlie laughed. "Just get in the car."

"Why don't you crash at my place tonight?" Allison said. "We'll come back in the morning for the cars."

"Oh good. That means I won't have to clean my toilet. You know that's where we're both headed, right?"

"Yep."

———

ALLISON HAD GONE THROUGH THE ENTIRE CHARADE WITH Laura Young in an attempt to determine whether Tracy Diaz had ever made mention of Tommy Boyce. So far, that was still up in the air.

"Thanks for doing this with me tonight. We'll pay for it tomorrow but we're getting closer to finding answers," Allison said.

"It doesn't feel like it." Charlie walked to the fridge. "You want some water?" She grabbed two bottles and returned to the kitchen island, handing one to Allison.

"Thanks. I should let Shane know we're back and ask if he got the phone records. I think this will start coming together if we see that Tracy was working with Boyce. It could explain why they were killed."

"I don't doubt Tracy was murdered because of what she might've known about her husband. I'm not sure I feel the same about Boyce. Who would want to draw that kind of attention? Three murders? That's excessive even by corporate standards. Anything more than one is just asking for trouble."

Allison cracked a tender smile. "Maybe so. I thought that by getting Laura to talk she'd tell us more about Tracy's final few days. But she wasn't interested."

"Well, you did say she discussed their marriage and that Tracy thought she was in some kind of trouble."

"That's not enough." She pressed Shane's contact on her phone. "If Shane got the records it might not matter. We'll be able to see first-hand if the two were talking." Allison held the phone to her ear. "Hey, Shane. It's Allison. Charlie and I are back at my house."

"How did it go with the friend?" he asked.

"Not as well as I would've hoped. She mentioned Tracy was concerned about Carlos and felt she might be in trouble. But I'm kind of hoping you have something more concrete? Like her phone records?"

"I convinced Alvarez it was in his interest to share the details in exchange for the Boyce laptop," Shane replied.

"Really? I thought you were required to hand it over anyway."

He stammered. "I was. I did. Point being, Alvarez ponied up copies of the calls. I'm coming over now and I'll bring them with me."

Allison set down her phone. "He has a copy of some records. Didn't say if it was Tracy's or Tommy's but he's coming over to give us a look."

"Thank the Lord. I don't think I could handle going out with those ladies again. I have no idea how they could drink so much and not be flat out on the ground," Charlie replied.

"Because they're in their 30s. We're not," Allison replied.

"I feel like I'm 30. Does that count?" Charlie asked.

"Sadly, no." Allison's attention was diverted when Nolan shuffled into the kitchen.

He ran his hands through his thick wavy hair and squinted from the light. "What did you say, Mom?"

"Nothing, honey. I'm sorry we woke you up. Charlie and I are just sobering up. We had one drink too many."

"That's right," Charlie began. "We're a cautionary tale, Nolan. Take note."

"You said something about phone records or something. Whose? The guy you were working for?" Nolan grew more alert as he shuffled in. "What's going on, Mom? Are you in some kind of danger?"

"No. No, honey. We're not in any danger. Charlie and I were just talking about Mr. Boyce. What happened to him has nothing to do with me."

"Your mom's right. We're just talking," Charlie said.

Nolan delivered her a sideways glance before eyeing his mother again and a knock on the door seemed to preempt another line of questioning. "Who's that this late at night?"

"My friend, Shane. The detective? You remember him, right?" Allison started toward the door. "Nolan, honey, you should go back to bed. Please. Everything's fine."

"Your cop-friend is here and you're talking about a dead guy. I might be half-asleep but I'm not stupid, Mom. I'm not a kid anymore, okay? I'm staying right here." He dropped onto the kitchen stool and folded his arms in defiance.

Allison pursed her lips before approaching the front door to open it. "That was fast. We're having quite the gathering. I should've set out crudités."

"Cruda what?" Shane walked inside.

"Never mind." Allison walked back into the kitchen with the slightest sway in her step.

"Are you drunk?" Shane followed her.

"It's a long story," Charlie replied.

Nolan cleared his throat. "Um, hello? If I was drunk, you'd be having a hissy fit right now."

Allison peered at him. "First of all, I'm an adult who's old enough to drink. You're not. Besides, I drank for a good reason."

"Nolan, hey man. Good to see you." Shane offered his hand.

Nolan eyed him for a moment before accepting his greeting. "So you're in on all this too?"

"That depends. What do you know about it?"

"He doesn't know anything except that we're not in any danger." Allison walked to the fridge. "Beer?"

"Sure. Thanks."

"I'll take one too," Nolan said.

"Nice try, kid." Allison handed Shane a bottle of Corona.

Shane cast a tentative glance to Nolan and back to Allison. "So, can we talk about how things went tonight?"

Nolan pulled upright and spun around to him. "Yes, let's."

"Nolan, come on. This isn't something you need to be concerned with," Allison began. "I'd appreciate it if you let the three of us talk. I'm still your mother."

Nolan scrunched up his face and held her gaze before yielding. "Fine." He pushed off the stool. "But I swear, Mom, if I find out you're in some kind of trouble..."

"That's not going to happen, Nolan, okay? I give you my word," Shane said. "Your mom and Charlie are just helping me on a case and that's all this is."

"I guess I'll have to trust you then." Nolan turned away in a huff and retreated to his room.

"Okay, now we can discuss the reason you're here," Allison said. "I'll tell you what we know if you tell us what you know."

Shane pulled up a stool and retrieved the copy of Tracy's phone records. "I highlighted Tracy Diaz's calls to Boyce." He peered at Allison. "Take a look at the dates. The two were in fairly constant contact."

"Like they were hatching a plan," Charlie said. "It's like what Milo said, right, Alli? About the bribe?"

"This confirms it to me," Allison said. "That must have been how Boyce ended up with copies of the development contracts and that bank statement. She was feeding him details and he was taking them to Milo until someone put a stop to it."

"That was my first thought," Shane replied. "But since they're both dead we'll have to get the answer for ourselves." He turned to Allison. "How did it go with the girlfriend? What did you say her name was?"

"Laura Young. It went well enough, I guess. Could've been worse, but it does seem like Tracy was looking for a way out of her marriage and possibly with whatever it was she had set up with Boyce."

"What if this was all nothing more than an attempt at blackmail?" Shane asked.

"Possibly, but why involve Milo then? Unless she didn't know Tommy was taking evidence to the D.A.'s office. Laura said Tracy was afraid of Carlos. I asked if he abused her and she insisted it wasn't like that. But I'd say that it's pretty clear she was working with Tommy to either force Carlos's hand in a divorce or maybe..."

"Turn him in to the cops," Charlie finished.

"Something like that," Allison replied. "I have Laura's contact information and I'll be making a call to her tomorrow to set up a lunch. I don't want too much time to pass so I need to hit her hard for information quickly. I still think she knows more than she's saying. And it won't be long before Alvarez or Montoya discover what was on Tommy's laptop from his house. They'll start talking to everyone in Tracy's circle, including Laura Young. She might not say much after that especially if her lawyer has anything to say about it."

"How do you want to handle Milo?" Shane asked.

"He says he's working on something big and he told me what Tommy was doing for him," Allison began. "If the detectives do find what we think is receipt of a bribe on that computer, Milo will want to know about it. It could put an abrupt end to his investigation."

18

When Allison last spoke to Milo he pleaded for time and she obliged. Since that conversation, she had discovered that Tracy Diaz was looking for a way to get back at her husband and get out of her marriage. Boyce appeared to be the means to make that happen. Now that the Tampa PD detectives were on the verge of finding out what they both already knew; something was going to have to happen to drive this investigation to its conclusion. Whatever that might be.

Allison sipped on her iced tea and gazed through the restaurant window at the bay. A weary smile teased her lips when she spotted her friend. "Milo. I appreciate you meeting with me."

"I appreciate you coming here. It's best if our association stays outside the purview of the folks in my office. For the time being." Milo pulled out a chair and sat down across from Allison.

"Believe me I understand. I've done as we discussed, and I've told you what we know. Do you have anything for me?" she asked.

"I am grateful for the advanced warning of what our friends at the Tampa police department have in their possession."

"Milo, how much were you aware of what Tracy Diaz was trying to gather against her husband? And what part did Tommy play?"

The waiter interrupted. "Afternoon. What can I get you both?" The young bearded man smiled.

"I'll take the bacon cheeseburger with a side of fries," Allison said.

"That sounds good. I'll have the same. And a Coke," Milo added.

"Right away." With a smile, the waiter retreated.

"The time for stalling is over. Our time's up, Milo," Allison said.

"Here's what I can tell you. I was made aware of dealings from Carlos Diaz that were of an illegal nature."

"I'm familiar," Allison replied.

"Yes, but I've been working on this for some time. It was Tommy who kicked it into high gear when he did what I asked and went to work for Carlos. See, I needed him to get close to the man, as you know. Tommy was listening in on a conversation Mrs. Diaz was having on her phone. He'd been following her for days, handing over little tidbits of information to Carlos. You know, just enough to assuage him that Tommy was doing his job. Well, this particular conversation held some very juicy details regarding a payment Carlos had deposited into a bank account Mrs. Diaz had previously not been privy to. I don't know how she found it, but she seemed quite a resourceful woman. Tommy knew then he was going to have to work his way into meeting Mrs. Diaz. And as always, Tommy executed his duties with supreme aptitude. He gained her trust and the two started working together to get proof of this money and well, as they say, the rest is history."

"Was Harlan Goodfellow the one who told her about this money?" Allison asked.

"I'm of the opinion that yes, he must've been. As you know, Harlan Goodfellow, who was Carlos's CFO and closest confidant, was very much in-the-know and most likely relayed everything to his mistress."

"I see. And Tommy came to you with the details?"

"He did. He knew what I was trying to build against Carlos. So, he played into Tracy's insecurities and her fear of being found out. He befriended her, honestly. He convinced Tracy Diaz that he would help her use this evidence in the divorce proceedings and..."

"And for you in a criminal one," she replied.

"As I said, this had been months in the making, Allison. A detailed operation involving Tommy and myself along with a man by the name of Franklin Perry."

"Wait. His prints were found at Tommy's office. How does he fit into this?"

"He was a previous business partner who we discovered was also involved in a few shady deals. Franklin offered to cooperate to help us get Carlos with the understanding my office would be lenient toward his own shifty dealings."

Allison leaned over the table. "Milo, how confident are you that Franklin Perry's people weren't the ones who killed the happy couple or Tommy Boyce?"

"You want the truth?" He leaned closer in response. "It is something that had crossed my mind a time or two. That said, I haven't found anything to prove it one way or the other."

"Doesn't mean it doesn't exist," Allison replied.

"No, ma'am. It does not."

———

MILO HAD DROPPED ANOTHER BOMB AND ALLISON WAS already shell-shocked. All she had been looking for was some extra cash until she could get her license and start her own agency. She would've laughed at the absurdity of it all had it not been so heart-wrenching.

Milo had handed her an opportunity to walk away right then and there. Insisting that he could take it from here and there was no need for her to continue going down this road. That would've been the smart thing to do since Allison was, without question, unqualified to handle the situation. But she couldn't do it. She was impelled by what Lucy had gone through and that outweighed concerns of being in over her head.

Allison pulled onto her driveway and noticed Leo's car in front of the house. "Leo." No doubt he was there because she hadn't had an opportunity to call him back on the multiple occasions he had phoned over the past two days. He was indifferent to the fact that they were no longer married and still harbored unnecessary responsibility for Allison. What he didn't seem to understand was that it still hurt her. He thought he was being a stand-up guy, but he only made it harder for her to pull away from him. She stopped the car and walked to the front door that was unlocked. "Hello?"

Leo emerged from the kitchen with a half-eaten sandwich in his hand. "Hope you don't mind. I helped myself to some lunch. I thought you would show up eventually."

"What are you doing here, Leo?" She walked inside and checked the living room. "Where's Nolan?"

"Still at school."

"And why aren't you at school?" Allison started into the kitchen and noted his lunch. "Luckily, I've already eaten."

"It's my break. I thought I'd stop by seeing as how you haven't returned any of my calls for the past few days." Leo set down his sandwich on the counter. "I needed to know that you were okay. With everything going on..."

"I'm fine. It's not your job to check up on me," Allison replied.

"Sorry if I still give a crap about my wife."

"*Ex*-wife." She opened the fridge and grabbed a bottle of water. "As you can see, everything is fine. I'm fine. The kids are fine. So, you can go back to work with the knowledge that you did your duty."

"Alli, come on."

Charlie was the only person who called her Alli except for Leo. The familiarity it conjured was distressing. She had been married to Leo for twenty years and it had taken every bit of the last five to put enough distance between them so as to feel whole again. Leo was well aware of the feelings it brought up when he addressed her that way.

"Sorry. I'm just worried about you, Allison. You're the mother of my children and you've turned your life completely upside down. You're involved in something that, honestly, scares the hell out of me."

"I know it does, Leo. And if I'm being honest, it scares me too —a little. That said, I can do this. I know I can."

"But this? Really?" Leo pleaded.

"It's too late and you have no say. I'm in it. And I'm going to do what I have to do to find out who killed a good man."

"How do you know this Tommy Boyce was a good man? You knew him for 5 minutes."

"Because Milo Nash said he was, and I trust Milo."

"Okay fine. I can see I won't be able to change your mind." He put his plate in the sink.

"Is that why you came here? To try to change my mind?" Allison chuckled. "Since when have you ever been able to do that?" She noticed the look of concern on his face and approached him. "Leo, I already told you I'm taking precautions. I'm not being stupid. I need you to trust me. Please. And I also need you to give me some space, okay? You can't just show up, let yourself in and expect that to be perfectly normal. This isn't your house anymore."

Leo held her gaze. "You're right. It's not my house and you're not my wife—anymore. I'm sorry to have bothered you." He headed to the door. "Tell Nolan I'm sorry I missed him and I'll see him this weekend."

His ego had been bruised but Allison didn't have time to coddle him today. "Nolan has that tryout with the Triple A team," she began. "You'll be there, right?"

"I'll be there. I'm still his father." Leo closed the door on his way out without another word.

Allison stood alone in her foyer, dumbstruck. Leo was using the same old tactics he employed when they were married. Yes, he was afraid for her and while she never intended to make him feel that way, worrying about his feelings wasn't her problem anymore. This was about her now, not him. If Allison ever hoped to move on with her life, she had to remember that he couldn't put that emotional hold over her anymore. It wasn't fair. There would come a time when he would realize it. And for Allison, it couldn't come soon enough.

She walked into the living room and opened her laptop. There was much more for her to do and now that she'd overcome one problem, it was time to tackle the next.

Milo was forthcoming with several details about his investigation and how it involved Tommy and Tracy. When Allison insisted that she wasn't going to stop trying to find Tommy's killer, he relented. Milo enlisted her to continue the forward momentum until such time as Montoya and Alvarez gathered enough evidence to arrest whoever murdered the three victims. Neither was confident that would happen anytime soon.

Allison learned through Milo that Tracy Diaz held a board position with a charity that helped local youth. She was about to research this charity because the more she learned about this woman who had been an adulterer and possible blackmailer, the more she realized Tracy Diaz was desperate to get out of her marriage to a wealthy and powerful man. Allison had nothing in common with that life.

As it turned out, Laura Young was a well-respected contributor to this same charity. It was a detail Allison could exploit at her next meeting with Laura to convince her that "Emma" had been a friend to Tracy Diaz. And that meeting was conveniently scheduled for happy hour this evening. The woman liked to drink. So, Allison was going to have to drink too, even if she was still recovering from the other night's alcohol consumption.

Charlie was given a separate task. Her job was to find out where Finley Dawson was going today. According to Shane, Alvarez had discovered several phone calls between Fin and Tommy in the days leading up to Tommy's death. Shane promised to come to Alvarez with anything he might find so long as he steered clear of Carlos Diaz. Alvarez appeared to be more willing to play ball than his counterpart, Montoya.

Fin made no mention of speaking with Tommy so close to his death which was cause for concern. So Charlie was going to follow him to see who else he might be in contact with. Allison suspected there could be more than met the eye with Finley Dawson.

———

JOINING FORCES WITH HER DEAREST FRIEND, ALLISON, HAD been the biggest decision Charlie had made since leaving her husband. But it meant leaving the comfort of a secure job. Charlie's job with the state was lucrative in the form of benefits and the pay was decent enough to allow her a modest home in a nice part of town. Thank goodness, because she got exactly squat in her divorce 8 years ago. Her ex-husband couldn't hold down a job to save his life and she was used to pulling double-duty where income was concerned. She had already been paying for most of the bills. And forget child support. Her kids were teenagers now, only a few years left until they turned 18, so she had that going for her. But there was so much more to her than filing away claims for the state, and Allison had confidence in her. That alone was enough to move ahead with the proposition.

Now Charlie found herself sitting in her car several yards away from Fin Dawson's home, waiting for him to surface. She knew whose side she was on. Now it was time to find out where Dawson's allegiances lay.

The bronzed blonde-haired man, who was too attractive for his own good, walked out of his house. Charlie dropped her head below the steering wheel, and since she was vertically challenged, it wasn't that tough.

He stepped into his Jeep Wrangler.

Charlie scoffed. "Could this guy be any more of a cliché?"

Fin backed out of his driveway and Charlie waited for him to get far enough away that she could safely trail him without being spotted. The rule was at least two cars between them. She had no idea where that rule came from, but it sounded reasonable.

Where he was headed was the unknown variable in this equation, but she would tail his butt for as long as necessary. Understanding his role, if any, in what happened to Tommy Boyce was necessary to consider how best to handle him from this point forward.

Charlie eyed his Jeep as it prepared to make a right turn and she followed but dropped back to allow another car in between them. He was heading north.

She peered at the time on her phone for an instant before returning her eyes to the road and to the Jeep. It had been almost ten minutes and she was at a loss as to his intended destination but would stay the course no matter what.

After another two miles, Charlie got a sense of where Fin was headed but it didn't seem logical. As she drove, hanging back as far as she could, she found herself approaching a suburb where the very wealthy lived. A coastal community lined with mansions and guarded gates.

"No. No friggin' way." Charlie dropped back because the closer she got to this place, the fewer cars were available to hide behind. Soon she would have to fall back altogether. There was no chance she'd get past the approaching guard shack and she wondered how it was possible that Fin would.

Charlie stopped along the side of the road fronting a home that was outside the gate and not nearly as extravagant as the ones behind it.

Fin entered without a single hiccup. They just let him on through.

"What in the world?" Charlie reached for her phone. "Hey, it's me."

Allison answered. "I'm just heading into the bar to meet Laura Young. Is everything okay?"

"I lost him."

"Oh no. That's okay, Charlie. Why don't you just head back?"

"I said I lost him but Alli, I'm pretty damn sure I know where he was headed."

"How?"

"Because I'm sitting in front of the community gate where the mayor lives."

"Wait. Hold on a minute. Are you saying Fin is headed to see the mayor? How can you be so sure?"

"Well, I'm not sure. In fact, there's a high probability I'm wrong but something in my gut says I'm not. Why would that beach bum, Dawson, have any reason to be in this neighborhood? Only corporate execs, state senators and the mayor live here. Everyone knows that."

"There must be another explanation. Maybe this was a bad idea," Allison continued. "Just come back and we'll regroup when I'm done here."

"Alli, I realize this is a stretch, but I think it's a stretch worth looking into. Don't you?"

19

Allison was sidetracked by the idea Charlie had asserted. It was like a jagged pill that stuck in her throat. Tommy Boyce had known Finley Dawson for years, had introduced him to his daughter. It seemed unlikely Tommy could be duped but maybe he had been. It was beginning to sound like Fin had an agenda just like everyone else.

He hadn't disclosed that he had been in touch with Tommy in the days leading up to Tommy's death. He had a key to Tommy's office and he still had the surveillance footage Allison had trusted to leave with him. Come to think of it, she didn't know if he had made any progress on finding the owner of this silver Mercedes. Her focus had been on Laura Young and she had let Fin Dawson fall through the cracks.

Allison sat in her car with her hands on the wheel and stared at the restaurant. A bevy of ideas swam in her head. There was still a chance she and Charlie were jumping the gun but why else would Fin be in a neighborhood like that? Could he have been there to see the mayor? Maybe she was making too much out of this. Fin had other clients. Some of them were bound to be wealthy, not unlike Tommy's client, Carlos Diaz. Yes, that was the only reasonable explanation.

She collected herself and stepped out of the car, shaking off the diversion and refocusing her efforts on extracting information from Laura Young. The casual bar was just ahead, and Allison made her way inside.

"Afternoon. How many?" A petite hostess wearing denim shorts and a black shirt smiled.

"I'm meeting someone." Allison surveyed the dining room. "I think that's her over there. Thank you." She made her way to the booth where Laura sat alone. "Hi. It's good to see you again, Laura. How are you?" Allison sat down.

"I'm doing a little better each day. And you?"

"I suppose about the same." Allison feigned an appropriate amount of grief. "So, have you ordered?"

"I was just about to." Laura raised her hand to gain the attention of the waitress. "Hi, I think we'd like to order."

"Of course. What can I get you ladies?"

Allison's attention drifted away once again. She was concerned about Charlie sitting there out in the open. What if someone was watching her? What if she was in danger? She reached for her phone but was stopped short.

"Ma'am? What can I get for you?"

"Oh, sorry. I'll have the chicken Caesar and a water. Thanks," Allison replied.

"Nothing to drink for you?" Laura appeared puzzled.

"Oh, did you order one?"

"I'm having a Mojito."

"I'll have one of those." Nothing sounded worse to Allison right now than booze. The thought of it made her stomach turn sour.

"I'll be right back." The waitress walked away.

"You seem distracted," Laura said. "Is everything okay?"

"Oh yeah. I just need to send a text to a friend. I forgot to tell her about an appointment. I don't mean to be rude. You don't mind, do you?"

"Not at all."

Allison typed the message to Charlie. *"Don't wait for Fin to leave. Just get out of there before you're seen."* She pressed send and returned her phone to her purse. "There. All taken care of. Now, where were we?"

———

CHARLIE HAD OPTED TO PULL DOWN A SIDE STREET JUST before the gated entrance into the community filled with lavish homes. Her car was facing the main road. She planned on waiting it out and following Fin when he reappeared. That was until she spotted the text arrive from Allison. She studied the message and pursed her lips. "That's not the right call, Alli. Come on. I need to know where he's going after this." Charlie peered at the gate once again. It had been almost 30 minutes since he went in. Surely, Fin wouldn't stay much longer. She peered again at the message and set down her phone. "Just a little while longer."

With the engine off, Charlie rolled down the windows and prayed for a breeze, but none came. The air was stagnant and thick, but she would wait because this was her job now. She considered herself Allison's partner and the notion Finley Dawson was a bald-faced liar was starting to piss her off. Allison was doing her part and it was Charlie's turn to step up.

A glimmer in the distance caught her eye. It was coming from behind the gate. This could be it. She waited for the gates to open. "Come on. I'm going to get a heatstroke out here." A cunning smile arose at the sight of Dawson's car. "There you are." Charlie waited for him to exit through the gates and head back out onto the main road where she would tail him once again. And more importantly, find out who he might be going to meet.

When he drove out onto the road, Charlie slowly pulled out and followed him from a safe distance. She wanted to message Allison again, but her eyes needed to stay fixed on Dawson. He was entering the highway and headed south. "Home?"

Several minutes passed and it had appeared Dawson was returning to his beach-side shack. It would be tougher for her to blend into the background when they entered his street. She might have to hang back until he parked and then approach, staying a few houses down. If he was only going back home there might not be a need for her to continue trailing him, but she would give it some time to see how it would pan out.

He'd done as she predicted. Finley Dawson arrived at his house and parked in his driveway. Charlie held back, waiting for him to go inside before she drove to a stop three houses away. "Okay. Let's just see if you decide to take off again." She stopped the engine and crouched low. Her phone rested on the passenger seat and she considered letting Allison know what was going on. But disrupting her evening with Laura Young might be a problem and she didn't want to interrupt whatever momentum Allison may have built.

"Well, hell. Maybe there's not much point in staying." She was about to start the car again when she noticed another car pull onto Fin's driveway right behind his Jeep. Her pulse jumped. She knew this car. She'd seen it on a video only days ago.

An older man stepped out from the driver's seat wearing a pair of jeans and a short-sleeved button-down shirt. He looked like the same man from the video, but it had been grainy, and her eyes were too old to be certain. The man continued toward Dawson's front door. She reached for her phone and snapped pictures of the car, including the plates. "That might come in handy."

He went inside and Fin closed the door.

Charlie kept her eyes glued on the house. "What do I do? What do I do?" She still held her phone and pressed on Allison's contact.

A crack of gunfire exploded. Charlie bounded from the driver's seat and dropped her phone into the footwell. Her eyes sparked fear as she looked for the source. Her heart raced. "It was just a car backfiring. That's all it was." But when her eyes searched for the offending vehicle, there was not one to be found. "Oh, no. No, no, no. This isn't happening." She reached into the footwell to get her phone as it wedged between the gas pedal and the floorboard. "Come on. Come on." Her fingers stretched; her neck craned but she couldn't reach it.

Charlie returned her sights to the home where the sound of a car's engine roared. The Mercedes peeled out of the driveway and onto the road driving opposite from where Charlie waited. A stroke of luck if there ever was one.

"Fin." She pushed open her door and jumped out, reaching deep into the footwell to grab her phone still wedged beneath the gas pedal. When she grasped it with her fingertips, Charlie slid it out and finally got a good grip on it. She pulled upright and surveyed the street. Either the neighbors weren't home, or they were and didn't care about the noise.

With time running against her, Charlie jogged to the front door. It was closed but unlocked. She turned the handle and slowly pushed it open. "Hello? Fin?" Her heart was in her throat and she tried to swallow it back down. "Fin? Are you okay?"

That was when she heard the moan. "Oh, God." Charlie rushed toward the back where she'd been only a few days earlier under much different circumstances. She heard him moan again. "I'm coming."

Fin was on the floor of his office. Blood pooled around his chest. "Fin!" She knelt beside him. "I'm calling 911 right now!" She dialed the number and couldn't take her eyes off him. He was bleeding out. "I need help. A man's been shot. He's bleeding. Please hurry!"

"I have your location, ma'am. We're sending someone right now. Stay with me, okay?"

Charlie nodded as if the operator could understand.

"Ma'am? Are you still there?"

"Yes. I'm here. Hurry, please. He's lost a lot of blood."

Fin snatched her free wrist. Blood spilled from his mouth as he tried to speak. "She's in danger," he muttered.

Charlie still held the phone to her ear and furrowed her brow as if that might help her understand him. "What did you say? Fin, what did you say? I can't understand you." Her tone raised to a shout.

"Allison. Danger."

"What? From who?" Charlie demanded. "Fin? Fin!" She shook him but he didn't respond. "No. No. You can't die. Hang on, help's coming."

Sirens sounded in the distance.

"You hear that? They're coming, Fin. Hang on." She shook him harder this time, but he didn't move. "Fin, please." Her voice cracked and her eyes reddened.

The clatter of paramedics rushing inside didn't alarm her. Charlie was frozen, one hand on the phone and one hand on Fin Dawson.

"Ma'am. I need you to step back now." One of the paramedics muscled his way next to Fin. He placed his fingers against Fin's neck. He looked to his colleague, who pulled Charlie back, and shook his head.

The phone slipped from Charlie's hands as she thrust her palms against her mouth. It bounced at her feet and landed on its face.

"Ma'am, come with me, please. I need you to tell me what happened."

When Charlie turned to see who was yanking her away from Fin, she realized it was a cop.

"Are you okay? Are you hurt?" The officer's eyes raked over her.

Charlie's face was void of any reaction when she turned to the officer. "Is he dead?"

"I'm afraid so, ma'am. Can you tell me what happened?" the officer asked again.

She slowly turned her head and gazed at Fin's body while the paramedics prepared to place him on a gurney. "He was shot. I heard the noise and I came inside."

"Do you know who shot him, ma'am? Did you see anyone? It's important we understand what happened."

She looked into the officer's eyes. They appeared kind, concerned, and sympathetic. It was comforting. Charlie's mouth was dry, but her nose ran, and she didn't care. "A man walked inside and shot him."

"Can you describe him for me?"

She nodded and in a monotone voice, replied, "Older. Fifties. He wore jeans and a red shirt. He was overweight."

"That's very good, thank you." The officer studied her again. "Are you a friend of his?"

She cast down her gaze and pondered the question.

"Ma'am? What's this man's name?"

"Finley Dawson," she replied.

"Are you Finley's friend? Is that why you're here?"

Charlie turned her gaze upward again, shaking her head. "We aren't—weren't—friends. I worked with him."

One of the paramedics approached her. "Excuse me, does this phone belong to you?"

She looked at it. "Yes. That's mine."

"I'm sorry, but it looks like it broke when you dropped it." He handed it back to her.

Charlie turned it over in her hands. The screen was shattered.

"Is there someone I can call for you, ma'am?" the officer said. "Someone who can take you home?"

"No. My car is here."

"Forgive me, ma'am, but you don't appear capable of driving. I think it might be best if someone comes to get you," the officer said. "What's your name?"

"Charlotte Wells."

"Ms. Wells, please let me call someone for you."

"I have to go now." Charlie stepped away from the officer and headed toward the door.

"Ms. Wells, please. I'm going to need you to come into the station and make a statement."

Charlie stopped at the door and turned back. "Now? I have to go now?"

"It would be best for your friend while it's fresh in your mind. We need to find the man who killed him. I think you can help with that."

Charlie stood at the door, half in and half out. Fin's words reverberated in her ears. *Allison. Danger.*

"Ms. Wells?" The officer approached. "I think it's best if you come with us now, but if there's anyone you'd like to have meet you there, that's perfectly fine."

"What about my car?" Charlie felt as though she was about to shatter like the screen on her phone.

"You can come back for it later." The officer reached for her arm and gently held it. "Please, Ms. Wells. Time is not on our side."

———

ALLISON HAD FINISHED HER FIRST DRINK BUT HESITATED TO order another. Meanwhile, her newfound friend, Laura, was on her third. The good news was that she'd learned a lot about Tracy Diaz.

"Aren't you going to have another?" Laura asked.

"I can't. I have to see my son later and I have to drive," Allison said. "But don't let me stop you. I'd enjoy another if I could." She wouldn't have, but she was playing a part and needed to sound convincing.

"If you insist." Laura gained the attention of the waitress and ordered another drink before casting her sights to her cell phone perched on the edge of the table. It appeared as though a text had arrived. She picked up the phone to view the message and her expression hardened.

Allison noticed the marked shift in Laura's demeanor. "Is everything all right?" She strained to see the sender of this message, but Laura pressed the button to darken the screen.

She cleared her throat and returned to Allison. "So, like I was saying, Tracy and Carlos, they were always fighting about something. Where to go out, what friends to see. You name it. Honestly, I don't know why she married him."

Allison's nerves tingled as Laura's voice suddenly dripped with contempt. Whoever sent that message had clearly knocked Laura for a loop. "I'm sure they must've been happy at first."

"Maybe." Laura sipped on her drink and seemed to return to normal. "I'll tell you one thing, though. It wouldn't surprise me one bit if Carlos was behind it, you know?"

This was new. Up to now, Carlos had just been the crooked developer-husband. Now Allison was seeing something she hadn't seen in Laura earlier. "Her murder?"

Laura glanced around the restaurant before looking back at Allison. "Oh yeah. And Harlan. Money was the only thing that mattered to Carlos. More than Tracy, that's for damn sure."

"So, do you know if she was doing anything to protect herself?"

"What do you mean?" Laura asked.

"I mean, like, did she have protection. A bodyguard or heck, I don't know, was she working with anyone to help her?" Allison did her best to appear both impartial and compassionate.

Laura knitted her brow and examined Allison with great concern. "I'm not sure I get what you're asking. Carlos would've ripped a new one in any other man who tried to protect her. I mean, like I said before, he never physically abused her..."

"But you say it wouldn't have surprised you if he did it. Killed both of them."

Laura took a much larger gulp this time. "Look, I get this is all sensational, you know? Intriguing. But Tracy was my friend. And I know you understand what a kind person she really was. You said you knew her from her charity work."

"That's right," Allison replied. "The children's charity. We met a few times at some of the functions."

Laura nodded. "Right. Of course. Well, I don't know anything about her getting help from some outsider. I wish I did." She raised her index finger from the glass she held. "Hang on a minute. There was someone she mentioned. I don't recall a name." She gazed upward as if thinking hard. "Damn. Who was that?" When she returned her sights to Allison, she continued. "I don't remember, but I bet if she was working with someone, it would be on her phone."

Allison nodded as if the whole thing was only mildly interesting. She knew that Boyce had some sort of arrangement with Tracy. And then there were the calls from the records Alvarez offered to Shane.

"Oh, you know what," Laura began. "It was that guy, that surfer guy. Tracy met him at some function the mayor was holding. God knows what a guy like that was doing with the mayor, but she came back all excited that he said he could help her."

"Help her with what?" Allison asked.

"I don't know. I assume with getting out from under Carlos. I told Tracy he was only looking to get in her pants and she already had enough men doing that."

"A surfer guy, huh? Interesting."

"I know, right? I saw him once. He was pretty hot. Blonde hair, super tan. Pretty typical. He had a cool name. I think...that's right I remember her mentioning his name was Fin, which I thought was cool for a surfer name, right? I mean, how perfect, you know?"

Allison's heart skipped a beat. "And you think he might've helped her sort of keep things on the down low with Harlan or something? What was he, some kind of cop?"

"No, he wasn't a cop. I don't know what he was doing to help her out. Maybe getting dirt on Carlos? She probably figured if she could get something on Carlos that hit his wallet, that would hurt him more than her having an affair."

Allison strained to think of what business Fin Dawson had with Carlos or the mayor. She instantly recalled Charlie telling her Fin was driving to a house who she believed belonged to the mayor. It seemed so out in left field but maybe it wasn't.

"Well, I guess it doesn't matter." Laura finished the rest of her drink. "Nothing matters now that she's dead. All I know is that Carlos better go to prison for taking her away from me. No matter what anyone says, he was behind her death. I just know it. Maybe I should tell the cops about this Fin guy?"

"I know the cops have a lot of people working on this. I'm sure they'll figure it all out. We should both just focus on celebrating Tracy's memory."

"You know what, Emma, you couldn't be more right."

20

It was like a horror movie that ran on a loop inside Charlie's head. Finley Dawson splayed out on the floor of his home, gurgling his words while blood spilled out. Then he just stopped moving. For almost two hours Charlie had waited at the police station and she couldn't escape the grisly scene.

Charlie was nothing if not tenacious. Hell, she managed to claw her way out of an abusive marriage and come out stronger on the other side, but this...this was going to haunt her for some time.

"Ma'am." The officer returned to his desk. "You can go now but please understand that it's possible you'll be called on again. Can I count on your cooperation?"

"Of course." Charlie was slow to rise from the chair. Stiffness had settled in her bones.

"And you're sure there's nothing else?" The officer asked. "Nothing else you can remember?"

Charlie looked away. "No, sir. Nothing else."

The officer appeared unconvinced. "Okay, then. We'll be in touch."

Charlie reached for her handbag and started to leave and as she returned to the lobby, a friendly face appeared. She wasn't close to Shane Sullivan the way Allison was, but he knew what they had been up to and that he could be trusted. Her eyes immediately welled. "Shane."

"Charlie, what are you doing here?" He hurried toward her. "Are you okay? Did something happen?"

Her eyes darted back and forth, confirming the officer wasn't watching. "He's dead, Shane. Fin's dead."

"What?" He lowered his tone and pulled Charlie aside. "How? When did this happen? Where's Allison?"

Charlie shook her head erratically and her voice cracked. "I don't know. I don't know."

"It's okay. Just calm down. Come here." Shane led her toward an empty corridor near the restrooms. "Charlie, start from the beginning and tell me what happened."

"There's no time. We have to find Alli. She's in danger."

———

THE EVENING CLOUDS ROLLED OUT, LEAVING BEHIND A twinkling sky as Allison made her way home. Drinks with Laura Young ran long and now her belly rumbled, but the end result had been worth it. Allison was armed with new information on the Tracy Diaz front.

The moment Allison left the bar, she tried to call Charlie but didn't get an answer. Now that she was home, she would try again. Allison pulled to a stop on her driveway and stepped out of the car. The sound of an engine racing echoed in the distance but was approaching quickly. Allison spun around. "Shane? What in the world?"

He slammed on the brakes and stopped inches from her car before he jumped out. Charlie crawled out of the passenger side.

It only took a moment for Allison to see on Charlie's face that something had gone terribly wrong. "What's going on? Charlie, are you okay?"

"We tried to call you, but you didn't answer," Shane replied.

"You did?" Allison reached for her phone. "Oh no. It's been on silent. What happened? You're both scaring me."

"Let's go inside. No need to draw attention." Shane ushered Allison and Charlie to the front door and waited for Allison to open it. "Is Nolan here?"

"No. He has baseball practice tonight." Allison walked in. "Please tell me what's going on. I'm starting to freak out."

Shane waited for Charlie to enter before he closed the door. "You want to tell her since you were there?"

Charlie nodded and looked at Allison. "It's Fin Dawson. Alli, he's dead. He was shot almost right in front of me."

"What?" She stumbled back. "You were there? Jesus, are you hurt?"

"No. I'm fine," Charlie said. "I should've listened to you. I waited for Fin to leave and I followed him back to his house. Just as I was about to give up, the Mercedes, the one we saw at Boyce's office on that video—the one you think drove by you that night. Alli, whoever was driving that car killed Fin."

"Another officer arrived on the scene and brought her in to make a statement. I saw Charlie as she was leaving and she told me. I brought her straight here," Shane replied. "Let's all just sit down. We need to clear our heads and figure out what the hell is happening." He walked into the kitchen and snatched bottles of water from the fridge. "Okay, now we know the Mercedes is the key."

Allison pulled out a dining chair, scraping its legs across the hardwood floor before sitting down. "That damn Mercedes." She turned to Charlie, who sat next to her. "Did you see the plates?"

Charlie pulled her damaged phone from her purse and set it on the table. "I took a picture of it. But then I dropped my phone when I saw..." She turned away.

"That's okay. I'm sure we'll be able to pull the information from this, right?" Allison looked at Shane. "You have people who can do that?"

"I do, but Allison, how do you think the department is going to react to the news that Charlie had this information and didn't disclose it to the officer who brought her in? It'll look bad."

"You're right," Allison replied. "Well, this has gone far enough." She grabbed her phone and waited for the line to answer. "Milo, we need to talk. Now."

———

THE DOOR OPENED AND MILO STOOD ON THE OTHER SIDE. "How are you holding up, kid?"

Allison exhaled a weary breath but managed a tender smile. "Me? Not great. Charlie? She's in bad shape."

"I'd say that's because this is bad, Allison. Really bad." He stepped inside.

"I'm glad you're here. We all are. Come in." Allison led the way into the kitchen and walked toward the window in the break-fast nook, peeking through the blinds. "At what point do we throw in the towel and tell Montoya and Alvarez what's happened up to now? We've been skirting around them as much as legally possible while Milo works to build his case. I'm afraid our time's up and it will be Shane who suffers the greatest fallout if we choose to keep quiet. So Milo, you're here to tell us which direction to take. This was your deal. Your's and Tommy's. We've lost Tommy and now Fin. If we don't come to a consensus, one of us could be next."

Milo studied the people around him. "I am not oblivious to the impact this has had on each and every one of you. I, too, am shaken up by what's happened. Allison came to me and I asked her to keep a lid on things as much as possible while I worked to finalize my investigation into Carlos Diaz. Although that hasn't changed, the circumstances certainly have. Especially for you, Charlie. What you saw today—it never should've happened."

"Did you have any idea someone was out to get Fin Dawson? Was it because of his relationship with Tommy Boyce?" Charlie asked.

"I had no idea something like this could've happened to him. Dawson was a good kid, but he had his own agenda."

"Surprise, surprise." Allison traversed a path around the kitchen. "You knew him better than just some guy who worked with Tommy, didn't you? Who was he really?"

Milo eyed her. "FBI."

"Christ on a cracker." Charlie dropped her head into her hands.

"And now that he's gone, they're going to be all over this," Milo added.

"But I thought he and Tommy worked together for the past few years? I don't understand," Allison replied.

"They had worked together, on occasion. The deal was if Tommy caught wind of something Dawson might be interested in, they'd share information. And that was what happened with the Diaz case. Dawson got his license, and from an outsider's perspective, he was a P.I. You could say it was his cover."

"Why did Dawson go see the mayor?" Charlie asked.

"When did he do that?" Milo asked. "I wasn't aware."

"Today. I followed him to the neighborhood where the mayor

and a bunch of rich people live. I couldn't get inside the gates but why else would Dawson have been there?"

"He must've been there to see someone else. How can you be sure it was the mayor?" Shane asked.

"Well, I can't, I suppose. But who else?"

"Charlie, a lot of wealthy and influential people must live there," Shane added.

"She might be right," Allison interrupted. "I was with Laura Young earlier tonight. She mentioned Fin. Tracy knew him and it sounded like they had met at a function hosted by the mayor. Laura said Tracy thought Fin could help her. I didn't get much more than that."

"Well, whoever he was meeting in that neighborhood, it was someone who mattered. I followed him back home and within minutes, that silver Mercedes pulled up and the man got out and killed Dawson," Charlie replied. "What's worse was that his last words to me were to the effect that Allison was in danger."

"Great. So now we have to keep Allison safe. Maybe the rest of us are in their sights too," Shane said.

"We have proof of what appears to be a bribe accepted by Carlos, thanks to what you guys have done," Milo began. "I've been working on exposing the name of the payor to see where it came from, although, I suspect it's someone with ties to the city. So Charlie, I gather you have pictures of the Mercedes. Let's pull them off that damaged phone and see if we can get a plate. It's time to find this car and whoever was driving it. I have a feeling it could be someone who knows the mayor."

"He was a good guy, Charlie," Allison began. "Fin Dawson was on our side and I didn't trust him. Now he's dead.

And what could've happened to you...I don't want to think about it."

"I'm okay, Alli. Not right now but I know I will be. Fin didn't deserve to die for this. For some bribe or whatever it was. Neither did Tommy Boyce."

"You're damn right they didn't." Allison peered through the front window while Charlie sat on the sofa.

Charlie reached for Allison's hand. "Hey, we've done all we can do for now. You told them what you knew about Tracy from her friend, and I gave Milo my SD card so they could get the pictures. What more is there?"

"I want this to be over." Allison dropped the blind and returned on the sofa. "I promised Lucy I would find out who killed her father. In all honesty, I don't care about Tracy Diaz or her boyfriend, or the fact that her husband was on the take. Tommy Boyce was trying to help Tracy and it got him killed. Fin might've been trying to help Tracy and it got him killed too. I love Milo, Charlie, you know that, but he's wearing blinders. He has his sights on something that means absolutely nothing to me."

"It's not fair to put that on him, Alli. Milo has a good heart and good intentions."

"Don't we all." She gathered her thoughts. "Here's what I'm going to do. I don't expect you to follow along this time and I wouldn't blame you one bit if you chose not to. After what you saw today..."

"What is it? I'll stand with you. Always have. We're partners, aren't we?"

Allison smiled. "Yeah, we're partners."

"What's your plan, Alli? I can see the wheels spinning. There's nothing we can do for Fin. But we're still here. We can make this right—for Lucy."

Allison walked to the front door where her car keys hung on a hook. "If you want to do this, I'm leaving now."

"Where are we going?" Charlie pushed off the sofa and caught up to her.

"We're going to Fin's house."

Charlie stopped dead. "I don't know if I can do that. Besides, the cops are bound to still be there."

"If they are, then we'll just drive on by. If not, then we go in and figure out what got Fin killed. He had to have something. We need to know what that was. I know in my heart that whoever killed Fin, killed Tommy. And until Milo and Shane get a hit on that license plate, we're dead in the water." Allison walked out into the night and the scent of damp earth filled the air. She reached her car and opened the driver's door. "You don't have to do this. I'll understand. This is your call, Charlie."

Charlie walked to the passenger door. "What are you waiting for? Evidence isn't going to just fall from the sky."

Allison slipped onto the driver's seat and turned the engine, and it promptly stalled. "Damn it." She tried again, this time, pressing on the gas pedal. The engine fired up.

"You really should consider buying another car," Charlie said.

"Sure. Right after I win the lottery." She thrust the gearshift into reverse before pulling out of the driveway. Allison slammed on the brake and whipped her head toward Charlie. "Nolan should've been home by now."

"Give him a call. This can wait until you hear from your son," Charlie said.

Allison reached for her phone and made the call. When the line picked up, a notable sigh of relief escaped her. "Nolan, where are you? Practice ended hours ago."

"Sorry, Mom. I'm out with some of the guys. Are you at home?"

"I am, but Charlie and I are heading out. We won't be gone long. Are you coming home soon?"

"In a few hours."

"Okay, hon. Just making sure. I'll see you later. Bye." She turned to Charlie. "Now we can go."

"You're a good mom, Alli." Charlie turned her sights toward the passenger window.

"So are you. Don't ever forget that." Allison made her way onto the main road and toward Finley Dawson's house. "I wish Fin had just been upfront with me, you know? About being a federal agent."

"It was his job to make us believe he was just some P.I. who liked to surf. I guess he was pretty good at it. What worries me the most is just where this all leads. I mean, are we talking about a corrupt city official?"

"I don't know." Allison kept her hands on the wheel and drove on. "Milo seems to believe this goes pretty high. It's still hard to face the idea that Fin's gone."

"Yeah," Charlie replied.

Allison made the final turn down Fin's street. "The good news, if there is any, is that I don't see any cop cars. Do you?"

"Not yet. Wait until we get to his house. They could be in the driveway."

"Ever the optimist, Charlie." Allison slowed as she neared the home and flicked off her headlights. "We might have ourselves a window of opportunity. I hope we can squeeze into it. Not a cop car in sight." She pulled to a stop two doors down from Fin's house. "I know it won't be easy for you—going back inside there. And I'll be honest, I don't know if the cops turned his place upside down or not. If they did, we'll have to hope for the best. It's gotten us this far. Are you ready?"

"I'm ready." Charlie opened her door and stepped out.

Allison caught up to her and gently took her arm. "You're sure you can do this?"

"I appreciate your concern, Alli, but I'm wearing my big girl pants today."

Allison kept up with Charlie's determined pace and began, "I want to go in through the back. He has a path along the side of his house. I remember from when I was here before looking for him and found him on the beach. That path will take us around back and to his gate. We'll be able to get in from there."

"You don't think it could be locked?" Charlie asked.

"If it is, I'm sure we'll figure out a way to get inside."

They arrived around to the back of his home. The sound of the waves crashing on the shore echoed in the distance. It was too dark to see the water, though a breeze carried the salty air and it was much cooler than inland.

Allison reached the gate first and pulled it open. "Voila." She walked through and Charlie followed. French doors were just ahead that opened into Fin's office. "What are the odds his computer is still sitting on his desk?"

"About as good as our odds of being mistaken for a couple of Millennials. Are we going to take it?" Charlie asked.

"If it's there, we're taking it. And anything else we can get our hands on that could help." Allison grabbed the door handle and turned. "Tonight's our lucky night."

Charlie scoffed. "Lucky for us. Not for Fin."

21

The coquettish wit and easy-going vibe that epitomized
Fin Dawson was nowhere to be found in this empty
house. Although, Allison speculated those traits were
part of his cover. She didn't really know who Fin was, except that
he was FBI. There was nothing carefree about that. Still, she
regretted doubting his intentions.

"Alli." Charlie tapped on her shoulder. "Where's the light
switch?"

"Huh? Oh, it's over here." Allison felt along the wall and
turned on the light of Fin's office at the back of his home. Sand was
still scattered on the tile floor and only a few feet away were signs
of the violence that had taken his life.

"They haven't bothered cleaning it up." Allison looked at
Charlie who only stared at the bloodstain. "Hey. It's okay if you
want to wait outside."

"No. I'll be fine," Charlie replied. "I just want to do what we
came here to do."

"If you're sure. We'll need to be quick." Allison hurried to the

2-drawer filing cabinet next to his desk. "I'll look in here. Maybe you can check the files on his desk? It doesn't look like the cops have touched any of this yet." She peered around. "I don't see his laptop. They must've taken it."

"Doesn't that seem strange to you? All this stuff—files, paperwork—they only took his laptop?" Charlie started her search of the desk.

"Now that you mention it, yeah. Like the cops knew he was a federal agent and they decided to wait on those guys to come and collect the files." Allison pulled out the top drawer and thumbed through the folders. "Taxes, receipts, a few case files. Any luck at his desk?"

"Not yet." Charlie continued rifling through his things. "Cripes, Alli, who would've wanted him dead? I mean, he was here one minute and the next..."

"I don't know, but I'm sure it has everything to do with Carlos Diaz and whatever deal he struck. Someone dropped a lot of money in his lap. What if it was someone with the city, like the mayor? If it was a legal payment, it wouldn't have been made anonymously." Allison continued to study each file in the drawer. "I don't know what the hell I'm looking for in here."

"Proof, I guess. Evidence of someone who had reason to want him dead." Charlie's eyes narrowed. "Hey, Alli? You might want to see this."

Allison drew up from the file cabinet and approached Fin's desk. "What did you find?"

"You remember when Fin said he wanted time to finish reviewing all of Tommy's surveillance footage and that he thought he could narrow down the owner of the Mercedes?"

"Yeah, of course. So?"

Charlie held a thumb drive between her fingers. "Well, I saw him put that drive in his desk drawer before we left."

"Is that what you have in your hands?" Allison asked.

"That one's gone. It was white with a black cover. This is different and it was in the pencil drawer tucked into the back. It has writing on it. There could be something on here."

"That means somebody took the one with Tommy's office video."

"Or Fin turned it over to someone," Charlie added.

Allison swung around at a noise coming from the front door. "Charlie!" she whispered.

"I heard it. Someone's here."

Allison pulled at Charlie's arm. "Bring that drive with you." She pushed open the French doors that were still ajar and stepped quietly out into the backyard.

The voices grew louder and Allison led the way to a grassy shrub planted on the side of the double doors. "Get down." Allison pressed her index finger against her lips as they crouched low.

"We need to go through this shit again before the cops do."

A man's voice, deep and gravely, arose from inside Fin's office. Allison strained to listen.

"Sadler wants us to bring anything we find straight to him."

This was a different man who spoke. His tone was higher pitched and less intense. But it was the name he used that mandated fear to shoot across Allison's face. When she turned to Charlie, she had heard the name too.

Charlie started to push up from the ground.

"No," Allison whispered. "They'll see us."

When Charlie squatted again, she shook her head. "I was right."

Clay Sadler was the mayor of Tampa. Charlie was right on the money about where Fin had been earlier in the day before being gunned down where it appeared the mayor's friends were now searching. But what were they looking for?

Papers rustled and drawers opened and closed, but that was all they could hear from behind the bush. The men spoke to one another in a low and indiscernible fashion. Almost as if they'd moved to the back of the room or to another room in the house. Allison had no way of knowing what was going on inside or if the men would wander out back where they had taken cover. "Cover" seemed too generous to describe where they were currently holed up.

"How are we going to get to the car?" Charlie uttered.

The car was parked in front of another house, which as luck would have it, turned out to have been a wise decision.

"Even if we could get to it, they'll hear it start up." Allison felt trapped and had dragged along Charlie for good measure. She had pushed things too far and the end result could be disastrous. "Listen, I have an idea, but you're going to have to follow my lead."

"Whatever you say," Charlie replied.

In a low voice, Allison began, "We're going to walk out through the back gate and onto the beach."

"What?" Charlie's eyes bulged into great white orbs. "Are you serious? They'll see us."

"Trust me." Allison pushed off the ground with some discomfort. Her knees threatened to buckle from the undertaking. When she returned to full height, Allison offered her hand to Charlie.

Charlie gazed up at her with uncertainty, but she surrendered and placed her hand in Allison's and heaved. Charlie managed to get herself off the ground with minimal cries of agony.

A low wooden gate several feet ahead was their only means of escape. If Allison could get them to the other side, they would be in the clear. The idea was that if they were seen from that point, it could be played off as two women strolling along the beach, possibly ending up at the wrong home in the dark of night. No harm, no foul.

"Now." Allison started toward the gate about twenty feet away.

As they ventured out, the light from the home diminished and spotting the gate against the black of the ocean was difficult. They had to just keep going.

"Ouch!" Charlie threw her hand over her mouth and winced in pain.

Allison whipped back.

"My foot." Her face writhed and she pointed at a jagged rock jutting from the sandy ground.

Allison checked the doors leading to Fin's office and shadows crossed in front of it. "They're coming. Go!"

They hurried toward the gate. Charlie hobbled but was doing her damnedest to push through the pain. Allison reached for the latch and pushed it open. She ushered Charlie through first then followed quickly behind. She turned to close it again when the unknown men appeared outside.

"Hey! What are you doing?" One of the men, the heavyset one with the deep voice, jogged toward them.

"Who are you?" The other man, who appeared much younger, rushed to his partner's side.

Allison and Charlie stopped in their tracks. They were on the other side of the gate—the ocean side. That was the easy part.

Allison glanced to Charlie, who was white with fear or pain, she wasn't sure. She had to think fast, or they were going to end up like Fin. "Who am I? Well, who are you?" Her words were slurred and her body swayed just a little.

"What are you, drunk or something, lady?" The gruff-looking man with a voice to match moved closer. "And who are you?" He peered at Charlie.

Allison looked at her. Charlie was paralyzed. Allison got them into this jam, it was up to her to get them out. "We're just having a nice stroll along the beach and were walking back to our house." Allison narrowed her eyes and placed her hands on her hips. "Wait a minute. This isn't my house."

"Lady, you and your friend better get the hell out of here. Go sleep it off, yeah?" This time, the younger man spoke. His tall and slender build with a long face didn't match his falsetto tone.

The older man grabbed his cohort's arm. "Wait a minute." With his squinty eyes, he stepped up to the fence. "You live around here?"

"Uh-huh." Allison raised her arm and pointed to her right. "Down there. I think." She gazed up at the dark sky as if uncertain.

"Do you know the man that lives here?" he asked, still appearing unconvinced. "You say you live around here. Maybe you seen him, huh?"

"Maybe once or twice. Some kid, I think. Surfer," Allison replied.

"That's right. You know where he's at now?"

"Should I?" Allison asked.

The man held her gaze with a lethal stare.

Allison's heart raced in her chest and she held onto Charlie's hand. Both had turned clammy. Fear crawled up her spine and she wondered if this plan was going to work.

"Just thought you might know your neighbors. You ladies should go on home. It isn't safe to be out here alone and especially seeing as how you've had too much to drink. Drinking and the ocean don't mix. You catch my drift?"

There was no doubt in Allison's mind what he meant. "You gentlemen have a good night. Come on, Sue, let's go home." She pulled Charlie's hand and they started along the beach, walking outside the properties that lined the way.

The men watched and Allison needed to keep up the ruse.

She was going to have to enter someone's property or those men would surely follow. "We're going in here. It looks empty."

"Just get us out of here, Alli, before I crap my pants." The color returned to Charlie's cheeks.

You and me both." Allison tried the gate of a house down from Fin's. It unlatched. "Oh, thank God."

When they were out of sight of the men, they nearly collapsed in the backyard of a stranger's home.

"I thought we were done back there." Charlie turned to Allison. "That was him. The fat guy. He killed Fin." She leaned against the wall of the house and pulled up her leg for a better look at the injured toe. "I think it's broken. I knew I shouldn't have worn sandals."

"They were the same guys from the video of Tommy's office too. I didn't see their faces that clearly, but one of them was chubby and the other was thin."

"They're working for the mayor. You see that now, right?" Charlie's lips quivered.

"Yeah, I see it." Allison draped her arm over Charlie's shoulder. "We're okay now. We're safe." She pulled back to examine the house. "Unless whoever lives here is a psycho killer."

"Don't you jinx us, Alli, I swear to God."

———

THE GREY LIGHT OF DAWN CLIMBED IN THE SKY AND ALLISON and Charlie had returned home.

Allison slipped her key in the lock and opened her front door. And after Charlie entered, Allison quickly secured the deadbolt. "Just in case."

"Just in case," Charlie replied. "Hey, look here." She pointed to the living room where Nolan was asleep on the couch. "I bet that kid waited up for you."

"I'm sure. I replied to his text once we got to the car. He sent half a dozen."

"Alli, you're going to have to tell him what's been going on. If you don't and something happens..."

"Nothing's going to happen, okay?" She walked quietly to the kitchen. "We made it out safely."

"By the skin of our teeth," Charlie walked behind her.

"Yeah, well, it was my idea to go there in the first place. I take the blame."

Charlie held up the thumb drive. "It was a good call, regardless of how it could have turned out. We can't dwell on that."

Allison smiled. "Thank you, Charlie. And I'm sorry about your toe." She peered down at it. "It does look broken."

"What do you want to do with this? We know it was the same men who were at Boyce's office and the big guy was the same man I saw at Fin's. Alli, we both heard the name. This implicates some serious VIPs. Milo must've suspected that was the case. That was why he needed to buy time—to prove it."

Allison walked to the coffee maker and started a pot. "It's 4:30 in the morning. Right now, I need coffee before I can consider the ramifications of all this."

"I hope you're making a full pot."

Allison walked around the kitchen island. "I'll go get my laptop. It's upstairs. Let's see how much more trouble we can get into." She placed her hand on Charlie's shoulder and smiled before walking into the living room. Nolan was spread out on the sofa and Allison draped a light blanket over the top of him.

"Mom? You're home." He roused from his sleep.

"I'm sorry to wake you, honey. Maybe you should go sleep in your bed. This couch isn't very comfortable."

"I was worried." He sat up. "I got your text. I think that was when I fell asleep out here. Where were you?"

"I was working. Charlie was with me and as you can see, we're both just fine."

Nolan peered into the kitchen and spotted Charlie. "When is this going to be over?"

"Soon. It'll be over soon, I promise. Now go on. Go sleep in your own bed before you get a neck ache out here."

He stood. The full height of his frame towered over her. He leaned in and kissed her cheek. "You should get some rest too, you know."

"Are you playing the parent now?" she asked.

"Only if I have to." He shuffled to his room and closed the door.

22

The sun burned through the morning clouds, but dew still clung to the windows of Allison's home. She and Charlie had been reviewing the contents of Finley Dawson's flash drive since before the sun arose.

Allison tipped her mug and noticed not a drop of coffee remained. "I'm out." She pushed up from the kitchen chair and swiped the mug from the table. "I'm going to make another pot. Do you want a bagel or something? I'm starved."

Charlie rubbed her eyes and released a heavy sigh. "Sure. Why not?"

"So far, we haven't found squat that'll tell us why Fin was murdered. Or what he was doing for the FBI." Allison stood at the coffee maker and filled the carafe with tap water.

"Just a bunch of old case files," Charlie began. "Why he would've kept them on here and not a server, I don't know. I mean, who keeps a flash drive without juicy details on it, you know? That's kind of the point of them."

Allison pressed the button to start the machine and reached

into the breadbox for the bagels. "We're not done yet. We just have to keep looking. People are getting picked off one by one and I don't want to know who might be next."

Charlie clicked on another file. "Looks like this one is a video. Come take a look."

Allison walked back and leaned over her shoulder. She peered at the thumbnail image. "It looks like video from his laptop camera. Press play."

Charlie started the video and turned up the volume.

Fin sat at his desk, the laptop's camera capturing him with a beam of light bouncing off his cheek. A knock sounded and Fin stood, walking out of the frame. He returned to his chair and was back in the picture, but someone was with him. Someone they couldn't see.

"Who's there?" Allison asked.

"I have no idea," Charlie replied.

Their eyes fixed on the video as it continued to play, and the man spoke.

"*So, you weren't told about the deal? I figured a man in your position would've been privy to that sort of information.*"

"*A man in my position?*" Fin had answered. "*I don't think so. Sadler doesn't say more than he thinks I should know. I don't have his trust yet. That's something I'm working on.*"

Allison shot a look to Charlie. "Sadler. Fin knew about Sadler."

"I was right. He did go see the mayor. And then he was killed," Charlie replied.

The video continued.

"*Last I heard, Diaz and Sadler were chummy until last week. I have no idea what happened at that point,*" Fin continued.

"*Look, Dawson, you're going to have to come up with something better than that. Nash wants Carlos Diaz and without you getting details from your relationship with Sadler, I don't know how long he can keep up the charade. Something's gotta give. Boyce is getting close to the wife, but Nash needs more."*

The video ended.

"That's it?" Charlie said. "That's all we're going to get?"

"Milo. They were talking about Milo. Maybe there's more. Go back into the files and look for more video," Allison said.

Charlie opened the file finder again. "I'm looking, just hang tight." She continued to click through the files. "Here's another one."

The video loaded and this time Fin was in his office alone. His cell phone buzzed on his desk. *"Yeah. Dawson here."* He nodded and stared at his laptop while he listened to the caller.

"He doesn't seem worked up or upset about anything." Allison folded her arms and looked on.

"Give it a minute," Charlie replied.

"That's what I told him, man. I'm telling you, he's reluctant. He doesn't fully trust me yet but given time..." Fin jumped in his chair. *"What the hell!"* He whipped his head toward the French doors, which were out of view.

"What's he looking at? What happened?" Allison dropped onto the chair next to Charlie, her eyes never leaving the laptop screen.

Charlie shook her head in reply and kept her sights glued to the video.

Fin set down his phone on the desk and walked toward the sound of the noise and then he was out of the frame. But only a moment later, he returned with a large stone and a note. He retrieved his phone. *"Do you know what the hell just happened?"*

"He's worked up now," Charlie replied.

"Someone just chucked a rock through my window. Can you believe this shit? And there's a friggin note attached to it." Fin

nodded. *"Yeah, a note. Says we know who you really are."* His voice trailed off and his face turned deadpan.

"Oh no. Whoever it was, the mayor's people or whatever, they figured out he was FBI," Allison said. "Look at his face."

"I see it," Charlie replied.

Fin appeared to regain composure. *"No, I'm not shitting you. Dude. What is this, some 1930s Al Capone bullshit?"*

Fin was silent again while whoever he was speaking to continued talking on the other end of the line. *"They figured it out. I'm going to have to see Sadler and convince him I'm not who they say I am."* He paused again. *"Just be there if I need backup, you hear me? Thanks, man."* Fin closed the lid on his laptop and the video ended.

"Oh, God." Allison looked at Charlie. "He had been threatened. Charlie, the mayor threatened him. That's why he kept this video. It was like his insurance so we would know what really happened."

"We know people came back, either the cops or his FBI buddies, and searched his house. They took his laptop and the flash drive with Tommy's surveillance footage. But they didn't know about this."

"And then Sadler's people came looking to cover their asses," Allison added. "We can have Milo make a call to the FBI field office and tell them about this. My God. How could I have not seen it sooner? Those men, they must work for Clay Sadler."

"It's looking more and more like whoever paid Carlos that cash is someone tied to the mayor. Why go after Tommy Boyce? Why go after Fin Dawson if it wasn't all the same bad guys trying to cut loose ends?" Charlie asked.

Allison shook her head. "This video, the money that went to Carlos, and Fin's murder, probably Tommy's too. This all goes back to the mayor, you're right about that." She held Charlie's gaze. "These are dangerous men who will stop at nothing to protect their boss. I think it's time we get Lucy out. Get her some-place safe."

"Where can she go?" Charlie asked.

"She has family who lives out of state. I know she has school here, but maybe she needs to make a trip to visit that family."

"Do you think she'll go?"

"We have a compelling argument. She's 19, she's scared. I don't think we'll get pushback." Allison grabbed her phone and keys from the counter. "Bring the flash drive. We can't let that leave our sight."

"Where are we going?" Charlie stood from the chair and pulled the USB from the laptop.

"To see Lucy."

———

THE SUN WAS JUST ABOVE THE HORIZON WHEN ALLISON AND Charlie arrived at Tommy Boyce's house.

"I don't want to scare her, Charlie, and right now the look on your face says, 'run for your life,'" Allison said. "Why don't I do the talking?"

"Probably best," Charlie replied.

Allison rang the doorbell. "I have no idea if she's home."

"Do you have her cell?"

"I do." Allison stood a few steps from the large oak front door with her hands clasped at her front. "Come on, kiddo. Please be home."

"It's not looking good, Alli. Should we call her?"

Allison held the phone to her ear and waited, still peering at the door in the event it opened. Not only did it not open but the call also went straight to voicemail. "No answer on her phone."

"What do you want to do?" Charlie asked.

Allison gazed out across the neighborhood streets in search of inspiration—anything that would tell her what she should do. She checked the time on her phone. "Okay, it's almost 8. I'm sure you're exhausted, but..."

Charlie raised a hand. "No buts. I'll stay here and wait for her. You go."

"The school isn't far. I doubt she's there, but it's worth a shot."

"Just call me when you find her," Charlie said.

"I will." Allison started toward the car again but looked over her shoulder with some concern.

"Go!" Charlie demanded. "I'll be fine here." She sat on a bench at the entry and waved goodbye.

Allison pulled away from the curb, double checking Charlie once again before turning her sights on the road ahead. The community college was familiar grounds for Allison. Nolan attended the same school. Lucy wasn't at home and wasn't answering her phone. Before panic erupted, this was Allison's last-ditch effort.

The college was in sight and Allison pulled into the administration parking lot, jumping out and almost forgetting to lock her door. There were plenty of times when she prayed someone would steal that heap of crap, but today wasn't one of those times. She pushed through the double doors and approached a woman behind the desk. "Excuse me, I need to find one of your students, Lucy Boyce."

"Are you family?"

"No. My name is Allison Hart. I'm not sure if you're aware, but Lucy has suffered a loss in her family and I'm helping her with the arrangements. And I'm afraid I can't locate her, which is concerning given her state of mind. I don't know if she has returned to school or not. I hope you can help."

"Lucy has made us aware of her personal situation. It's very unfortunate. That young lady has been through a lot. However, as you're not a member of her family, I'm afraid I can't give you any information about her. Unless..." The woman typed something on her computer. "No. Sorry. I thought you might be on the list of contacts but you're not. I wish I could help."

Allison wore defeat. "Of course. No, I understand. It's just. Well, she's not answering her phone. She's not at home. I was getting worried. That's all. But I do understand." Allison dropped her shoulders and turned on her heel to walk away.

"Hold on," the woman said.

At this, Allison held a glimmer of hope and turned back. "Yes?"

"I can't tell you her class schedule, however, I can tell you that she is not here today."

"She's not?" Allison asked. "But she has been back to school since—the incident?"

"I'm afraid not. That's all I can tell you and I've probably said too much."

"Thank you. I'll take it from here. Thank you very much." Allison pushed through the doors and hustled back to her car.

Before stepping inside, she grabbed her phone from her purse. "Let's try this one more time." She waited for Lucy to answer. "Where are you, kiddo?" But as the line continued to ring and eventually went to voicemail, Allison sighed. "Damn." She dialed Charlie and expected a better outcome. "Well, at least you're answering. Any luck?"

"By your question, I assume Lucy's not at the school," Charlie replied.

"Nope. I tried her phone again and still no answer. We need to find her."

"Does she have a job? Part time or anything?"

"I don't know. But I have a feeling if she did, she probably didn't show up there either. The school said she hadn't been back."

"Should we tell Shane?" Charlie began. "I know he's going to be pissed about what we did last night, but this isn't about us. It's about Lucy's safety. That takes precedence over our choices."

"You mean, my choice." Allison stepped into the car. "No, I agree. I'm on my way back to you now." She set down her phone in the center console and started the engine. Charlie knew when to call it and she was right. Shane was going to have to know what was on that flash drive and along with that, he would want to know how they got it. To say he would be pissed was an understatement. What she did—and with Charlie—wasn't smart. But what was done was done and now they had compelling evidence against Clay Sadler.

Allison returned to the Boyce home and still there was no sign of Lucy's car. "I can't catch a break today." She stepped out and walked to the front door. "Charlie?" Allison looked around. "Charlie? I'm back. Where are you?" She moved beyond the cover of the patio. "Charlie?" Fear exploded in her voice and lodged in her throat. "Oh God, Charlie, please answer me." Allison walked onto the sidewalk in front of the house. Her hand clasped over her mouth and she choked back her welling tears. Then a hand pressed against her shoulder.

"Alli."

Allison spun around. "Charlie! I've been calling for you. Do you have any idea...?"

"Someone was here." Charlie's eyes darted up and down the street. "I heard a car just after we got off the phone and I thought it might be Lucy. I stepped out from under the porch and saw a black car. At first, I was just so damn glad it wasn't the silver Mercedes, but I was afraid to stick around to see who stepped out of it. I flew like a bat out of hell looking for cover."

"Someone came looking for her. After I promised her she would be safe." Allison examined Charlie. "But you're okay? They didn't see you?"

"No."

"You're sure?" Allison asked.

"I'm sure. The bright side is no one else seems to know where she is either."

"Always looking at the bright side. But that makes it all the more urgent we find her."

"It's time to tell Shane," Charlie said.

Allison nodded. "I'll drive."

23

Shane perched on the edge of his desk and rubbed his chin. "I can't believe you would do something so completely reckless, Allison. And you, Charlie? I would've expected more from you. Instead, you both risked your lives and for what?"

"For damning evidence that the mayor had a hand in the death of not only Tracy Diaz and Harlan Goodfellow, but it's looking like he also played a part in the murder of Tommy Boyce and now Fin Dawson. At least, based on what's on that flash drive. The bodies are piling up, Shane. We thought we were doing the right thing." Allison spoke with dogged conviction. "But Lucy—she's who I'm worried about now."

"Charlie, you're sure it wasn't the men from Dawson's house who showed up at the Boyce residence?" Shane cast a wary eye toward potential eavesdroppers. "The men you say work for Mayor Sadler?"

"It definitely wasn't," Charlie said.

He pushed off the desk and sat down at his computer. "Hand over the flash drive. You do have it with you, I hope?"

Charlie opened her handbag and retrieved the storage device, handing it to Shane. "Here. See for yourself. It's really bad."

"Your most insightful comment of the day." He inserted the drive into his computer.

"It's the file third from the bottom. Recorded September 8th at 2:45pm. There are two. The first one doesn't give away much, but the second, that's the valuable piece," Charlie replied.

Allison looked at Shane. "Can we get a number for her out-of-state relative? I have the man's name written down. It would be a good idea to either let him know she might be coming or to call us if he hears from her."

"Give me the name and I'll look into it," Shane replied.

She retrieved a sticky note with the name of the relative. "I should've kept in closer contact with her. She's all alone."

Charlie placed her hand on Allison's arm. "This isn't your fault. I don't want this to sound callous, but she is a grown woman."

"Charlie, she's 19," Allison replied.

"And she has street smarts thanks to her dad. I'm just saying, you can't shoulder responsibility for everything. You couldn't with Micah and you can't with Lucy."

Allison shot her a stern look. "That was different."

"Was it?"

"Okay, I see what you guys were looking at," Shane interrupted. "I can't argue with the fact this puts Clay Sadler in a negative light." He swiveled toward them. "But if you think he doesn't have a boatload of people in his pocket, then your ideas on politics are severely misguided."

"We aren't operating on ill-advised ideas, Shane. And when you see the next video, that's when you'll understand that this is so much bigger than we thought," Allison replied.

Shane frowned before returning to the screen. "Show me."

Allison played the file and sat back, waiting for him to see what they were up against. When the video played out, she continued. "Now you see? Fin was an undercover federal agent. Milo knew it and so did the man he was talking to. If we can find out who he is, we might be one step ahead of Sadler," Allison replied.

"How do we bring down Sadler without risking Lucy's life in the process?" Charlie asked.

"Well, I don't know who that man is Fin was talking to, but I'll bet Milo does. He's only told us what we needed to know. Maybe he thought he was protecting us," Allison said.

"What we did last night was illegal," Charlie began "And so is the evidence Shane currently has in his police-issued desktop computer. Montoya and Alvarez will have our heads on a plate and Allison won't stand a chance at getting a P.I. license. I realize that's not the priority here. I'm just saying. We broke the law. There will be consequences."

Shane nodded. "I am going to have to hand over this flash drive, but I can protect you both by insisting it was turned over by an anonymous tipster. It won't come back to either of you if I have my way."

"So you're going to have to lie for us?" Charlie shook her head. "That's not right, Shane. We can't let you do that." She looked at Allison. "I know you agree with me. Look, we did it and we'll have to suffer the repercussions. Maybe, once all this comes to light, we'll be given leniency, you know, for exposing a corrupt government official. But I can't—we can't, in good conscience, let you lie for us."

"She's right," Allison added. "We'll just have to deal with that when the time comes. I'd rather the detectives know what they're up against and maybe be able to save some lives—including Lucy's."

"What I want is for you both to go home and get some sleep,"

Shane said. "You've been up all night on this and now it's my turn. I'll run this up the flagpole and I'll get the contact information on Lucy's relative. When I have something, I'll call you, okay?"

"Got it." Allison stood from the chair. "Come on Charlie, I'll take you home."

———

THE PENTHOUSE APARTMENT WHERE CARLOS DIAZ NOW resided alone was where he had been holed up since the funeral. He was hiding out to avoid the press, his friends, and his board of directors. They blamed him for the death of his wife. He saw it in their eyes. It didn't seem to matter to any of them that she was having an affair with his CFO, Harlan Goodfellow.

"I didn't kill them." Carlos tossed back the rest of his Jack and Coke, his third of the day and it was only 2 pm. But then most of his days were spent in a state of intoxication.

The money had been moved and there was no evidence he'd ever received a payoff from Clay Sadler's campaign slush fund. It was now sitting in an offshore account that if the FBI got involved, it would no doubt be easily traced back to him.

Carlos walked to the window and stared out across the bay. "How did this get so out of hand?" He loved Tracy and never wanted to see her dead. He had gotten in up to his eyeballs with the mayor and his people. There seemed to be no way out. If only Tracy had kept her mouth shut. "Christ." Carlos walked toward the kitchen and poured himself another drink. He had to be prepared for Franklin Perry. The two were set to meet inside the hour. Carlos refused to leave the apartment, so Perry was coming to see him. It seemed every time he left his house, some idiot member of the press hounded him. Someone was bound to make the connection sooner or later. That was the reason for Perry's impending visit; to formulate a plan.

Carlos diverted his attention when the knock came, and he opened the door. "You're early. Come in."

"Couldn't be helped. Something came up and I needed to move our meeting. But I see you're not busy." Franklin Perry entered.

"How could you have let this happen?" Carlos downed another swig of his drink. "Did you know that guy was FBI?"

"No. Neither did Clay. His boys weren't supposed to do anything to the kid. I don't know what happened, but Clay is looking for answers. That's why I'm here. We need a way out because when the FBI gets here, there's no protecting any of us." Franklin took a seat on the couch, crossing one leg over the other. "What about the account? Is it closed?"

Carlos nodded as he joined Franklin in the living room, dropping onto a chair across from the sofa. "Nothing will trace back to me or to Sadler."

"Or me?"

"You're in the clear too."

"Good. That's a start," Franklin said. "Where is it? The money, I mean."

Carlos eyed him. "I said it's safe."

Franklin turned serious and leaned over with his elbows resting on his knees. "I'm making sure you didn't spend it, that's what I need to know. All we need is the cops finding some major purchase with no way to answer for it. Look, I'm trying to help you, man. I'm not doing this shit for my health, you got it?"

"Got it." Carlos raised his hands in defense. "It's in an offshore account. I'm not an idiot. I know the cops were at Tracy's funeral. They're watching me like a hawk. I can't even leave this place

without someone following me. Don't suppose you can do something about that?"

"You're better off here anyway. Let them believe you're in
mourning."

"I am," Carlos insisted.

"Sure you are. You should know that I'm not the only one who
noticed you didn't attend Harlan's funeral. That doesn't put you in
a favorable light, my friend."

"The guy was screwing my wife. You think any man would
have blamed me?" Carlos replied. "Look, why are you here? To
remind me that the noose around my neck is tightening?"

"The federal agent. That's why I'm here. Carlos, the cops and
the feds are going to come to you with this. The man who was
killed had close ties to Tommy Boyce, the P.I. you hired. Sadler
wants to be sure you'll do the right thing."

Carlos scoffed. "The right thing? And what might the right
thing be in this torrent of shit I'm standing in?"

"You're to keep your mouth shut about the kid—the fed. You
don't know anything about him or his association with Boyce,"
Franklin replied.

"That shouldn't be too hard since I didn't know him."

Franklin stood. "Just so we're crystal clear on this point,
Carlos, am I to understand that you will do as you're told?"

"I said I'll be your Huckleberry."

Franklin started toward the door. "That's all I needed to know.
You have a good evening, Carlos. Try not to drink yourself into a
stupor." He opened the door to leave.

Carlos watched him close the door behind him. "Asshole." He
returned to the chair and eyed his cell phone before finally
retrieving it. Clay Sadler was his top contact and so he called his
friend and cohort. When the line answered, he began, "Clay, it's

Carlos. I think it's time we sit down for a talk. Perry just left my place."

"Not over the phone," Clay replied.

"Then we need to meet. Now."

"The boat. Thirty minutes."

———

THE TIME IT TOOK FOR CARLOS TO MAKE ARRANGEMENTS FOR a clean getaway from his apartment and the drive to the marina took longer than the thirty minutes on which Clay had insisted. But Carlos wasn't worried. He had the mayor dead to rights and Clay knew it. Sending Franklin over did nothing but stoke Carlos's anger. He was a man with nothing left to lose and could take down all the players with a single visit to the Tampa Police Department.

Carlos understood that ultimately this situation had been of his own making. Hiring Tommy Boyce to get the goods on Tracy was one thing, but then she went and told the private detective about the money, the deals, all of it. When Clay caught wind of it, well, she'd signed her death warrant, and Harlan's. Franklin refused to give a name, though he knew who killed her. It was a process of elimination and Carlos figured it out, even if he had no proof.

There were moments when the grief swelled in his chest from out of nowhere and as Carlos walked along the dock toward the slip where the yacht waited, one of those moments struck. But he couldn't show Clay any weakness, not when he was about to use everything in his arsenal to protect his own skin. He pushed back his shoulders and raised his chin in defiance.

"You're 10 minutes late." Clay Sadler, the distinguished mayor of Tampa, stood on the deck of his 100-foot yacht with a glass of wine in his hand. "Well, are you coming aboard or not?"

Carlos stepped on the ladder and climbed onto the luxury boat on which he had been a guest many times before. One of the perks of dealing with a crooked city official. "I apologize for my delay. It's been difficult keeping the media off my back. I'm sure you wouldn't want any of them to track me down here, Mr. Mayor."

"If I didn't know any better, Carlos, I'd say that was a thinly veiled threat." The short man with a medium build and dark olive skin moved toward the leather-wrapped bench along the side of the bow. He sat down and stretched his arm across the railing, peering at Carlos with acute brown eyes.

"I'm not threatening you, Clay." Carlos approached him. "I'm simply stating a fact." He eyed the wine.

"Oh, where are my manners? Would you like a glass?" Clay returned to his feet and walked down into the living quarters.

Carlos followed him.

The mayor retrieved a glass from the dark cherry cabinets that lined the galley and pulled the wine from the refrigerator. "This is an excellent year. It won't disappoint." He handed the glass to Carlos.

"Thank you."

"So, you called this meeting; insisted on it, actually." Clay emerged from the galley and met Carlos at the dining table. "Please, sit down. What would you like to discuss?"

After taking a seat, Carlos sipped on the wine, savoring both the flavor and the building of anticipation. "Franklin Perry paid me a visit."

"Yes, I know," Clay replied. "I asked him to see you, to see how you were holding up."

"Holding up, or holding up my end of the bargain?"

"I believe you know the answer to that. Let's not skirt around the issue. I don't have the time. Why don't you get to the matter at hand?"

Carlos sat fully upright and captured Clay's eyes. "You understand that by removing the federal agent, you cast a bright spotlight in my direction."

"First of all, I'm not sure to what you're referring. Secondly, I don't see it that way at all, Carlos. I see it as Mr. Boyce, a man you hired, had an associate. That associate, who happened to be an undercover agent, was ensnared in a situation beyond the reach of either of us. It was an unfortunate episode and that is what you will tell the police when they come to you, which they most certainly will, given your association."

"Of that, I have no doubt," Carlos replied. "But this will go well beyond the local city police force and we both know that. The FBI doesn't like it when one of their own is murdered. Whatever Finley Dawson was working on will come to light and I honestly don't know how to keep my end of the bargain because I can't imagine what he had to do with you or our arrangement."

The mayor smiled and cocked his head as if convinced he had Carlos pegged. "Ah, I think I know what this is about. Given your elevated risk, you believe you should be compensated. Well, I can't say I disagree with you, Carlos. But as you know, your finances are sure to fall under great scrutiny. A transfer of any kind right now would be unwise."

"Clay, cut the shit. This isn't about money. Not anymore. Whatever deal we had regarding the revitalization efforts is long over. This isn't a game. Lives have been lost and I know I'm not responsible for that."

"Aren't you?" Clay began. "It was your wife who confided in the P.I. who in turn brought in the undercover agent."

"I think you might have that backward. That agent was doing work for you and you didn't know anything about him. Yes, he knew Boyce, but that appears to have been a coincidence. Clay, I believe we are at the end of our arrangement and I'm afraid there seems to be no way forward."

"You know, Carlos, I don't believe in coincidences. And there's always a way out. Dawson is gone and so is any connection to me he had. They can't connect us and it will stay that way as long as you keep to the story. The feds will come, yes. But they won't connect the dots. Not on this."

"I truly hope you're right." Carlos stood. "I won't take up any more of your time, Mr. Mayor. I do appreciate you taking a few moments out of your busy schedule."

"Anytime, Carlos. We're in this together. Have a good day and try to get some rest. Just know that Tracy is in a better place."

Carlos stopped on the polished cherry steps leading topside. He turned to face Clay. "Don't think for one minute I don't know what you did."

"Me?" He placed his hand on his chest. "You have that wrong, Carlos."

"I don't believe I do, Mr. Mayor. That's something you would do well to remember." For a moment, Carlos expected to hear the sound of a gun being cocked into position. It must've only been in his head. He continued up to the deck and disappeared.

Clay Sadler waited until he was certain Carlos had left before reaching for his cell phone. "Franklin, it's Clay. Listen, what we discussed before, I think the time's come for you to handle it. He's backed me into a corner, and you know how I hate that."

24

Franklin Perry ended the call and turned his sights to Milo Nash as they sat in his office. "I think we got him."

"That was Sadler?" Milo asked from behind his desk.

"Yep. He says he wants me to take care of the problem. That problem is Carlos Diaz."

"It's about damn time," Milo said. "We can finally put an end to this."

"When I met with Carlos, I could see he was losing it because of what happened to Dawson. He must've gone straight to Sadler and Sadler apparently didn't like what he had to say."

"It's a damn shame about Dawson, though. I thought the kid had his buddies covering his back. If I would've known he was exposed, we could've protected him," Milo said.

"The real question is, how did he get made? Last I talked to him, he was still cozying up to Sadler, but Sadler had reservations. And after Boyce was killed, I think Dawson was afraid of who to trust. He stopped coming to me or you. Decided he would take the situation into his own hands. The feds will come after Sadler and his people, but we need to find them first if we stand a chance at making any charges stick."

Milo nodded. "When that's done, I want to bring Lucy Boyce home."

Franklin eyed Milo with concern. "I agree. And what about your friend, Hart? Have you been able to keep her on a short leash?"

"I haven't heard from her in almost 24 hours. I'll rectify that here shortly. Don't worry about her. She's got a good nose for things, but she won't get in the way of what we're trying to do."

"Good." Franklin started to leave. "I'll be in touch after I meet with Sadler."

"Hey, Franklin, don't go in there wired, okay? I know we're close to nailing him, but people are dropping like flies."

"How else am I supposed to get something we can use?"

"Just find out where his people are. We find them, we'll bring them in. Sadler won't be far behind," Milo replied.

"If you say so. This is your operation."

Milo waited for Franklin to leave before picking up his phone. He double-checked the time noting that it was later in the day than he thought. With the phone to his ear, he waited for her to answer.

"Milo," Allison began. "You have no idea how good it is to hear from you."

"Allison. Am I disturbing you? You sound half-asleep."

"It's been a long day and I didn't sleep last night, so I was just closing my eyes. There are things we need to discuss and…"

"Listen, something's about to happen and I need to make sure you and Charlie don't get caught in the middle of it."

"What do you mean? What's going on, Milo? Because last night, well, let's just say Charlie and I came across some men who we're pretty sure were responsible for the murder of Finley Dawson."

"Wait. Hold on. What?" A heated flush crawled up his neck and landed on his rounded cheeks.

"I couldn't just sit and wait for you and Shane to track down the Mercedes. We needed to know if there was anything at Fin's house that would explain his connections and if it related to Tommy Boyce. I understand it was dangerous..."

"No. No, you can't be serious. Criminy sakes, Allison. Do you have any idea what could've happened to you two? There are people embroiled in this that you wouldn't want to cross paths with, you understand?"

"I know. I know. But Milo, hear me out," she pleaded. "We found something. Charlie found it. It was a flash drive. Some man I don't know, but it seems you might, was on that video and discussed the mayor, Clay Sadler. Then there's video proof that the mayor's people threatened Fin. It had to have been Sadler's people who killed Fin and probably Tommy, too. Milo, you said you were working with Tommy to help bring down Carlos Diaz. You knew what Fin was doing, too, didn't you? After you sat there and told me he and Tommy were just helping each other out."

Milo inhaled a breath to tamp down his anger and guilt. "I didn't know everything Dawson was dealing with, but I knew it had something do with my investigation. He was FBI. I didn't get in his way. But how could you go back to his house? Allison, the FBI is going to be all over this."

"No doubt. But you're missing my point. We have evidence that the mayor threatened Fin."

"Indirectly," he shot back. "Things are going on behind the scenes that you have no idea about."

"Then maybe it's time you fill me in because here I thought we were on the right track. And now Lucy Boyce is missing. Did you know that? That's what Charlie and I have been doing most of the day—trying to find her."

"I know where she is," he interjected. "She's safe and far away from here. My God, Allison. Why didn't you come to me with any of this? The risks you took. I told you I've been working on something."

"You took her? Milo, I've been worried sick that she was in danger."

"Hey, the last we spoke, you were cozying up to Tracy Diaz's friends who you thought might know something. Allison, you said nothing about the rest of it. I thought I could trust you to do what you set out to do, not get sidetracked and risk your life and Charlie's."

"Yeah, I went my own way, but Milo, it paid off. Tell me this video evidence will help bring down the mayor, Carlos Diaz and whoever else is wrapped up in this insane investigation. And then, you can tell me when you're going to bring home Lucy."

"Do you have the flash drive?" Milo asked.

"I left it with Shane. He was going to take it to Detective Montoya."

"When?" Milo jumped in.

"Now, I imagine."

"I have to go." Milo ended the call and grabbed his keys, rushing through the door of his office. He picked up his cell phone again and pressed Shane's contact. "Sully, did you hand over the flash drive Allison gave you?"

"You know about that?" Shane asked.

"Did you turn it over?" He demanded.

"I was going to but Montoya's out. Due back inside the hour. I didn't tell him about it over the phone because I didn't know who he was with or who else might be listening. What's going on, Milo?"

"Sit tight. Don't do anything. Don't hand over that flash drive. I'll be there in twenty minutes." Milo ended the call and headed straight into the parking lot.

The sun had set, and the street lamps flickered on. Milo fidgeted with his keys before pressing the button on the fob to unlock his doors. The pearl-white Lexus sedan flashed its lights and clicked open. He slid onto the ivory leather driver's seat and pressed the button to start the engine. With the Bluetooth button on the steering wheel, he made the call to Franklin.

"Milo, long time, no hear," Franklin joked.

"We have ourselves a real problem, Franklin. I have people going rogue on me and now I have to find a way to stop them before it hits the fan."

"I just left you. What happened?"

Milo turned the wheel and peered over his shoulder before merging onto the highway. "I'm headed to the police station to see Detective Shane Sullivan. Allison found some new information and I need to make sure it doesn't implicate you."

"What the hell are you talking about?"

"My friend, Allison Hart? She broke into Dawson's home hours after he was murdered. Long story short, she found video evidence of a threat to Dawson's life on the order of Clay Sadler. And there's another video too. I won't know until I see it, but I have a feeling it's you talking to Dawson two days before he was killed."

"Shit."

"Yeah. I'll get with Sullivan and clean this up."

"Milo, whatever evidence he has will need to be put on hold until we find Sadler's men. Forget about what he's got on me. If not, and the cops go after Sadler, his people will scatter in the wind. We'll never learn if there's anyone higher on the food chain involved and we'll never put those men in jail for the murders."

"Believe me, I am well aware of that, which is exactly why I'm going to talk to Sullivan now. I'll keep you posted. Stick to our initial plan."

"You know I will," Franklin replied.

Milo pressed the end-call button and drove hastily toward the station. His anger at what Allison had done masked his true feelings. She could so easily have been scrubbed the same way Dawson had been. And it would have been Milo's fault. He put her in the line of fire the moment he facilitated an introduction to Tommy Boyce. "But it was just supposed to be pictures." He shook his head knowing that it had gone so utterly cockeyed that he'd lost control of the situation. And it could have meant Allison's life and Charlie's. That was the reason he directed his anger toward her. Fairness didn't play into it.

Milo pulled into the parking lot of the station and started inside; his soft belly bouncing as he hurried.

"Hi, Milo. What are you doing here?" The officer behind the admin desk smiled at him.

"Can't talk now, Reese. Need to find Sully."

She pointed toward the bullpen. "He's at his desk."

"Thanks." He waved without stopping and marched onward to Shane's desk. "We need to talk."

"Good evening to you too, Milo," Shane replied.

"You still have the flash drive?" Milo dropped into the chair across from him and was out of breath.

"Right here." He held the drive between his index finger and thumb. "I hope you have a good reason for asking me to hold onto this."

"Buddy, you have no idea."

———

Allison sat on the edge of the sofa reflecting on what Milo had said. Maybe she wasn't cut out for this line of work. Her disregard for her own safety was bad enough, but then to drag Charlie into it made it that much worse. Milo had trusted her to follow the leads they discussed. And she had until a wild hair crawled up her backside and led her in a different direction. One she thought would end it. Instead, it seems to have compounded whatever situation Milo was handling.

She eyed her car keys on the side table near the front door. Then she eyed the hall toward Nolan's bedroom. Tomorrow was his big chance and she couldn't miss it. He would be trying out for the Triple A team. What a strange thing to think about and how entirely normal in her current world filled with murderers and crooks.

"It's almost over." She tried to convince herself it was true. Allison marched toward the door, swiped the keys from the table and walked out. She was going to the station.

Allison stepped into her faded blue Honda and keyed the ignition, reversing out of the driveway. Glare from the streetlamps shone through her back window as she made her way onto the road causing her to squint, but her eyes quickly sharpened, and she headed toward the station.

The bridge was just ahead, and Allison caught sight of headlights in her rearview mirror. She glanced at the vehicle but continued. It wasn't until she realized that at each turning, the car seemed to follow. Allison paid closer attention. "Don't be paranoid like the last time. Stay calm," she told herself.

Allison slowed and the car slowed behind her. She sped and the car followed. "The Mercedes." She pulled off the road, diverting from her intended destination and instead headed toward Downtown where lights were abundant. She eyed her cell phone in the center console. Help was only a phone call away if she needed it. But she wasn't about to alert anyone until she knew for certain this was actually happening.

"You want to follow me? Come on, then. I'll lead the way." She peered through the rearview mirror again and headed toward the well-lit area of bars and restaurants. The car followed and it didn't take long to see what she initially suspected. "I figured that was you. How did you find me?" She rummaged through the past few days' memories and thought she had been careful to avoid detection. But then how to explain this? Something she did or something she said brought the men in the Mercedes to her now and while drilling down for an answer was important, perhaps she was overlooking the significance of this event. Allison could be in real trouble. And she was reminded of Fin's haunting words of warning.

It was time to double back and go to the police station. They were trying to intimidate her, which was working, but she wasn't about to engage these dangerous men.

Allison stopped at the next light and turned left. The Mercedes followed. She continued until reaching the bridge. On the other side of that bridge was the police station—only a few minutes, ten at most, away from her current location.

She leaned over and opened the glove box, and as it dropped down, her gun fell forward. Allison started carrying a gun after a case a couple of years ago. A man who had for years been defrauding the system to pull in tens of thousands of dollars in disability payments didn't take too kindly to Allison confronting him on that mild winter's day.

The man had rushed toward Allison and shoved her against her car. He then used his forearm to press on her neck. She'd never been so afraid in her life. When the man finally calmed down and God only knew why he did, he released her. From that point on, Allison carried a gun. She'd been trained and wasn't afraid to use it. Though she hoped it wouldn't come to that tonight. "Stay in the car. Go to the station." Her words of assurance were doing little to calm her nerves.

Unless these men were crazy, which was a possibility, they wouldn't follow her to the stationhouse. She would be safe and now could identify them without a doubt. Maybe that would be enough to both smooth things over with Milo and help put them in jail for murdering Fin Dawson and probably Tommy Boyce, too.

With the gun resting on her lap, Allison drove on, keeping one eye on her rearview. So far, they weren't leaving. "You're going all the way, huh?"

When she made it across the bridge, the Mercedes roared toward her, inching so close she could have sworn it was about to hit her bumper. Her heart raced and her pupils shrunk into tiny specks. With her attention diverted from the road, the bumps along the shoulder sounded as her tires veered toward them. "Shit." Allison pulled back, nearly overcorrecting. The Mercedes continued to ride her tail. Now it was time to panic.

Allison held the gun in her right hand and kept her left hand on the wheel. She thought about Nolan and the prospect she would miss his tryout tomorrow. Allison was first and foremost, a mother. Thinking about her children even in the face of danger couldn't be helped.

The car swerved to the side and pulled up next to her. The man in the passenger seat glared.

Allison recognized him immediately. The man who was at Fin's home. It was the younger one, the one who didn't say much. But at that moment, Allison realized he identified her as well. His eyes sparked with that flash of recognition and suddenly, Allison felt like this was it. This was how it was going to end.

"No!" She slammed on the brakes and dropped back, far back from the men who were after her. With a sharp pull on the wheel, she spun around and started in the opposite direction. There was another way out and it came to her in an instant. She reached for her phone and while trying to keep ahead of the Mercedes before it turned around, she called Shane. Relief swelled in her chest the moment he answered.

"Oh, thank God. Shane, I'm in trouble. I'm being followed by the Mercedes."

"Where are you?" Shane's tone was sharp with worry.

"Downtown. I'm on my way to see you..."

"Allison, listen to me, drive to the nearest station. There's a substation 4 blocks from the business district, off Granby Street. Go there—now!"

"What if they follow?" Her voice cracked.

"I'm going to tell them you'll be there any minute. Someone will be outside. No way those guys will get that close, not unless they're stupid. And somehow, I don't think they are. Put me on speaker and set down your phone. I'm not leaving you."

Allison placed her phone on speaker and listened as Shane used his landline and made the call to the substation. She was close and knew the street but couldn't recall the police station. A quick check in her mirror; they were gaining on her. "Come on. Come on!" She slammed down the gas pedal and the 4-cylinder engine whined.

"Allison, I'm on my way. They know you're coming. Stay on the line," Shane said.

She could hear Milo's voice in the background. What was he doing there? It didn't matter. What mattered was that she made it to the station in time.

"How close are you, Allison?" Shane asked as he started the engine of his car.

"Close. A block, maybe two. They're still on me and coming up fast."

"Stay calm. We'll be there soon."

Allison recognized this new voice. "Milo, is that you?"

"I'm here with Shane. Just stay focused, okay? Get there as fast as you can."

Allison nodded and remained eagle-eyed on the road ahead. "I see it! I'm almost there." She dared to allow a hint of relief, but this wasn't over yet. "Come on baby, just get me there," she said to the car.

It was just ahead now—a few hundred yards, at best. The Mercedes roared up to her once again. When she peered into the rearview mirror, it seemed to drop back. Its headlights became smaller as it fell farther away. "They're leaving. Oh my God. They're leaving." Allison pulled to a stop directly in front of the station where two uniformed officers stood outside.

She thrust the gearshift into park and leaped out of her car.

"Are you Allison Hart?" One of the officers asked.

"Yes. They're gone. They saw me coming here and they're gone now." She turned back just to be certain.

"Come inside. Detective Sullivan is on his way."

"Hang on. I need to grab my phone." Allison returned to her car only a few feet away and spotted her gun on the floorboard. It was only the second time she thought she might actually use it. She yanked her phone from the console and stored the gun in the glovebox once again. "Okay. I'm coming."

25

The doors of the police substation burst open and Shane and Milo hurried inside. The small outpost was virtually empty and it was easy to spot Allison.

"Thank God you're okay." Shane rushed to her side before turning his sights to the officer at his desk. "Did you get the plates?"

"Running them now," he replied.

"It was the same one, I know it was," Allison said.

"I know. We just have to be sure," Shane added.

Milo, who caught up to them, put his hand on Allison's shoulder. "I'm glad you're safe."

"They're behind all of it," Allison began. "I don't know who they work for, but it has to be..."

Milo raised his hand to stop her. "We'll find them, don't you worry about that."

The other cop who had waited outside approached with a piece of paper in his hand. "I got a hit on that plate. Care to take a look?"

Shane took the paper from him and studied it with Milo peering over his shoulder. "Matches what we found on Charlie's phone." He looked at the officer again. "Did anything come up on this name? Criminal records?"

"No, sir."

Shane nodded. "Yeah, we didn't have much luck on that front either. Okay, thank you. We have some work ahead of us. This car has been involved in other investigations. This is good work."

"I'm glad we could help." The officer turned to Allison. "You're a gutsy woman, Ms. Hart. Most people would've panicked, but you stayed clear-headed and knew where to go."

"Thank you. And if you two hadn't been standing outside, I'm not sure I would've made such a clean getaway." She offered her hand. "I appreciate the help more than you know."

"Let's let these good men get back to work," Shane began. "Nash, you mind driving Allison's car and she can ride with me? We'll head back to the main station."

"You sure I can't put out a BOLO for you?" the officer asked. "That would seem to be the most logical step."

"It would seem to be, yes, but as I said, this car has been involved in ongoing investigations. I think it's best we find them on our terms. Any BOLO might send them into hiding," Shane replied.

"I understand. If there's anything else I can do, please don't hesitate." He turned to Allison. "That goes for you too, ma'am."

Shane nodded and placed his arm around Allison's shoulder. "Goodnight, officers." He led her outside and opened the passenger door. "Why don't you get in my car? I'm going to have a word with Milo."

Allison stepped inside and watched through the sideview mirror as Shane approached Milo at her car. She couldn't hear what they were saying and suspected Shane wasn't giving her the full story. Allison was growing tired of people withholding information when she was at the center of this scheme. They appeared to have lost faith in her and it hurt. The concept of running her own agency grew dimmer by the moment. And that was assuming she would make it out of this alive.

Shane slipped behind the wheel of his car. "He's following us. I hope that's okay."

"Fine by me. He'll sweat his nuts off, but what the hell do I care anymore?" Allison peered through the passenger window.

"You're angry and you're right to be but Allison, this thing as I've been told, is about ensnaring some high-ranking government officials."

"What is Milo withholding, Shane?" she shot back. "Why can't we go to the house where the car is registered and bring in the jerk who drives it? I got a good look at both of them. They were the same men who were at Fin's house. And the same men I saw on the video at Tommy's. I can ID them with no problem. Let me do that so we can get them off the street and in jail where they belong."

"Just take a breath, Allison. After what you just went through, I understand where you're coming from. Milo is aiming for the..."

"The mayor. Yeah, I already know that."

"Then you should know that Milo also has a man working for him. A man by the name of Franklin Perry. Name sound familiar? The one whose fingerprints showed up at Boyce's office? He's a developer, same as Carlos Diaz, but he came to Milo when Diaz offered him a little something extra to look the other way. The two have been building a case against Diaz ever since and it led him to the mayor. This flash drive you gave me," Shane turned to her. "Milo says we have to sit on it for a while. Just a little while. Until he can get Carlos Diaz on the hook hard enough that he can't wiggle off of it, you understand?"

"No," she pleaded so as not to lose this battle. "We have enough to bring in the men in the Mercedes. We probably have enough to catch the mayor and Carlos Diaz too."

"Probably. But Allison, I'm telling you, Milo insists he needs more. He's the lawyer. We have to trust he knows what he's doing. You and Charlie have to back off. Milo is a day, maybe two, away from bringing all of them in. You can't be involved anymore. Not only is it too dangerous but it could blow up in your face and destroy all that Milo has been working toward."

Allison kept quiet for the rest of the drive back to the station. Even if Shane was right, it didn't feel right. She helped get them this far and she wanted to see it through for Lucy. But Allison wasn't in charge and this was a stark reminder. Authority wasn't hers to assume.

The only way to make them see her side was to approach this calmly or risk alienating herself from both of them who had been her close friends for years. She needed a clear and logical argument. And on their return to the station, she refocused her thoughts and knew what she had to do.

"Let's go into the conference room." Shane led the way to an intimate space where a round table and four chairs were placed in the center and a television was mounted on the wall.

Allison waited for Shane and Milo to sit down. She was ready to present her argument. "Montoya and Alvarez need to be told about this, Milo. I don't see any other way. We're all on the verge of obstructing an investigation right now. You're the prosecutor and you should realize that."

"I have someone who's doing the work that needs to be done and if those detectives are let loose on this, he won't be protected. Dangerous people are out there, and I think they made it clear tonight that none of us is safe." Milo eyed Allison. "Not you, maybe not even your family."

"That's enough talk like that, Milo. Come on," Shane said.

"I'm being upfront and honest, which is what I should have been all along and for that, I'm sorry, Allison. I screwed up. Look, I'll run it by the captain. He'll be irate as all hell, but if he understands what's at stake, he'll keep his people in check. They've been so focused on Carlos Diaz that they haven't put in much groundwork on his business dealings."

She studied each of them. "I appreciate that you both have been trying to protect me. And I'll agree that I should've kept to my part of the plan. I didn't. Nevertheless, what we have on the mayor is huge. I don't care about money Carlos Diaz took from the city. I don't care that his wife and her lover were murdered." Allison raised her hands. "I'm sorry. I know how that sounds, but it's true. What matters is that the mayor instructed his men to kill a federal agent. They killed Tommy Boyce too and that is what's important to me. And now I can identify both of the mayor's henchmen because they just tried to kill me." She took in a breath to make sure she was clear on this final point. "I don't want to wait until someone else is killed. I want to get Montoya and Alvarez—maybe the entire Tampa Police Department—to bum rush the mayor's house and bring him in and his men."

"Please, Allison," Milo began. "Just take a step back. Realize what it is you're saying."

"I know what I'm saying. What I don't know is why you aren't listening."

"What you have," Milo began. "What we have is damning, but it isn't proof the mayor ordered the deaths of those people you just mentioned. These men, they were careful. They left nothing behind on Tracy Diaz or Harlan Goodfellow. No DNA, nothing."

"We're still waiting on the ME's report to come back for Tommy and Fin," Shane said.

"You have an eye-witness sitting right here in front of you," Allison said.

"What I'm telling you is that I need more time. Maybe only hours. I have Franklin Perry headed to see Sadler now. He'll find out where his men are and listen while Sadler buries himself with threats against Carlos Diaz. We think there could be others too."

"Who else do you suspect is in on this?" Shane asked.

"It's looking like it could go up to the state senate."

Allison shook her head. "I'm glad you want to bring down a corrupt state government, Milo. Honestly, that's a good thing. But I want to bring justice for Lucy Boyce." Allison stood up. "Please. You know me. Both of you do. You know I can't sit here and do nothing." She started to leave.

"Where are you going?" Shane asked.

She reached the door but stopped and turned back. "I'm going to let you two find a solution. You're the law. I'm not. I do hope you'll think about my side of this and come up with something that will finish this once and for all. You're my closest friends and I don't want to be in fear of these men anymore. I need you both to fix this." She opened the door and walked out.

Milo stood. "I can't argue with the lady. I cast a wide net. Everyone associated with Carlos Diaz and the mayor, in spite of the case I have staring right at me. Tommy Boyce was a good man. He deserves justice and so does Finley Dawson. Allison's right. It's time to put an end to this before someone else gets hurt. Get with Montoya and whoever else you need to get with and give them the details on the Mercedes. It's time to find them and bring them in."

"What are you going to do?" Shane asked as he stood at the door, ready to leave.

"I'm going to meet up with Franklin Perry before he moves forward with his plan and we'll both pay a visit to Carlos Diaz. He'll talk now. I'll offer up a sweet deal to go turncoat on the mayor. We'll see what happens after that. Go talk to Allison. Let her know. I need to get with my man before it's too late."

"Thanks, Milo." Shane left the room and jogged to catch up to Allison as she made her way into the parking lot. "Hey! Allison, wait up."

She turned. "That didn't take long. What's the verdict?"

"He conceded, Allison. He agrees it's time to end this even if he doesn't get the people he wants most."

"Really? He said that?"

Shane nodded. "He said that. You convinced him. I'm going to Montoya. You want to come with me?"

She wore a smile. "You bet your ass I do."

SHANE PREPARED FOR THE VERITABLE BEATDOWN HE WAS going to suffer at the hands of Detectives Montoya and Alvarez. It had been less than a week but in those few days, Allison and Charlie had uncovered details that should have been communicated immediately to the authorities. Montoya would be right to have him suspended or even fired.

"I think you'd better let me talk, Allison. Montoya isn't going to be happy when he learns what has happened," Shane said.

"I understand. But he has to know we were acting with caution and not out of recklessness."

Montoya hurried through the hall with his face buried in a file. He caught sight of them and stopped. "Sully, what are you doing here? Shouldn't you be busting some kid for boosting a car or something?"

"Probably. However, what we have to say, you're going to want to listen to. Allison has uncovered evidence in your double homicide."

Montoya glared at her. "Oh, are you a detective now, Ms. Hart?"

"No, but Tommy Boyce was a friend and his daughter asked for my help. Detective Montoya, I have evidence that Boyce was working with Tracy Diaz to prove Carlos had received bribes from who we believe was a high-ranking government official."

He eyed them and turned on his heel to head back toward his desk. "Where is this evidence?"

Allison hurried to keep in step. "Before I get into that, I also know that the men I saw drive past me the night of the double murder—they came after me."

He stopped and his once smug expression was replaced with concern. "They came after you? When?"

"Tonight," Shane interrupted. "She managed to shake them off and we directed her to the substation in the business district. You're welcome to contact the officers who secured her safety when she arrived."

Montoya dropped the file on his desk and sat down. "Sounds like you both have been very busy on an investigation that I've been working. It wouldn't be a stretch to say you're undermining me, Allison." He spit out her name like venom. "And you, Sully. Withholding evidence? Boy, I'd say that could get you in a whole lot of trouble."

"I wasn't exactly withholding evidence. The laptop from Boyce's home. I turned it over to Alvarez a day ago. I just failed to mention what was on it. My intention wasn't to undermine, you, Montoya," Shane said.

"And I certainly wouldn't want Sully to get into trouble because of anything I've done. He's not responsible for that. Last night, I took it upon myself to go to Dawson's home."

Montoya licked his lips and held his contemptuous gaze. "You contaminated an active crime scene?"

"Yes. But what I found is evidence that the city mayor is corrupt and might be responsible for the murder of Tommy Boyce and Fin Dawson."

Montoya nodded. "I see. And do you have this evidence with you?"

"I do," Allison replied.

Montoya's brows raised and appeared almost clown-like. "So, you're telling me the mayor, Clay Sadler, is responsible for murdering two people. One who just so happened to be an FBI agent."

"She's telling the truth, man," Shane said.

The detective's face no longer smiled. He pulled upright in his chair and directed his full attention to Allison. "Ms. Hart, you'd better tell me everything and I mean everything."

26

Franklin Perry faced the window in his office with his back to Milo. "It's too soon. We don't have enough to bring down the mayor."

Milo approached him. "That's where I think you could be mistaken. We have the flash drive that almost cost Allison Hart and Charlie Wells their lives."

"It's a verbal threat by a third party." Franklin turned to him. "It's nothing. Carlos Diaz has what we need. The payoffs, the deals."

"We're out of time, Franklin. Too many people have died. The detective on the double homicide is being briefed on everything as we speak. It's time for you and me to meet with Diaz and bring him in. I'll be the first one to say that I believe we have enough, circumstantial though it may be."

Franklin shoved his hands in his pockets and cast his eyes to his feet. "We're risking everything and for what?"

"I know you have risked your company, your standing and

your life to help me get Diaz. That won't be forgotten. Franklin, I need you to make the call and set up the meeting."

He retrieved his phone, pressing on Diaz's number. "Carlos, it's Franklin. I know it's early, but I need to see you. Can you meet?"

Milo looked on as Franklin appeared to wait for a reply. He knew the time had come and there would be a price to pay for his decision to wait this out. To not bring in Diaz when he knew he should have.

"Thank you. I'll see you in 30 minutes." Franklin ended the call and turned to Milo. "The marina. Half an hour."

———

When Allison finished explaining all that had happened and what brought them to this moment, Montoya appeared stunned, and more than a little riled.

"I'll give you credit, Ms. Hart, you've got bigger balls than a lot of cops I know. But make no mistake about it, you're lucky to be telling me the tale, you understand?"

She couldn't refute the facts and felt reduced to that of a child being scolded by a parent. But rather than defend her indefensible actions, she allowed him to vent.

"You and your friend," he pressed on. "I don't condone what you did. In fact, Sully here should never have let it get that far. But what's done is done and you have evidence that points to men who appear to work for the mayor." Montoya pulled up in his chair. "Here's what we're going to do. I'm going to put together a team and we'll go to that address. Whether one or both of those men will be there, I don't know, but if they're not, we'll issue a BOLO and we will find them."

"What about bringing in help from the FBI's field office? They lost a man too," Shane said. "They have resources."

"I don't want to get into bed with them right now. The death of one of their agents is going to bring in a gaggle of them. We're out of time as it is, and I can't focus on that." Montoya looked at Allison. "I'm going to have an officer posted at your house until this is over. Those people found you once; they'll find you again."

Allison was ready to protest but relinquished. "I understand."

"Then let's move." Montoya picked up his landline. "Better get Alvarez in on this too."

Shane turned to Allison. "Let's pick up Charlie and bring her to your place."

"She has two boys."

"If they're with her, we'll get them too." He started to leave and turned back when Allison hadn't caught up to him. "Allison, it's time to go. Let Montoya do what needs to be done to finish this."

She turned on her heel and caught up to Shane. "Yeah, okay."

———

THE MARINA WAS STEEPED IN FOG AS THE BREAK OF DAY GOT off to a sultry start. Milo Nash wiped the sweat from his neck with a handkerchief he kept in his pants' pocket. Franklin was steps ahead as they continued along the dock toward the boat that belonged to Diaz. Milo's phone buzzed in his pocket and he took hold of it to view the incoming text message. It was Sully and he indicated Allison and Charlie were safe and at Allison's house. He also mentioned that a patrol car was on its way to help them bring in Carlos. "Hey." He caught up to Franklin. "Tampa PD is sending a cruiser now."

"Don't let them jump the gun, Milo. We need Carlos to go in

willingly. No struggles or this thing could turn ugly. He's a man with nothing to lose."

"I couldn't agree more. I'll pass along the information," Milo said. "Isn't that Diaz's boat up ahead?"

"You mean, yacht? Yeah, that's his. I can't see him through this fog," Perry replied.

"He's probably inside. It's a sauna out here."

Franklin approached the vessel before turning back to Milo. "Are you feeling good about this? Because I'm not."

Milo walked near the boat and began, "Carlos Diaz?" He waited, but there was no answer.

Franklin grabbed his cell phone and called him. "Let me see if he answers." The line rang. Once, twice. "Come on, man." On the third ring, the voicemail message began. "Shit. He's not answering."

"We're already here." Milo stepped onto the boat. "We'll find him."

Franklin followed him onto the yacht's bow. "Carlos? It's Franklin Perry. Are you here, brother?" Dread masked his face as he turned to Milo. "How are you feeling about things now, Milo?"

Without answering, Milo started down the steps and into the living quarters. The luxurious wood surroundings and leather furnishings appeared immaculate. "Carlos Diaz?" He continued toward the sleeping quarters and peered inside. The king-sized bed was made. Everything appeared untouched. Milo turned and started back toward the living area where he spotted Franklin. "It looks like we might have lost our chance. I think Carlos has flown the coop, my friend." Milo picked up his phone. "Sully, we have a problem. Diaz isn't where he said he would be. Have you heard anything?"

"Detective Montoya is putting a team in place to raid the

house where we think the Mercedes owner is. He thought it would happen by around 7am. What's the time now?"

"It's 5:30. What do you want to do?" Milo asked.

"You've tried to contact him?" Shane asked.

"Of course we have. The call went to voicemail. Your patrol car is on the way. Man, we're standing on his boat, for Pete's sake."

"Milo!" Franklin shouted from the deck. "Milo! Get the hell out here."

"Damn. I have to go. I'll call you back." Milo ended the call and rushed up the stairs. "Where are you?"

"The stern." Franklin's voice came from the back of the boat.

Milo hustled toward him. "What is it?" But he didn't need to be told. It was in front of him, plain as day. "No." His shoulders sank.

Franklin shook his head. "He's gone, man. Someone got to him."

———

ALLISON SET DOWN HER CUP OF COFFEE ON THE KITCHEN island. "What happened?"

"That was Milo. They were expecting to meet Carlos Diaz. I don't know what happened, but he said Diaz wasn't there as planned," Shane replied.

"Should we tell Montoya?" Allison asked.

"What good would that do?" Charlie added.

"Charlie's right," Shane said. "His priority is to bring in the driver of the Mercedes. Let's give Milo a chance to work this out first."

Allison peered through the kitchen window as if considering a plan. "You know, there's one person who might know where Carlos is."

"And who's that?" Shane asked.

"Laura Young." Charlie looked at Allison. "She does seem to have an inside track on Carlos Diaz."

"She's mentioned multiple times that she was certain Carlos had a hand in Tracy's murder. Then there was her odd behavior at the funeral. I don't know. Something about her has been gnawing at me for a while," Allison replied. "I have no doubt Laura said those things to me for a reason."

Shane nodded. "To shift blame? She's the only one, so far, whose hands have remained clean where the Diaz's are concerned."

"I don't know if she was trying to shift the blame. I think it was more like she was trying to point out that Carlos's business ties were worth looking into," Allison said. "I don't know how she would've known that without having seen first-hand what those dealings were. Maybe Tracy let her in on some of it, but there could be more. I say it's worth talking to her again. Right now, she's the only other person who knows about any of this."

A text message buzzed on Shane's phone and as he viewed it, his mouth fell agape. He turned the screen to Allison. "You can talk to Laura Young until you're blue in the face. It won't matter. We're too late. Carlos is dead."

Allison closed her eyes. "Clay Sadler must be getting desperate. He must know his time's up and now he's cleaning house."

"That would mean he knew Carlos was meeting with Milo and Franklin Perry. Who would've told him that?" Charlie asked.

"Laura?" Allison asked. "If you wanted to get back at someone, what better way to do it?"

"It's starting to make sense." Charlie peered at them. "How else would Sadler have known about Tracy Diaz meeting with Harlan Goodfellow the night of their murder? We all know Carlos had insisted he wasn't responsible for their deaths. Is it possible Laura Young tipped off Sadler?"

"She's the only connection I know of," Allison regarded Charlie and Shane. "I say we get to her before anyone else does."

––––––––

CARLOS DIAZ WAS THE OBVIOUS LOOSE END IN MAYOR Sadler's plan. The only reasonable deduction Allison could muster was that Laura Young had a hand in it. Now she wondered just how close Laura had been to Tracy Diaz. Because it was starting to look like she'd cozied up to someone else and now Carlos was dead. "She lives here." Allison pointed to the high-rise just ahead.

"Is it just a coincidence that she lives in the same building as Carlos Diaz?" Shane asked.

"A coincidence, maybe," Charlie said. "But it would explain how Laura Young came to know the Diaz's."

"She said she knew Tracy since before she married Carlos," Allison began. "It's possible Tracy helped her get a place in here. I don't know, but it doesn't look good for Laura."

They walked toward the lobby.

Shane stopped and turned back to them. "Let me do the talking, okay?"

Allison and Charlie nodded.

"Good morning." Shane approached the reception desk and held out his badge. "I need to see Laura Young. I understand she lives in one of these units?"

"I'm sorry, but is she expecting you?" The slim man in the three-piece suit eyed them. "We have some follow up questions regarding the murder of a friend of hers. I'm sure you must know.

Tracy Diaz? Wife of Carlos Diaz, who I believe also resides here if I'm not mistaken. It's imperative we speak to her."

"And you two?" He eyed Allison and Charlie. "Also police officers?"

"They're with me. Both are assisting in the investigation."

"Shall I call up to Ms. Young and let her know you're here?" the man asked.

"You could, but I wouldn't," Allison said.

"Well that didn't take long," Shane muttered before regaining control of the situation. "Ms. Young could be in danger. You wouldn't want anything to happen to her, would you?"

"No. Of course not. She's in unit C-335 on the 3rd floor."

"Thank you." Shane walked to the elevators and pressed the button.

When the doors parted, Allison stepped in and held the doors for Shane and Charlie. "I didn't mean to overstep back there, Shane. It's just..."

"You didn't, Allison. Don't worry about it. Although, I am starting to think you should look into a career as an interrogator."

As they stepped off the elevator on the third floor, Allison led the way to unit C-335 and knocked. "I don't know if she's home—or sober."

"It's like 8 in the morning," Charlie said. "Who the hell's drunk at 8 am?"

Laura opened the door. "Emma. What on earth are you doing here? Were we supposed to meet this morning?" And before Allison could answer, Laura's eyes shifted to the others and her brow furrowed. "Charlie. Nice to see you again. I'm afraid I don't know your friend." She peered at Shane.

"Laura, can we come in and talk?" Allison asked.

Shane leaned into Charlie and whispered. "Why did she call her Emma?"

"It's a long story," Charlie replied.

Laura's teeth clenched and her stance firmed. "What's this about? What happened, Emma? Why are they here?"

Allison remained poised, almost indifferent. "We need to talk about Carlos."

Laura flinched and tried to recover. "Why would I care what happens to that man? Is that why you're here?"

Allison sighed. "Laura, he's dead."

27

Detective Montoya secured his tactical gear while surrounded by his hand-picked team of four others who were doing the same, including Alvarez. Conducting raids were usually outside of their periphery. It was a task generally left to the specialists, SWAT, and other trained officers. However, Montoya wasn't going to hand over the reins entirely. Two of the four were SWAT members.

"It's time to head out." Montoya placed his gun in its holster. "We bring the men in and have the Forensics team tow the car as soon as possible. Any evidence we can get from that car will only firm up our case." He spotted Milo Nash and Franklin Perry in the distance. "What are you doing here?" He aimed his sights on Milo. "As you can see, I don't have a lot of time right now."

"We found Carlos Diaz dead on his boat," Milo replied. "It was called in only minutes ago, and by the look on your face, I can see you haven't heard about it. An officer met us out there and he's the one who called it in. I assume others are headed to secure the scene."

Montoya turned straight-faced. "What were you doing on his boat?"

"We had a meeting with him this morning," Milo replied. "When we arrived, we found him already dead. He was shot in his chest."

"You gotta be shitting me. Carlos Diaz held all the cards. Christ, what if word already reached the men responsible for the other murders?" He looked at Alvarez. "If we don't do this right now, it's game over."

"If they were the ones to kill Carlos, we've already lost," Milo said.

Montoya returned his attention to Alvarez. "Let's contact the responding officer and have him pull surveillance from the marina. Get a forensics team out there and scour the scene."

"They're still reviewing the footage from the day Boyce was murdered," Alvarez said.

"Then they'll have more to examine."

And the raid?" Alvarez asked.

"It's our last hope at finding them." Montoya started toward the lobby. "We're doing this and we're doing it now."

Milo stood by as the team of officers filed out of the building and disappeared.

"This was what you wanted, right?" Franklin asked.

Milo looked on. "Sadler's cleaning house. If the men in the Mercedes aren't dead yet, they will be by day's end."

Laura Young perched on her sofa, still and beautiful like a figurine. "I just can't believe it. Who would do that to him?"

"You didn't seem to care much for him the other night," Allison said.

"Maybe not. But I know he didn't kill Tracy or Harlan. He didn't deserve to die."

"And how do you know he's innocent?" Shane sat down next to her. "It's time for you to be honest with us. What is the nature of your relationship with Clay Sadler?"

Her brow creased and her lips raised in a tenuous smile. "What? The mayor? You think I have a relationship with the mayor of Tampa?"

"Alli, we don't have time for this. She's going to need to speak to Montoya. We're wasting time here," Charlie said.

"Who's Alli?" Laura asked. "You?" She pointed to Allison. "You said your name was Emma Stone, like the actress."

Allison dodged her gaze. "I needed to get close to you. And I couldn't risk you finding out I was working with Tommy Boyce."

"You lied." Her eyes narrowed with anger.

"Ms. Young, I need you to come with us." Shane held out his badge. "We're going to need to know where you were this morning and last night."

"Oh, wait. You think I killed Carlos? Are you crazy?"

"If you don't come to the station, I will have officers escort you. I'm sure you won't want to make a scene in front of your neighbors," Shane said.

"Fine." Laura surrendered. "But you'll hear from my lawyer and you'll realize you're making a colossal mistake. If anyone should be taken to jail, it should be her." She pointed to Allison. "You lying bitch. I trusted you!"

"Let's go." Shane picked her up off the sofa and led her to the door. "You might've had a better chance if you didn't live in the same building. And your friendship with the victim makes it all the more plausible."

Allison and Charlie followed behind and waited while Shane

loaded Laura into the car. When he closed the door, Allison approached him. "Can we search her place?"

"Not if you want to use anything you find in court. Allison, let me take it from here. If she was responsible for Carlos's death, Montoya will get it out of her."

"What should we do in the meantime?" Allison continued.

"Go home. I'll call you later after I hear how the bust went." Shane opened his car door and peered at them one more time. "Go home. It's the best thing you can do right now."

Allison and Charlie stood on the curb and watched as Shane drove away.

"He could've offered to drop us off," Charlie said.

"I don't think we should leave right now," Allison replied.

"How did I know you'd have a plan? Just know that you're risking your relationship with Shane. You need him to trust you."

Allison eyed the doors leading back inside the building. "I saw something. It was on her side table. I don't know if she realized I noticed, but I don't think so. Otherwise, she would've done her best to hide it."

"Why didn't you say anything to Shane?"

"Because I didn't want to alert her. We had no warrant. I guess I have learned a thing or two hanging around the station." She watched Shane's car disappear around the corner. "Look, it'll only take a minute and I have a feeling, after watching her get hauled out of there, the guy at the front desk will let us back inside."

"Five minutes. Then we do as Shane said and go home, and wait by the phone," Charlie replied.

"Sure. We'll do that." Allison started back inside the building and approached the man who stood behind the desk. "I'm so sorry, but I left my phone inside Ms. Young's apartment. Could you let us back in for just a moment so I can grab it?"

He gazed at her with reluctance. "I suppose that would be

okay. Seeing as how Ms. Young might not be back today." He walked around the desk and led them back to the elevators. "Just for a moment, though, I'm afraid."

"Of course," Allison replied.

The man opened the door to Laura's apartment. "Please, go inside. I'll wait here."

They entered the apartment once again and Allison made a beeline for the item that she was sure would give them the answers they needed. She swiped the burner off the table. "See?"

"Oh my God." Charlie hurried to her side. "How did I not see that? How did Shane not see it?"

"I had a chance to walk around the place. Shane didn't. He moved in next to her right away. We'll take this to the station and hand it straight to Montoya when he returns. There could be calls on here about or to Carlos Diaz."

"I think you would've made Tommy Boyce proud."

"I hope so." Allison led the way out of the apartment, holding her cell phone. "I got it. Thank you very much for your help."

"Glad I could be of assistance." He started into the hall again. "I do hope Ms. Young has nothing to do with Mr. and Mrs. Diaz. That would be a genuine shame and especially after all the trouble that has befallen Mr. Diaz. Poor man."

"Yes. It's been an unfortunate situation," Allison replied. "Thank you again for your help, sir. You have a good day."

———

"The car's in the driveway. That's a bonus." Montoya peered through the windshield of the van that now sat outside the home of Victor Esposito, the lead accomplice of Clay Sadler. "At least we have something breaking our way this morning."

The SWAT officer, Lieutenant Hoffman, was in the driver's

seat of the tactical van and he pressed on the radio. "Let's get into position. Our target's in sight." He turned to Montoya. "You and Alvarez need to hang out here until we secure the scene and have the man in custody."

"You got it. This is your show," Montoya replied.

"Then let's do this." Hoffman jumped out of the van and the other officers surrounded the home.

Montoya and Alvarez looked on.

Hoffman gestured for his team to move into position. He pointed to the front door and two men with a battering ram appeared. There would be no talking, no negotiating. That Mercedes had been identified at multiple locations near where the murders had taken place. The time for pleasantries was over.

The front door burst open, falling off its hinges. Hoffman, gun at the ready, yelled. "Victor Esposito, Tampa Police. We have your house surrounded." He motioned to his team to search the rooms.

A man emerged from inside the hall closet with his hands in the air. "Don't shoot. Don't shoot."

"Victor Esposito, you're under arrest for fleeing the scene of the murder of Tracy Diaz and Harlan Goodfellow." Hoffman approached him with handcuffs. "Where's your partner?"

"I'm sorry, who?"

"Don't get cute. We know you were both in the car."

"I have no idea who you're talking about, man."

Hoffman sneered. "Whatever you say, pal. We'll find him. But you're coming with us." He led the way outside.

"I see one of them." Montoya drew up in the seat and peered through the windshield. "That's Esposito. Where's the other?"

"It was a longshot to think he'd be here," Alvarez said. "We're going to have to track him down before he learns that we have his buddy in custody."

Montoya watched as the lieutenant led Victor to the rear of the van. He jumped out to meet up with them.

"Who the hell are you?" Victor asked.

"The man who's going to put you behind bars for the rest of your life." He smiled and patted him on the shoulder. "Now be a good boy and tell us where we can find your boyfriend."

Victor pulled back and lunged with a mouthful of saliva that splattered across Montoya's face.

He wiped it away and smiled. "I hope you'll be more cooperative at the station." He turned to Hoffman. "Will your men stay here until the forensics team shows up for the car?"

"Yes, sir."

"Good. Then we'll ride back with you."

———

THE CAB PULLED UP ALONGSIDE THE FRONT OF THE STATION. "Thanks for the ride." Allison closed the passenger door and helped Charlie out of the back given her broken toe that still caused her pain. "I want to see Shane before we take this to Montoya."

"I bet Laura Young won't talk without her lawyer." Charlie closed the door and hobbled alongside Allison until they entered the building.

"I don't see him." Allison surveyed the bullpen before turning to another officer nearby. "Have you seen Sully?"

"Interrogation Room 3," the detective replied.

"Thanks." She and Charlie walked back. "I see him." Allison gazed through the window. "I need to get his attention."

"Call him," Charlie said.

"And that's why you're my partner." Allison grabbed her phone. She spotted him glance at his phone and he answered.

"Where are you?" he asked.

"Here. Outside with Charlie. Shane, I have to show you something and it's important."

He looked at the window, which was a two-way mirror from inside the room, and then cast his sights to Laura Young. "I'm coming." He ended the call. "Would you like a glass of water, Ms. Young? A coffee, maybe?"

"Water, please. Thank you."

Shane nodded. "I'll be right back." He left the room to find Allison and Charlie in the corridor. "What is it? What did you find?"

Allison held out the phone. "This was in Laura's apartment. I have a feeling it's a burner."

"A burner." He examined the phone. "You found this in her apartment, which means you went back after I said not to. Come on Allison, cut me some slack, would you?"

A guilty expression cloaked her face. "I've apologized so many times, I'm sure you don't care to hear it again, but I went back in because I saw this on her side table when we went in the first time. I didn't want to say anything in front of Laura, which is why we—I did what I did."

"I'm not excusing your behavior, but I can't argue with your results. We'll still need her to unlock it," he replied.

"Yeah, well, here's the thing. I'd like to go in there with you and ask her about it."

Shane groaned. "I can't let you do that, Allison. You're not a cop, you're not a lawyer. There's no legitimate reason for me to allow you inside."

"Sure, I get it." Allison scratched at the bun on top of her head. "But I know her better than you. I think I can get her to talk and especially if I show her the phone. I'm telling you Shane; she'll sing like a bird."

"This isn't the 1950s Allison. We don't say things like that anymore," he replied.

"Sounds cool though," Charlie said.

"Two minutes. Any ammo we can get on her will only help Montoya."

"That's all I need," Allison replied before walking into the room. "Hi, Laura."

"What the hell are you doing here?" Her eyes were puffy and her forehead was lined with bands of sweat.

"I wanted to ask you about this." She sat down and placed the phone on the table. Her attention was diverted for a moment when Shane entered.

"It's a phone." Laura shrugged.

"Yep. I found it in your apartment. It was on your side table in the living room."

A hint of worry lined Laura's eyes.

"I assume this is a spare phone. What we in the law enforcement industry call a burner. You know, a phone no one else knows you have. One that you get secret calls and texts on." She examined the phone. "What do you think Detective Sullivan might find if he were to take a look at it?"

Shane leaned over the table and studied it. "I bet I'd find some interesting phone numbers. Maybe a voicemail or two. A couple of text messages." He eyed Laura. "Do you think I'd find something on here from Clay Sadler? Or I don't know, maybe Carlos Diaz? You were friends with his dead wife, right?"

"I didn't do anything, okay?" Laura demanded. "I told Carlos that some woman calling herself Emma Stone was asking a lot of questions about Tracy."

"They were watching you so that must have been how they found me," Allison said.

Shane pressed on. "Were you in a relationship with Carlos Diaz?"

"No. I mean, not at that time."

"But previously?" he added.

"Yeah. For a little while. It was nothing. Didn't mean anything."

"Did Tracy know you were sleeping with her husband?" Allison asked. "I was betrayed by my ex, you know. That kind of stuff starts to taint your idea of friendship and loyalty."

Shane peered at Allison with concern but quickly returned his attention to Laura. "What about Clay Sadler? Would I find anything on here from him?"

"No." Her tone softened.

"You sure about that? Someone must've known where Carlos would be this morning. That he'd be on his boat." Shane held her gaze. "Did you tell Sadler? Did he have something on you?"

Allison felt a wave of recognition. "You told Sadler about Tracy's affair with Harlan, didn't you? Of course, Carlos suspected it and told Tommy. But Sadler already knew where the two love-birds would be that night. Why would you do that?"

"I don't know what you're talking about," Laura replied.

"Oh, I think you do. I imagine you were introduced to the mayor through the Diaz's, seeing as how you were long-time friends and had slept with Carlos. Maybe you and Sadler struck up a little something. Got hot and heavy for a while."

"I didn't know about whatever deal Carlos had going with Clay. I swear it."

"Tracy didn't tell you? I thought she told you everything?" Allison waited but then continued. "I think Tracy told you about the deal Carlos struck with Sadler. The bribes. She knew you'd been sleeping with him and figured it would help in the divorce case she was building. How am I doing so far?"

"Really great," Shane answered, though the question hadn't been directed at him.

"I have a feeling you were helping Sadler control Carlos after Tracy was killed. You went back to Carlos and tried to offer comfort in the face of his grief. He must've mentioned he was going to the boat to meet with Franklin Perry. And that was a surprise to Sadler. Then bye-bye, Carlos."

Laura Young dropped her head into her hands and sobbed.

Allison stood from the table. "I'll leave the rest to you." She started to walk out but turned back. "It's a real shame you betrayed Tracy that way. With friends like you..."

28

The lieutenant who led the bust pushed through the back doors of the stationhouse with the detectives close behind. And Montoya was bestowed the honor of bringing in Victor Esposito in cuffs. Now was the time to put this investigation to bed, but there remained a missing piece; his partner whose name Victor hadn't relinquished. The younger accomplice was still on the lam and Montoya banked on Victor giving up his location in an effort to save his own skin.

But what Montoya hadn't banked on was Allison Hart. She emerged from the hall and stopped in her tracks at the sight of Montoya hauling in one of the Mercedes men.

She recognized him immediately and he recognized her. Allison gathered her wits before approaching. "Where's your friend?"

Victor captured her gaze with the look of a man who wouldn't hesitate to slash her throat if given the opportunity. He shrugged and broke away from her sights.

"What are you doing here, Ms. Hart?" Montoya asked.

"You should speak to Sully. He's in Room 3 with Laura Young."

"The friend of Tracy Diaz you spoke about?" he asked.

"Yes. She has some interesting information and a phone you should probably look at." Allison shot a glance to Victor once again. "The FBI is going to come after you with everything. You took one of their own. And I'll make sure you pay for killing Tommy Boyce too."

"I have no idea what you're talking about, lady," Victor replied sharply.

Allison returned to the lobby and waited for Shane to appear, and while it took the better part of an hour, he finally returned. She stood to meet him. "Well?"

Shane returned a calculated smile. "Well, Ms. Hart, seems this little piece of evidence is chock-full of details surrounding the murders of the Diaz's and Harlan Goodfellow."

"And Tommy Boyce? Did she have any information about him?"

At this, Shane cast down his gaze. "Nothing concrete. I'm not sure she knew much more than what she told you."

"She knew Tommy was helping Tracy Diaz but that's it?"

"That's how it seems, yes."

"Well, you might want to speak to Montoya. He just brought in Victor Esposito. I have a feeling he'll talk, especially if he wants a deal."

"He's here?" Shane asked.

"Montoya took him to Processing. The other one is still out there."

Shane nodded. "I'll go see him. It's all coming together, Allison. And Montoya will have you to thank. You and Charlie."

"I'm not going to hold my breath for any thank yous. Montoya is still pretty pissed."

"He'll get over it. You know, I had my doubts and you were reckless at times. You got lucky this time, Allison. I need you to see that. It won't always turn out this rosy."

"I know," Allison replied. "I won't make the same mistakes. Trust me when I say it won't happen again."

Detective Alvarez rushed by them. Shane whipped around and called out. "Alvarez, what's going on?"

The detective stopped and turned on his heel. "I just got a call about a car going down in the bay."

Shane's face grew pale.

"A silver Mercedes?" Allison asked, knowing Shane was about to ask that very same question.

"That's what we think. I need to see Montoya. Officers are on their way. We have no idea if there's anyone inside the car."

———

PATROL CARS WITH LIGHTS TWIRLING, AMBULANCE TRUCKS, fire trucks; they were all there on the road parallel to the spot where the car went down. Shane's car raced toward them. "Jesus. Look at this." He slammed the gearshift into park and jumped out.

Allison and Charlie followed Shane to the edge of the rocky shoreline. A crane was perched near the water and had been hooked to what looked like the car's bumper.

"I see it. They're pulling out the car now," Allison replied. "I can't believe this. It had to be Sadler's doing. He knew they were going to come for him and he was getting rid of evidence."

"What if that kid is in there?" Charlie asked.

"I hope not." Allison approached Shane as he spoke to one of the officers on the scene.

"You're telling me you pulled out the driver already?" Shane asked him.

"He's over there, under the tarp. You working this case?" the officer asked.

"No. Detectives Montoya and Alvarez are. That's them right over there." Shane turned to Allison. "Let's go see if it is who we think it is."

Allison didn't hesitate and marched toward the blue tarp covering the body on the side of the road. "I need to do this for Tommy and Fin."

"I know you do," Shane replied.

Allison stood over the lump beneath the tarp. She was more afraid than she thought she would be and the same hesitation she felt when looking at Tommy's body overcame her.

Shane squatted and pulled back the tarp to expose only the head and shoulders. "Is this the kid you both saw?"

Allison glanced at Charlie and the slight nod meant she knew the answer as well. When Allison turned again to examine the face, she began, "It's the kid we saw at Fin's house and the one I saw in the passenger seat chasing me."

Shane returned the tarp and pulled upright again. "That's all you need to do, Allison. They'll pull DNA and compare it just to be sure, but your part is done. Both of the men who had been following you are gone now."

"And what about Clay Sadler?" Allison asked him. "Is he finished now too? Will this be enough?"

"I hope so, Allison. I really do."

Montoya and Alvarez were quickly approaching the three of them. Montoya, who was winded, began, "Who's under there?"

"It's the kid," Allison said. "I've seen him enough times to know it's him. Victor Esposito will have to confirm the kid's name."

"I knew I shouldn't have left that house this morning," Montoya said.

"What are you talking about?" Shane asked.

"The car was there at the house when we brought in Victor. The officers on the scene assured me they would stay put until Forensics arrived where it would then be hauled in for processing."

"Then Sadler's reach is longer than we thought," Alvarez began. "He must've had someone on his payroll who made sure the car never made it to the impound lot. And the kid never made it out alive."

"Son of a bitch." Montoya shook his head. "We have enough to bring in Sadler and that's what we're going to do right now."

"Now?" Allison asked.

"You bet your ass," Montoya added. "That phone you swiped, the verbal threats. Ms. Hart, as much as I hate to admit it, you gave us what we need to bring down the mayor."

"It wasn't just me. Milo Nash knew Sadler was a bad apple. He started this. He and his buddy, Franklin Perry."

"That may be the case, but you risked your life. I can give credit where it's due." Montoya turned and shouted to one of the officers. "Over here. We need to get this body to the M.E. pronto!" Montoya turned his attention to Alvarez. "Let's get Nash up to speed and get an arrest warrant issued for Clay Sadler. The sooner the better."

"Do you think he's still here?" Allison asked. "With everything that's happened."

"If there's one thing I know about politicians, Ms. Hart," Montoya said. "It's that they think their shit don't stink. Pardon my French. What I mean to say is I can guarantee you he believes he can buy his way out of trouble. What he doesn't know, I have to assume, is that we have Laura Young up our sleeve. She's the key. Sadler won't get out of this."

"There's one other thing," Allison said. "We don't have conclusive proof as to who murdered Tommy Boyce. He's the reason I'm here and I have to give his daughter closure."

Montoya creased his brow and traded glances with Shane. "You didn't tell her?"

"Tell me what?" she asked.

"The Medical Examiner just came back with results of the autopsy. Ms. Hart, Tommy Boyce died of a heart attack."

"What?" She turned to Shane. "You knew this?"

"No. I'm sorry, I did see a message from you, Montoya, but I didn't have the chance to check it."

"A heart attack?" Allison continued, glancing to Charlie with uncertainty. "He was found at the docks floating in the water."

"That's right. We retrieved surveillance footage from the dock operator and found Boyce walking toward Carlos Diaz's boat. It was late at night. No one was nearby and he collapsed. The video shows him clutching his chest. Unfortunately, he writhed around, trying to pull himself up, but he ended up in the water and struck a large tiedown on the slip. That was why there was trauma to the skull. It was all a very unfortunate accident, I'm afraid. The security guard on duty at the time had walked away to take a leak. It happened so fast that when he returned, Tommy was already in the water. He had no idea."

"Oh my God." Allison's face masked in shock. "That was why he wanted me to take the pictures because he figured Carlos would be preoccupied and he could check out his boat. His phone. Tommy's GPS put him near Goodfellow's apartment 30 minutes before I arrived."

"Maybe the battery died before he reached the docks," Charlie said.

"I suppose. All this time, I thought it was Victor Esposito at the direction of Sadler. Have you told his daughter about this?" she asked.

"Milo Nash has her in hiding, which we agreed to. It was too risky with the evidence uncovered from his office. You might not have believed we were working this investigation, Ms. Hart, but I assure you we were. We'll relay to Nash that it's safe to bring her home. Alvarez and I will work with Nash to get her the details. Look, I hate to cut this short, but we have a high-ranking public official to bring in."

"Of course," Allison said. "Thank you, Detective Montoya, Detective Alvarez."

"At least you know." Charlie laid her hand gently on Allison's shoulder. "You got what you needed, Alli. It's time to go home now."

———

SHANE TOOK THEM BACK TO THE STATION SO ALLISON COULD pick up her car.

"Thanks for bringing us back," Allison said.

Shane peered at her. "You two did good, you know. Considering how all this started, you kept digging and you got answers. You should be proud."

"I guess so. But if we'd just waited for the Medical Examiner's report, we would've known about Tommy," Allison said.

He nodded. "Maybe so, but then we wouldn't have known about Laura Young."

"We'll see you later, Shane," Charlie said, stepping out of his car.

Allison stepped out and gazed at the sky for a moment. "What day is it?"

Charlie looked at her. "Saturday. Why?"

"Oh no. Today is Nolan's Triple A tryout. I promised I would be there."

"It's only noon. When was it due to start?" Charlie asked.

Allison reached for her phone and checked the emails. "He hasn't called me. I'm trying to find the email. Hang on." She continued to scroll through. "Got it. It started an hour ago." She waved back to Shane and jumped into her car.

Charlie hopped onto the passenger seat.

"If we leave now, we might not miss all of it." Allison keyed the ignition.

"Then step on it, lady."

Allison pulled out of the parking lot. "I can't believe I forgot about it."

"You've had a lot on your plate," Charlie replied.

"Yes, but I promised him I wouldn't let anything get in the way of my being there. Damn it."

"You haven't missed it yet. Just calm down. We'll be there soon."

"Yeah." She eyed her phone in the center console that buzzed with an incoming call. "It's Milo. Can you answer that?"

Charlie picked up her phone and answered the call, placing it on speaker. "Alli's phone."

"Who's this?"

"Hey, Milo, it's Charlie. Alli's driving. What's going on? We just left the station."

"I know. I just got here. They're headed to Sadler's home now. In an hour's time, the mayor of Tampa will be under arrest."

"Thank God," Allison said. "I'm here, Milo. Thanks for the heads-up."

"You got it. Hey, I also wanted you to know that we're bringing home Lucy Boyce in a few hours. I thought you might want to see her."

"Absolutely. I have some things going on now, but I'll be around later this afternoon. You want me to come by your office?"

"Actually, I'd like you to stop by her house if that's okay. I want her to be comfortable and try to find some sense of normalcy. Would that be okay? Say around 3 pm?"

"Yep, that'll work. Thanks, Milo. I'm glad you were looking out for her."

"And you. I have a feeling that kid's going to need some looking after for a while now that this is over. Maybe you can help out with that too."

"Whatever she wants. I'll be there for her," Allison replied.

"Good. I'll leave you to it then. See you this afternoon. Thanks, Charlie. Bye."

"Bye." Charlie ended the call and looked at Allison. "How do you think she's going to react to what really happened to her dad?"

"Honestly? Probably with a measure of relief. Just knowing that someone didn't take his life, that's going to mean something to her. I know it would mean everything to me." She made a final turn and arrived at the ballpark. "Here we are. I hope I'm not too late."

"Nolan will understand." Charlie opened her door to step out.

"He'll say he understands, but we'll both know better." Allison stepped out. "The email says they're on this field to the right. I should text Leo and see if he's here." She texted the information and waited for a reply. "Ah, I was right. They're over there. Leo says he's on the center stand halfway down."

They headed in that direction and arrived to find Leo, but he wasn't alone. Allison slid onto the bleachers and sat down next to him. Charlie was next to her.

"Please tell me I haven't missed everything?" Allison asked him.

"He was in the outfield first. You missed that, but he should be up to bat soon." Leo leaned over. "Hi, Charlie. Thanks for coming."

"Wouldn't miss it."

"You remember Jenny?" He leaned back and revealed his shiny new girlfriend. "Jenny, of course you know Allison, this is her best friend, Charlie."

"Pleased to meet you, Charlie." Jenny offered her hand that stretched across the laps of the formerly married couple.

Allison looked on and noticed how perfect Jenny's hair had been. Pulled back in a small, neat ponytail. The reddish-brown hue glistening in the sun. Her skin was pale, smooth and young. Allison smiled at her. "Nice to see you, Jenny."

"You too, Allison." Jenny returned to her position and watched the field.

"Why are you late? You know how important today is for Nolan," Leo asked.

"I'm well aware. It'll be on the news soon, I'm sure, so I guess there's no harm in telling you that Mayor Sadler is about to be arrested for murder, fraud, corruption and whatever else they can make stick to him."

"Oh my gosh," Jenny interjected. "You already know this?"

Allison nodded. "I do."

"Alli was the one who helped bring him down," Charlie said.

"We both helped." She turned back to Leo. "We've been at the station most of the morning."

Leo's face wore concern. "Sounds like things got very real for you. I hope you weren't in danger, but I have a feeling if you were, you wouldn't tell me." He held her gaze. "I'm glad you're here. Nolan will be glad too."

"I hope so."

"*And coming up next to bat, Nolan Hart.*" The announcer broadcasted over the loudspeaker.

Allison's eyes lit up. "This is it." She pulled upright, her back stiff, her eyes fixed on the batter's box. "Come on, baby. You can do this."

Nolan stepped up to the plate. His slim build was adorned in a black jersey and white pants. He tugged on his ballcap and took a couple of practice swings before getting into position.

Leo leaned into Allison. "He looks good out there."

"Yes, he does. We did good with that one." She patted his knee. "Wish I could say the same about the other."

"Oh, come on now. Micah will come around," Leo replied.

Allison continued to stare at Nolan as he stepped toward the plate. "It's been 5 years, Leo. She hasn't forgiven me yet."

"You weren't the one who did wrong. She knows that," he replied.

"Well, she blames me anyway. I can't think about that right now." She cupped her hands around her mouth. "Let's go, Nolan! You can do it!"

The first pitch was a curveball.

"Strike!" said the umpire.

"That's okay. You got this, buddy," Leo shouted.

Another pitch, a fastball.

"Strike two!"

"Damn. Okay. Okay. Don't worry about it." Leo appeared to be reassuring himself.

"He'll do it," Allison replied.

Another pitch.

"Foul ball!"

"Yes!" Allison said.

Nolan pounded his bat against homeplate a couple of times and took another practice swing. His weight shifted on his legs before he fixed his sights on the pitcher. His stance was perfect.

The pitcher threw another fastball.

Nolan took the swing and it connected with a sweet crack of the wood. He dropped the bat and bolted toward first.

"Yeah! Go, Nolan! Run!" Allison was on her feet.

Leo joined her and placed his fingers in his mouth, whistling as loud as he could. "Run, Nolan! You got it. All the way to third!"

Nolan hustled fast and hard around first base, then onto second. The outfielder picked up the ball and threw it to the second baseman. But Nolan blew past him before he caught it. He rounded to third and slid, reaching for the base with his fingertips. The third baseman caught the ball and tagged him.

"Safe!" the outfield umpire yelled.

"And that's a triple by the young Nolan Hart," said the announcer.

Allison jumped and shouted, shaking the stands. She threw her arms around Leo and both embraced with delight.

It took a moment, but they settled back down, returning to their seats.

"You raised a good ballplayer, you two," Charlie said.

The game finished and Nolan had made it onto base for nearly all of his at-bats. He made a few good plays as the short-stop and overall, had a good showing. But whether it was enough to make the Triple A league team was still undetermined.

They left the stands and waited at the locker room for Nolan to emerge. Allison and Leo stood side-by-side, ready to greet their son. Jenny fell back, appearing to understand that this was a moment for the parents, not the new girlfriend.

Charlie picked up on her reluctance and approached. "Hey, Jenny. That was quite a game. Nolan's a talented kid."

"He sure is," Jenny replied. "I'm glad he has such supportive parents."

"Me too. A kid needs that. I wish my ex was as caring as Leo. Things don't always work out the way you planned."

"No, they don't." Jenny held her gaze. "Thanks."

"For what?"

"Talking to me. Allison doesn't usually give me the time of day."

"She will eventually. They were married for 20 years. That's a long time in anyone's book." Charlie's attention was diverted when Nolan emerged, freshly showered and wearing basketball shorts and a t-shirt.

"There's my boy." Allison wrapped her arms around Nolan. "You were great out there, kiddo."

Nolan pulled away from the embrace. "I didn't see you when I was first in the outfield. Where were you?"

"Just wrapping up a few things. I'm sorry I was late. But I saw that triple you made. And the rest of it."

He appeared reluctant to forgive, but it didn't last long. A wide smile danced on his lips. "Yeah, I didn't think I was going to make it to third. Sheer luck."

"Not luck, talent." Leo patted Nolan on the back. "What's the good word?"

"I made it through the first cuts."

Leo pumped his fist. "Yes!"

Charlie walked to Allison and tapped her shoulder. "Hey, Alli, it's pushing 3 o'clock."

"What's going on at 3?" Nolan asked.

"You know what, I actually think you should come along," Allison replied.

Charlie creased her brow. "You sure about that, Alli?"

"What's happening at 3?" Leo asked.

"We have to be someplace. A girl I was helping." Allison turned back to Nolan. "You know her. Lucy Boyce? She goes to your school."

"Yeah, I might've seen her around."

"I just have to pop in at her place. I'd like for you to come with us. It won't take long, then maybe we could all go out for some food? A late lunch, early dinner?"

Nolan looked at his father. "Would that be okay with you, Dad?"

"Sure. I don't see why not. You should go."

"Will you meet us at the restaurant?" Nolan asked.

"Oh, you want us to eat with you?" Leo eyed Allison.

She nodded her approval.

"You got it, kid," Leo replied. "Text me where to go and we'll meet you there."

"Great." Nolan smiled. "That's great." He turned back to his mom. "I'd like to see Lucy. She just lost her dad, right?"

"She did. I think she'd appreciate having you there. Someone her age." Allison wrapped her arm around his waist. "We should get a move on though. I don't want to be late." She turned back to Leo. "We'll see you both later?"

"Sounds good," Leo replied. "I'm proud of you, son."

"Thanks, Dad."

———

ALLISON PULLED TO A STOP IN FRONT OF TOMMY BOYCE's house. She spotted Milo's car in front of hers. "They're here."

The three of them exited the car and walked toward the porch where Milo opened the door before they had a chance to knock.

"Sorry we're a little late," Allison replied.

Milo cast a glance to Nolan.

Allison saw his concern and intervened. "He was at a tryout and I asked him to come along."

"Okay. Come on in." Milo stepped aside and closed the door behind them. "She's in the kitchen."

"Does she know?" Allison whispered.

Milo nodded. "She's handling it pretty well."

Lucy spotted them enter and stood up. "Allison. You're here." She approached her and pulled her into an embrace. "It's so good to see you. I wish I could've told you they made me leave. I can't imagine how worried you must've been."

"It was nothing compared to what you've been through, Lucy. Don't you worry about it." Allison turned to Nolan. "This is my son, Nolan."

She nodded. "Yeah, you're the baseball player. I think we know some of the same people."

"I think so." He offered his hand. "I'm very sorry to hear about your dad."

"Thank you." Lucy turned back to Allison. "If your mom hadn't been so kind, well, I don't know if I would've made it this far."

Charlie smiled. "I'm sure you're glad to be home, Lucy."

"It's a mixed blessing," she replied.

"Of course."

Allison held Lucy's gaze for a moment. "You know, without you bringing your dad's case files to me, I don't think we would've found the truth. I have you to thank for that. Is there any way I can repay you?"

Lucy appeared to think about the question, fidgeting with her hands until she finally spoke. "I was actually thinking maybe we could help each other."

"Oh? How's that?"

"Well, my dad had a lot of clients. Good ones. And I kind of know how he did things."

"Okay," Allison replied slowly.

"I know you said you were planning on getting your license, you know, to do what my dad did. What if maybe I came to work for you? Maybe I could talk to the people who Dad did work for and tell them they could come to you. That I'd be helping out."

"Is that what you want?" Allison asked. "You want to do P.I. work?"

"I've been around that sort of thing my whole life. My dad was a cop too. It kinda makes sense to me. I could help you get started, maybe?"

Allison turned to Milo.

"I think that would be a fantastic idea," Milo said. "Allison, I knew you were capable of great things, but you exceeded my expectations. But a leg up, a helping hand, I think that could be the best thing to kick your agency into high gear."

"Well, it wouldn't just be my agency." Allison turned back to Charlie. "What do you think?"

"Hey, I'm all in. You know that, Alli. Where you go, I go. No questions."

Allison pondered the idea and cast her gaze to Nolan. "And you?"

"I want you to be happy, Mom. And it seems like you're good at it, so why not?"

"Okay. I still have the formalities to go through to get the license, but it shouldn't take too long." She regarded the people around her and turned back to Lucy. "Lucy, I'd be honored to have you on our team." Allison reached for Nolan's hand. "We were just about to celebrate Nolan's great day on the ball field. How would you like to join us? You should get to know the entire circus before deciding to join in."

Lucy smiled. "I'd love to."

"Then it's settled." She turned back to Charlie. "I guess we're going to really do this."

"You know it, sister."

THE END

ABOUT THE AUTHOR

Robin Mahle has published more than 40 crime fiction novels, many, of which, topped the Amazon charts in the US, Canada, and the UK. And most recently, she has delved into the world of psychological thrillers.

Also a screenwriter, she has adapted some of her works into teleplays, which have gone on to place in film festivals nationwide.

From detectives to federal agents, and from killers to corruption, her page-turning tales grab hold and refuse to let go. Throw in tense action and thrilling twists, and it becomes clear why her readers come back for more.

Robin lives in Coastal Virginia with her husband and two children.

If you enjoyed Ms. Mahle's work, please share your experience by leaving a review on Amazon.

ALSO BY ROBIN MAHLE

The Kate Reid FBI Thriller Series (17 books)

The Chef (stand-alone psych thriller)

The Man in My Attic (stand-alone psych thriller)

The Compound (standalone psych thriller)

The Remy Fontaine Fugitive Hunter Thrillers (4 books)

The Det. Rebecca Ellis Thrillers (5 books)

The Allison Hart PI Thrillers (5 Books)

The Lacy Merrick Thrillers (4 books)

**Visit Robin's website at robinmahle.com and sign up for her newsletter so you can stay up to date on her new releases, events, contests, and even exclusive new material!